VLADIMIR NABOKOV

The Original of Laura (Dying is Fun)

劳拉的原型(死亡是欢愉的)

弗拉基米尔·纳博科夫 著

德米特里·纳博科夫 编

谭惠娟 译

上海译文出版社

图书在版编目(CIP)数据
劳拉的原型/(美)纳博科夫(Vladimir Nabokov)著;
(美)纳博科夫(Dmitri Nabokov)编;谭惠娟译.—上海:
上海译文出版社,2018.6
(纳博科夫作品系列)
书名原文:The Original of Laura
ISBN 978-7-5327-7644-3

Ⅰ.①劳… Ⅱ.①纳… ②纳… ③谭… Ⅲ.①中篇小
说—美国—现代 Ⅳ.①I712.45

中国版本图书馆CIP数据核字(2017)第280198号

Vladimir Nabokov
THE ORIGINAL OF LAURA

图字:09-2008-038号

劳拉的原型	弗拉基米尔·纳博科夫 著	出版统筹 赵武平
	德米特里·纳博科夫 编	责任编辑 邹 滢
The Original of Laura	谭惠娟 译	装帧设计 @broussaille私制

上海译文出版社有限公司出版、发行
网址:www.yiwen.com.cn
200001 上海福建中路193号 www.ewen.co
上海信老印刷厂印刷

开本890×1240 1/32 印张9.75 插页2 字数80,000
2018年6月第1版 2018年6月第1次印刷

ISBN 978-7-5327-7644-3/I·4685
定价:48.00元

The Original of Laura (Dying is Fun)

劳拉的原型(死亡是欢愉的)

目 录

导 言

德米特里·纳博科夫

一九七七年，瑞士湖区进入乍暖还寒的春天。我从国外被召回到父亲的病床前。父亲当时正住在洛桑市的一个诊所，他在这里接受了一个普通手术后，显然是在康复期内感染了医院的杆菌，从而导致身体抵抗力大大减弱。他体内钠元素和钾元素含量骤降，这表明病情已恶化，却全然没有引起院方的注意。要想保住他的生命就得赶紧采取措施。

我们迅速将他转到洛桑市的沃州大学医院，为了找到可恶的病因，医生们展开了一场漫长而令人痛心的检查。

父亲闲暇时笃爱昆虫学，[①]有一次在达沃斯采集捕捉蝴蝶时，不小心跌倒，被卡在陡峭山坡上的一个险要处，他一边摇着捕蝶网，一边喊救命，坐在电缆车里的游客误以为是节假期间特意安排的恶作剧，都报以阵阵狂笑。官僚作风有时真让人感觉到世态炎凉。父亲好不容易由两位侍者搀扶着回到旅馆大厅时，又因走路不稳、衣冠不整而遭到旅馆工作人员的呵斥。

也许没有必然联系，但似乎就是一九七五年的这次意外使他病倒了一段时间，病情一直没有真正好转，直到后来在洛桑住院又发生了那次可怕的感染。不少人自作聪明地讲述父亲早期在蒙特勒皇宫酒店的生活，其中某部蹩脚的电子版传记更是勾起我无限的回忆，记得《洛丽塔》的成功并没有冲昏父亲的头脑，他继续住在一家*简陋的瑞士旅馆*。（变体是我所为。）

随着年龄的增长，纳博科夫年轻时的强健体魄确实开始丧失。他那六英尺高的身躯不再挺拔，他沿湖散布的步履不再矫健和稳重。

但他并没有停止他的文学创作。他在赶一部一九七五年就着手创作的小说。就在这个非同寻常的关键年度，天才大脑酝酿已久的一部杰作逐渐成形，他的这些卡片也由此产生并保留至今。他几乎不提及他的创作细节，但也许他已预感到机会不多了，他开始向母亲和我详细讲述他的某些创作细节。我们家庭的饭后聊天时间变短了，也变得不规律了，他一吃完饭即回到自己房间，好像急于要完成他的作品。

很快到了父亲最后一次被送进医院的时候。父亲的病情加重了。一次接一次的检查，一轮又一轮的诊断，站在病床边医生们流露出一副束手无策的表情，可见他们已回天无力了。雪上加霜的是，一个打着喷嚏的年轻护士离开时忘记关窗户，吹进来的风让父亲临终前受凉。我和母亲坐在他身边，眼睁睁地看着他喘了三口粗气后，因充血性支气管炎而停止了呼吸，我劝他吃的食物还堵在喉咙里。

医生几乎没有透露夺去父亲生命的病因。这伟大的辞世似乎

---

① 纳博科夫除了从事文学创作之外，还是著名的鳞翅目分类专家。对于写作和蝴蝶两者之间的关系，纳博科夫在其回忆录《说吧，记忆》中有详尽解释。

神秘地笼罩在尴尬的沉默中。多年过去后，我为了给父亲写传记，想把事情弄个水落石出，但通往他死亡细节的所有渠道依然不明朗。

直到父亲生命的最后一段岁月里，我才了解到某些极为隐秘的家事。其中包括父亲曾经明确交代，如果在他有生之年不能完成《劳拉的原型》，务必将其手稿销毁。对于这部未竟之作的种种猜想有如洪水泛滥，想象力贫乏的人也来凑热闹，急于发表其主观谬论：一个大限将至的艺术家首先会决定销毁自己的某部作品，不管出于什么原因，而不是让它活得比自己长久。

一个作家会病情严重，甚至危在旦夕，可他仍然会孤注一掷地与命运赛跑，直到终点线，他想战胜命运，但还是失败了。他也有可能会受到某种突发事件的干扰，或人为的阻止，纳博科夫早年就有过类似的经历，他已经走到了火炉边，要不是他妻子出手及时，《洛丽塔》的手稿早已烧成灰烬了。[①]

对于海滨城镇圣纳泽尔最令人难忘的物体颜色，父亲的记忆和我的有出入，当时我还只是个六岁的孩子，竟能从圣纳泽尔迷宫般纵横错综的建筑群中将它辨认出来，真是令人难以置信。那便是我们即将乘坐的“尚普兰”号巨大烟囱的颜色，我们就是要乘坐这艘船前往纽约。我记得烟囱呈淡黄色，而父亲在他的自传《说吧，记忆》结尾处的几行字中说它是白色的。

---

① 《洛丽塔》是写一个名叫亨伯特·亨伯特的中年男人与一个十二岁姑娘多洛蕾丝·黑兹的恋爱故事。纳博科夫当时是康奈尔大学俄国文学教授，他花了大量的时间在图书馆阅读心理学研究案例，以便更逼真地刻画书中的人物形象，这让纳博科夫遭受了巨大的精神折磨。在一九五〇年的一天，他决定终止自己的痛苦，将未完成的书稿和笔记卡片带到房屋后面的垃圾焚化炉准备烧掉，幸亏他的妻子及时阻止了他。

无论研究人员从法国海运公司色标的历史记录中翻阅到何种证据，我始终坚持我对烟囱颜色的最初记忆。我对于我们到达美国时，最后像做梦一样地在船上看到的各种颜色相当确定：纽约并非父母承诺的那样，到处是令人激动的摩天大厦，留在我梦幻般记忆中的是令人沮丧、深浅不同的灰色，到处坑坑洼洼、破败不堪。下船后，我们看到的美国也有两番不同的景象：海关检查时，一长颈瓶科涅克白兰地酒从行李箱中不翼而飞；另一方面，当父亲（还是母亲？——记忆经常会混淆他俩）拿出一张当时对我们来说也很新鲜的一百美元钞票给出租车司机时——诚实的的哥带着善意的笑容谢绝了。

在我们离开欧洲前那几年里，父亲具体在“忙”些什么，我不甚了解。我甚至对“作家”是什么都不太清楚。后来回想起父亲偶尔在我睡觉前给我讲的语言优美的短小故事，我才意识到我对他进行中的小说已先听为快了。在我父母朋友家书房的书架顶层，摆放着很多我喜欢的红皮革封面的巨著，我对书的理解与崇拜即来源于此。用俄语来表述，就是那些书对我来说“太吊胃口”了。然而，我第一次“读书”是听妈妈诵读爸爸翻译成俄语的英文小说《爱丽丝漫游奇境记》。[①]

---

① 纳博科夫翻译了英国作家刘易斯·卡罗尔的《爱丽丝漫游奇境记》。在翻译过程中，纳博科夫大胆采取各种归化翻译法，他将《爱丽丝漫游奇境记》译成了《安亚漫游奇境记》，小说中背诵莎士比亚作品的英伦少女爱丽丝变成了背诵普希金作品的俄国小姑娘安亚，英国的威廉大帝变成了基辅中世纪的伟大王子弗拉基米尔，英镑也兑换成了卢布。纳博科夫还采取归化策略翻译过许多英语诗歌和法语诗歌，包括莎士比亚、济慈、拜伦、丁尼生、叶芝及波德莱尔的诗歌。他这样做的原因也许在于，其译文的读者主要是那些失去家园、流亡欧洲的白俄群体，归化的翻译作品便于唤起他们共同的民族记忆，从而有利于加强流亡途中俄罗斯人的文化身份认同。同时，纳博科夫也能借此舒缓自己对母语被其他语言污染的恐惧。

我们去过里维埃拉的阳光沙滩旅游，而后最终乘船到了纽约。在那儿，当我第一天从现已不复存在的沃尔特·惠特曼小学放学回到家时，我向妈妈宣布我今天学英语了。我的确是踏踏实实、循序渐进地学习英语，英语也从此成了我最喜爱、最灵活的表达工具。然而，最让我引以自豪的是，我是这个世界上唯一跟弗拉基米尔·纳博科夫学习过基础俄语的人，教材词典一应俱全。

父亲当时正处于由使用俄语向使用英语转变的时期。父亲自小就是"能自如地使用三种语言的孩子"，[①] 可他发现，要为了一种新的语言而舍弃那"意蕴丰富、自由奔放的俄语"是个极大的挑战。这种新语言不是他与他那位以英语为母语的父亲在家里说的英语，而是一种如他运用熟稔的母语般富有表达力和诗意且能自如驾驭的工具。父亲在创作第一部英文小说《塞巴斯蒂安·奈特的真实生活》时，由于缺乏信心而倍受痛苦煎熬，毕竟他得放弃他钟爱的俄语，这一"世界上最温柔的语言"，他曾以此为标题写了一首英文诗发表于一九四七年的《大西洋月刊》。在他向一门新的语言过渡、也是我们即将启程来美国的这段时期，父亲完成了他最后一部用俄文创作的独立的重要抒情作品（换言之，它既非未完成的片断之作，也不是已有作品的

① 纳博科夫自小就会的三种语言是俄语、英语和法语。俄语是纳博科夫的母语。而据约翰·厄普代克为纳博科夫的《文学讲稿》写的前言称，纳博科夫的父亲有些亲英，也是一位狄更斯研究专家，他经常用英语给孩子朗读狄更斯的作品。在纳博科夫的记忆里，他孩提时代的英语就跟俄语一样流利。他甚至不无得意地宣称，英语才是他最先掌握的语言。纳博科夫一直怀念的家庭教师是一位法国小姐。因此这三门语言都是纳博科夫的日常生活用语。

俄文版)，它就是《魔法师》，该作品有似《洛丽塔》的前奏。他原以为这个短小作品的手稿已被他销毁，或已丢失，以为这部作品的创作精华已完全为《洛丽塔》所吸收。父亲后来回忆起巴黎的一个深夜，在以无声的语言抗议纳粹的轰炸威胁时，他曾将这部小说读给一群朋友听过。这份手稿最终失而复得，父亲在一九五九年与他的妻子仔细翻阅后作出了一个决定，如果"由纳博科夫夫妇把它翻译成英语"出版会更具艺术感染力。

那个决定直到父亲去世十年后才付诸实施，连《洛丽塔》都比它的前身《魔法师》问世得早。有几家美国出版社因担心《洛丽塔》的敏感主题会产生的负面反响而放弃了它。纳博科夫确信该作品将永远不会为世人所理解，便决定将手稿付之一炬，两次都是在薇拉·纳博科夫的竭力阻拦下，手稿才免于被扔进伊萨卡火炉烧为灰烬。①

最终，在对莫里斯·吉罗迪亚的奥林匹亚出版社的可疑声誉尚不知情的情况下，纳博科夫同意代理将书稿交给他们出版。②多亏格雷厄姆·格林对它褒奖有加，才使《洛丽塔》避免了《南回归线》与《北回归线》遭遇的恶评，没被视为吉罗迪亚继承其父的丰碑③，沿袭奥林匹亚出版社热衷于色情读物的老路推出的垃圾

---

① 纳博科夫当时正在位于纽约州伊萨卡镇的康奈尔大学任教，故有"伊萨卡火炉"一说。

② 巴黎的奥林匹亚出版社创建于一九五三年，创建人即莫里斯·吉罗迪亚。《洛丽塔》遭四家美国出版社拒绝后，一九五五年由该出版社出版。

③ 莫里斯·吉罗迪亚的父亲杰克·卡亨(Jack Kahane)就是在二十世纪三十年代出版亨利·米勒的《北回归线》和《南回归线》以及许多其他色情书的出版商。一九五三年，一文不名的吉罗迪亚决心效仿其父，在巴黎出版在英美遭禁的英文书，以此致富。其实，吉罗迪亚本人颇有文学品位，五十年代末他的书单上已经有了塞缪尔·贝克特、亨利·米勒、劳伦斯·德雷尔、威廉·(转下页)

之作，而是广受赞誉，被有些人视为有史以来最优秀的文学作品之一。①

父亲用纳博科夫特有的双关语和字谜，使美国二十世纪四十年代的高速公路和汽车旅馆，还有无数地名，都在这部原初公路小说中得以永生。一九六一年，纳博科夫一家入住瑞士蒙特勒皇宫酒店，刚住进去时的一个晚上，一位女服务员好心地将废纸篓中印有蝴蝶图案的东西倒空：那是一厚叠美国道路地图，父亲仔细地将他和母亲曾经去过的道路和城镇名称都标出来。父亲的即兴评论、蝴蝶的名字以及它们的栖息地都记录在那上面。令人何其悲哀！尤其是在好几个大洲的学者都在研究所有这类细节的今天。同样令人痛心的是，上有给我的深情题献的《洛丽塔》第一版，被人从纽约的一个地下室里窃取，以两美元廉价卖给了一位康奈尔大学的毕业生。

焚烧书稿的话题还将继续追随我们。纳博科夫受邀去哈佛大学做一个关于《堂吉诃德》的讲座，在肯定塞万提斯的某些优点的同时，他指责这部作品"粗俗、残忍"。多年后，人们用"批驳得体无完肤"来形容父亲对该书的评价，后来"体无完肤"又被那些半文盲记者曲解。他们后来还画了一幅漫画，上面父亲

（接上页）巴勒斯，以及琼·热内等人作品的英译本。正如他在《花花公子》上所说，他"有意如此，只是想对好书坏书一视同仁：唯一的标准就是他们的遭禁"。他的书单上四分之三是色情垃圾，他"自豪地欣然"接受了"色情书商"的称号。

① 纳博科夫并不知道奥林匹亚出版社当时还出版一套绿色封皮的色情小说丛书，他心爱的《洛丽塔》用的也是同样的绿色封皮。究竟有多少购书者被误导，我们不得而知。《洛丽塔》无声无息地与《罗宾逊的性生活》、《直到她叫春》等色情读物为伴近六个月，直到格雷厄姆·格林慧眼识珠，将它封为一九五五年最佳小说之一。

站在教室前面，举着一本燃烧的《堂吉诃德》，还伴有不失礼节的说教。

我们最后还是回到《劳拉的原型》，回到对焚书一事的思考。纳博科夫在生命中的最后几个月住在洛桑医院，狂热地创作着这部作品。外界麻木不仁者的嘲弄、好心人的关切询问、好奇者的凭空推断，以及自己身体的病痛，他都通通不予理会。他的病痛还包括脚指甲下面及周围没完没了的发炎。有时，父亲觉得宁可把他的脚趾全部剁掉，也不愿意接受护士们总在他身上进行试验性足疗。他甚至想纠正护士的错误，想去戳自己的脚趾以减轻痛苦。我们在《劳拉的原型》的好几个地方都能发现那种痛苦的痕迹。

看着户外明媚的阳光，父亲轻轻地感慨有种蝴蝶该已翩翩起舞了。但他手里拿着捕蝶网、脑海中构思着小说漫游于山坡草地的日子一去不复返了。书还在继续写，但只能整天待在病房，都要憋出幽闭症了，纳博科夫开始担心他的创作灵感和精力会输给每况愈下的身体。于是，他郑重其事地和母亲有了一次交谈，他明确交代，若临终前不能写完《劳拉的原型》，务必将其烧毁。

我曾收到过堆积如山的信件，其中有些心境狭窄的写信人声称，如果一个艺术家想销毁自认为不完美或不完整的作品，他理应提前考虑清楚并干净利落地处理好。然而，这些智者忽略了一个事实，即纳博科夫并不想无奈地销毁《劳拉的原型》，而是希望能活着将最后一些卡片整理完，这样至少可以完成一份完整的初稿。我们还可以推定，弗朗茨·卡夫卡故意将《变形记》的再版书，还有包括《城堡》与《审判》在内的其他已出版或尚未出版作品的销毁任务交给他的朋友马克斯·布诺德，就是因为他清楚地知道，布诺德无论如何也不会忍心把那些书烧掉。纳博科夫把销毁《劳拉的原型》一事委托给我的母亲时，也有过类似的推理。母亲是一个完美、英勇、值得信赖的受托人，她没能履行这一职责是源自拖延——由于年老体衰，还有无法估量的爱而造成的拖延。

就我来说，当这一重任落到我的肩上时，我确实想了很多很多。我曾不止一次用口头和书面的形式表示，对我来说，在某种意义上，父母从未离世，他们依然活着，冥冥之中我感觉他们就站在我身后关注着我，并在需要作出重大决定时给我以智慧与忠告，从一个关键性的准确措词到一些更为寻常的事情。我不需要从时髦的低能儿的标题中借用“优雅”（从而混淆视听），而是从源头就掌握了它。如果这一说法能让大胆的评论者欣喜地将之视为某种神秘现象，那就悉听尊便吧！在这个当口，在假定的回想中，我断定纳博科夫不会希望我成为“来自波洛克的人”，[①]也不会接受“小朱厄妮塔·达克”——因为那是早期的洛丽塔的名字，注定要消亡，要像现代的“圣女贞德”一样被烧毁。[②]

---

① 据说柯勒律治在创作《忽必烈汗》时被一个“来自波洛克的人”打断，导致《忽必烈汗》最终没能完成。纳博科夫在《洛丽塔》中也设计过这样一个人物，他以“来自英国波洛克的人”为名在宾馆登记入住，这个表达后被泛化为“不速之客”。

② 据《纳博科夫传记：美国岁月》记载，纳博科夫认为，年老男人娶年老的女人是想以此来接近她年轻的女儿，他第一次产生这样的想法是在二十世纪三十年代中期，在《天赋》的一个段落中；一九三九年他把这个段落扩展成了中篇小说《魔法师》（*The Enchanter*）；一九四六年他开始酝酿把中篇变成长篇。他给女主人公取名为朱厄妮塔·达克（Juanita Dark）、贞德（Joan of Arc）或简涅塔·达科（Joaneta Darc），这些女性人物的名字最终都为“洛丽塔”所取代。

父亲待在家里的时间越来越短，回家也越来越少，他每次回家，我们都会勇敢地继续着我们热闹的晚餐闲谈，但会对《劳拉的原型》的虚构世界只字不提。我想，那是因为我和妈妈对事态会如何发展已了然于心。

父亲去世一段时间以后，我才有勇气打开他装有索引卡片的箱子。在触摸这些父亲悉心整理的卡片之前，我的内心穿越了痛苦得令人窒息的障碍。几经尝试后，我终于在自己有一次住院时，首次阅读了这些用对纳博科夫来说已成为全新的"最温柔的语言"的英语创作的卡片，尽管不完整，其结构和文体却堪称史无前例。我着手整理和准备这些卡片，然后将初稿口述给我忠实的秘书克里斯蒂安·加利科。《劳拉的原型》在半明半昧中继续生存。只有在我鼓起勇气拿出来一点一点研读和编辑时，她才会浮出水面。她一边沉寂地躺在保险箱内，一边又萦绕于我心中，我逐渐习惯了这个似乎过着双重生活的令人不安的幽灵。我不再有烧毁《劳拉的原型》的想法了，我唯愿她能偶尔从幽暗中探出头来透透气。在那之后我提及这部作品的次数屈指可数，我能感觉到父亲并不反对。此外，从其他渠道也透露了些许消息，加上种种臆测，逐渐就出现了现在某家总在期待独家猛料的出版社关于《劳拉的原型》的一鳞半爪的溢美之词。

我说过，我不认为父亲，或者说父亲的在天之灵会反对《劳拉的原型》的问世，既然她已在纷纭嘈杂的议论声中幸存了这么长时间，或许是我促成了她的幸存，但我并非出于一时的兴致，也并非为了奇货可居，而是因为一种无法抗拒的其他力量的驱使。我是该被诅咒，还是被感谢？

可是为什么纳博科夫先生，你最终决定让《劳拉的原型》问世？

哦，因为我是个好人，看到全世界这么多人将心比心地同情我进退维谷的处境，我应该善意地减轻他们的痛楚。

鸣 谢

感谢以下人士给予的慷慨帮助和宝贵建议：

格纳迪·巴拉巴塔罗教授

布赖恩·博伊德教授

艾丽亚安·佐卡·科斯达克

阿勒克塞·坎诺瓦沃

斯坦尼斯拉瓦·沙瓦布利恩教授

罗恩·罗森鲍姆，即使事先有所计划，也不会有比他所做到的更出色的宣传了。

感谢全世界所有提供观点、评论和建议的人们——不管那是什么类型的建议，那些认为自己的观点——有时表达得十分巧妙——或多或少能令我改变看法的人们。

关于文本的注解

《劳拉的原型》一书排版时保留了弗拉基米尔·纳博科夫手写卡片的原貌。不规范的单词拼写（比如“bycycle”）与标点使用未作改动，文中的法语如果在卡片上没有加音符的话，排版时也同样处理。一些说明性的材料附在括号内或脚注中。

劳拉的原型

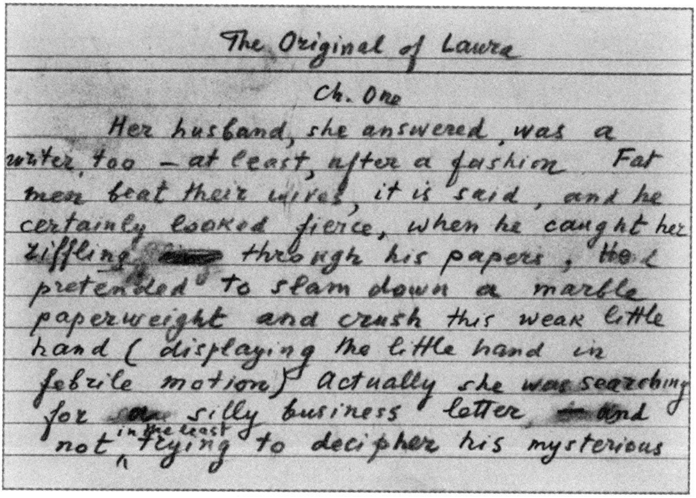

The Original of Laura

Ch. One

Her husband, she answered, was a writer, too — at least, after a fashion. Fat men beat their wives, it is said, and he certainly looked fierce, when he caught her riffling through his papers. He pretended to slam down a marble paperweight and crush this weak little hand (displaying the little hand in febrile motion). Actually she was searching for a silly business letter and not in the least trying to decipher his mysterious

THE ORIGINAL OF LAURA

Ch. One

Her husband, she answered, was a writer, too—at least, after a fashion. Fat men beat their wives, it is said, and he certainly looked fierce, when he caught her riffling through his papers. He pretended to slam down a marble paper-weight and crush this weak little hand (displaying the little hand in febrile motion) Actually she was searching for a silly business letter—and not in the least trying to decipher his mysterious

劳拉的原型

第一章

她回答说，她的丈夫也是一位作家，至少勉强算是。据说肥胖的男人会殴打自己的妻子，当发现妻子翻弄自己的手稿时，他肯定会火冒三丈，想出手打人。他假装气得把大理石镇纸一摔，然后握紧那只无力的拳头（摆出一副头脑发热要揍人的架势）。事实上她只是在寻找一份无聊的商务信函，毫无解读他的秘密之意。

(2)

manuscript. Oh no, it was not a work of fiction
which one dashes off, you know, to make
money; it was a mad neurologist's
testament, a
kind of Poisonous Opus as in that film.
It had cost him,
and would still
cost him, years of toil, but the
thing was of course, an absolute
secret. If she mentioned it at all, she
added, it was because she was drunk.
She wished to be taken home or preferably
to some cool quiet place with a clean bed
and room service. She wore a strapless gown

2

manuscript. Oh no, it was not a work of fiction which one dashes off, you know, to make money; it was a mad neurologist's testament, a kind of Poisonous Opus as in that film. It had cost him, and would still cost him, years of toil, but the thing was of course, an absolute secret. If she mentioned it at all, she added, it was because she was drunk. She wished to be taken home or preferably to some cool quiet place with a clean bed and room service. She wore a strapless gown

2

哦，不，要知道那份书稿可不是为了挣钱草率写就的小说，而是一位疯狂的神经病学家的遗作，类似那部电影中的某种"有毒作品"。它已耗费了他多年心血，并且还将继续耗费下去，当然，这事绝对是个秘密。她补充道，如果她提到那份手稿，一定是因为她已醉得神志不清了。她希望有人带她回家，最好去一个凉爽、清静，有一张干净的床，又提供送餐服务的地方。她身着无吊带礼服，

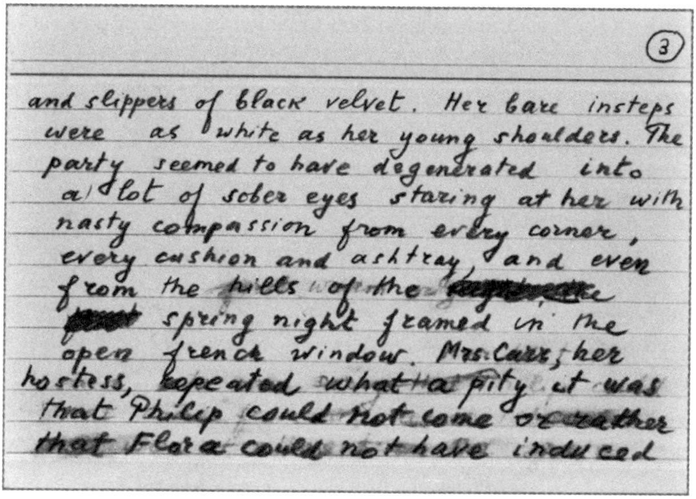

3

and slippers of black velvet. Her bare insteps were as white as her young shoulders. The party seemed to have degenerated into a lot of sober eyes staring at her with nasty compassion from every corner, every cushion and ashtray, and even from the hills of the [redacted] spring night framed in the open french window. Mrs. Carr, her hostess, repeated what a pity it was that Philip could not come or rather that Flora could not have induced

3

and slippers of black velvet. Her bare insteps were as white as her young shoulders. The party seemed to have degenerated into a lot of sober eyes staring at her with nasty compassion from every corner, every cushion and ashtray, and even from the hills of the spring night framed in the open french window. Mrs. Carr, her hostess, repeated what a pity it was that Philip could not come or rather that Flora could not have induced

3

脚蹬一双黑丝绒拖鞋。她裸露着的脚背和她充满青春活力的肩膀一样白皙。整个会场似乎蜕变出一道道冷静的目光，带着不怀好意的同情，从每个角落、每个坐垫和每个烟灰缸投向她，就连笼罩于春天夜色之中的群山也透过敞开的法式落地窗投来这样的目光。女主人卡尔夫人反复唠叨道，菲利普没来真是一大遗憾，或者说弗洛拉没能把他引诱来是一大遗憾。

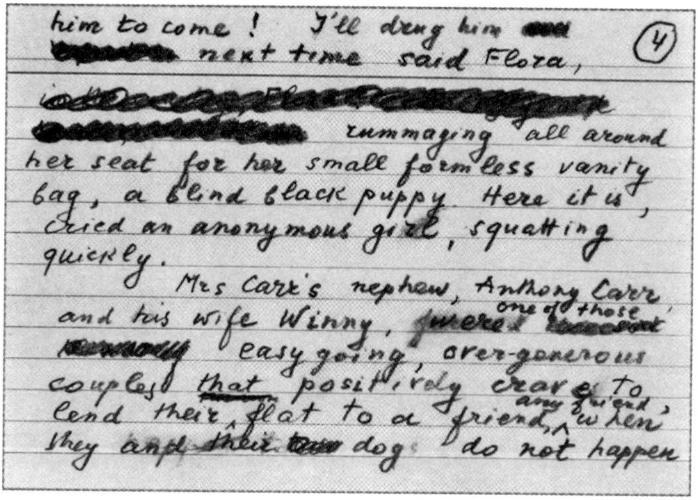

him to come! I'll drag him [redacted]
[redacted] next time said Flora, (4)
[redacted] rummaging all around
her seat for her small formless vanity
bag, a blind black puppy. Here it is,
cried an anonymous girl, squatting
quickly.
Mrs Carr's nephew, Anthony Carr,
and his wife Winny, [redacted] one of those [redacted]
easy going, over-generous
couples that positively crave to
lend their flat to a friend, any friend, when
they ~~and their~~ [redacted] dog do not happen

4

him to come! I'll drug him next time said Flora, rummaging all around her seat for her small formless vanity bag, a blind black puppy. Here it is, cried an anonymous girl, squatting quickly.

Mrs Carr's nephew, Anthony Carr, and his wife Winny, were one of those easygoing, over-generous couples that positively crave to lend their flat to a friend, any friend, when they and their dog do not happen

4

我下次把他麻醉后带来，弗洛拉一边说一边在她座位下面寻找她那个没有形状的小手袋，一只盲眼小黑狗。它在这里，一位不知姓名的姑娘迅速地蹲下去大叫道。

卡尔夫人的侄子安东尼·卡尔和他的妻子温妮性情随和，慷慨有加。只要他们两口子和他们的狗碰巧不在家，他们就迫不及待要把自己的公寓借给朋友住，任何朋友都行。

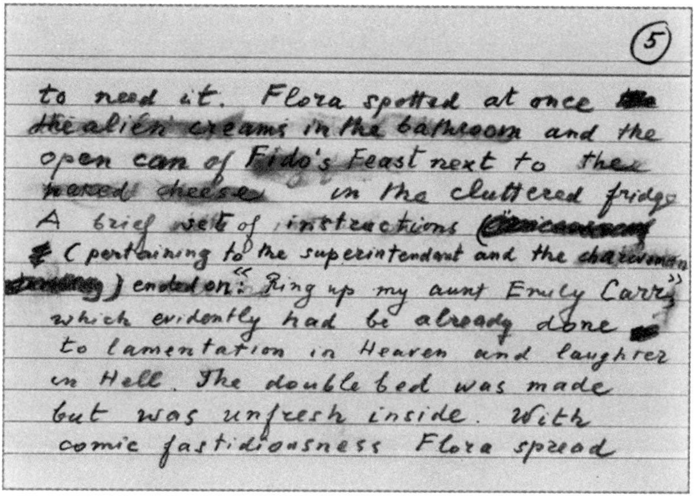

(5)

to need it. Flora spotted at once [illegible] the alien creams in the bathroom and the open can of Fido's Feast next to the [illegible] in the cluttered fridge. A brief set of instructions [illegible] (pertaining to the superintendent and the charwoman [illegible]) ended on: "Ring up my aunt Emily Carr," which evidently had be already done to lamentation in Heaven and laughter in Hell. The double bed was made but was unfresh inside. With comic fastidiousness Flora spread

5

to need it. Flora spotted at once the alien creams in the bathroom and the open can of Fido's Feast next to the naked cheese in the cluttered fridge. A brief set of instructions (pertaining to the superintend[e]nt and the charwoman) ended on：“Ring up my aunt Emily Carr,” which evidently had be[en] already done to lamentation in Heaven and laughter in Hell. The double bed was made but was unfresh inside. With comic fastidiousness Flora spread

5

弗洛拉一眼便看到了浴室里的进口乳霜，还有一盒打开的“非多牌”宠物狗罐头，原先就放在凌乱冰箱里没有包装的奶酪旁。还有一连串简短指令（给管家和女用人看的），最后一张上写着“打电话给我的爱米丽·卡尔姨妈”，这显然令人啼笑皆非。双人床已铺好，但被褥不是新的。挑剔得可笑的弗洛拉

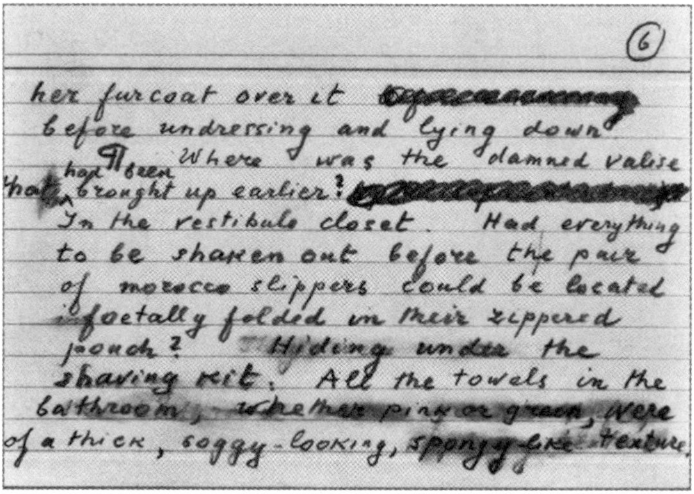
6

her furcoat over it
before undressing and lying down.
¶ Where was the damned valise
that had been brought up earlier?
In the vestibule closet. Had everything
to be shaken out before the pair
of morocco slippers could be located
in foetally folded in their zippered
pouch? Hiding under the
shaving kit. All the towels in the
bathroom, whether pink or green, were
of a thick, soggy-looking, sponge-like texture.

6

her fur coat over it before undressing and lying down.

Where was the damned valise that had been brought up earlier? In the vestibule closet. Had everything to be shaken out before the pair of morocco slippers could be located foetally folded in their zippered pouch? Hiding under the shaving kit. All the towels in the bathroom, whether pink or green, were of a thick, soggy-looking, spongy-like texture.

6

把自己的毛皮大衣铺在床上,这才脱衣躺下。

早些时候拎上来的那只该死的小提箱在哪里?在门廊壁柜里。那双摩洛哥羊皮拖鞋是否经过了彻底除尘,才折叠成胎儿形状放入带拉链的鞋袋,[①]藏在剃须工具包下面?浴室里所有的浴巾,不管是粉红色还是绿色的,全都很厚,看上去湿漉漉的,质地像海绵。

① 纳博科夫和卡夫卡都常用degenerate(蜕变,变异)或foetal(胚胎的)这类字眼来描述物体的变化及形态。纳博科夫还特别喜欢用双关语,比如此句中的pouch,有“育儿袋”和“鞋袋”两种含义。

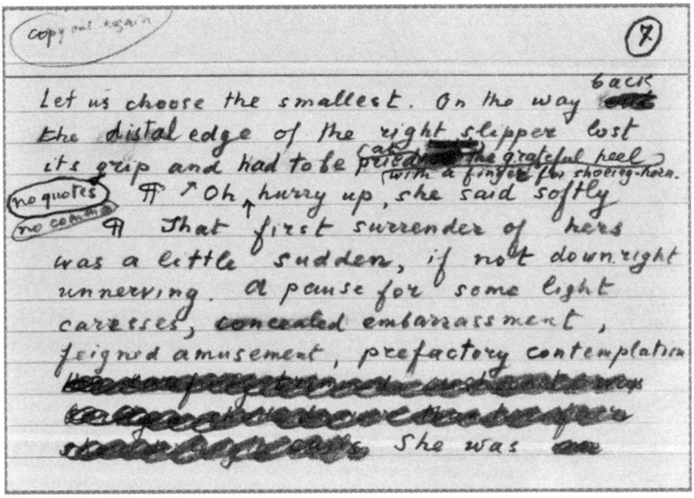
copy out again

7

Let us choose the smallest. On the way back [redacted]
the distal edge of the right slipper lost
its grip and had to be pried [redacted] the grateful heel
with a finger for shoeing-horn.
no quotes ¶ Oh, hurry up, she said softly
no comma ¶ That first surrender of hers
was a little sudden, if not downright
unnerving. A pause for some light
caresses, concealed embarrassment,
feigned amusement, prefactory contemplation
[redacted]. She was [redacted]

7

Let us choose the smallest. On the way back the distal edge of the right slipper lost its grip and had to be pried at the grateful heel with a finger for shoeing-horn.

Oh hurry up, she said softly[.]

That first surrender of hers was a little sudden, if not downright unnerving. A pause for some light caresses, concealed embarrassment, feigned amusement, prefactory contemplation[.] She was

7

我们选最小号的吧。在回来的路上，右脚拖鞋边上的鞋襻掉了，只得用一根手指在迷人的脚跟那里当鞋拔才能把鞋套上。

哦，快点，她轻声说道。

她的第一次屈从即使没有让人极度不安，也有点突如其来。停下来轻抚一番，掩饰尴尬的神情，假装快乐，开始陷入沉思。

(8)

an extravagantly slender girl. Her ribs showed. The conspicuous knobs of her hipbones framed a hollowed abdomen, so flat as to belie the notion of « belly ». Her exquisite bone structure immediately slipped into a novel – became in fact the secret structure of that novel, besides supporting a number of poems. The cup-sized breasts of that twenty-four year old impatient beauty seemed a dozen years younger than she, with those pale squinty nipples and firm form.

8

an extravagantly slender girl. Her ribs showed. The conspicuous knobs of her hipbones framed a hollowed abdomen, so flat as to belie the notion of "belly". Her exquisite bone structure immediately slipped into a novel—became in fact the secret structure of that novel, besides supporting a number of poems. The cup-sized breasts of that twenty-four year old impatient beauty seemed a dozen years younger than she, with those pale squinty nipples and firm form.

8

她是个极为苗条的女孩，肋骨历历可数。髋骨的明显突起令腹部呈凹陷状，平得真让人以为那不是肚子。她那精致的骨架顷刻间融入一部小说，事实上成为那部小说的神秘框架，还可以成为许多诗歌的素材。经过二十四年的成长，已经迫不及待地粲然怒放的两只杯口大小的乳房光滑坚挺，浅色的乳头微微探向一边，似乎比她还年轻十几岁。

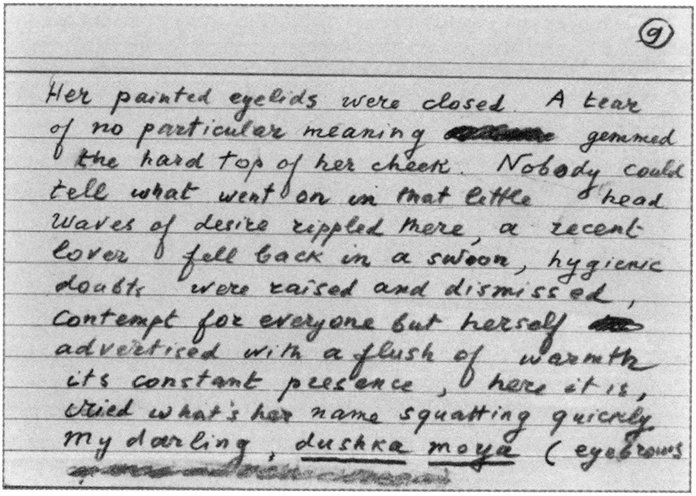

(9)

Her painted eyelids were closed. A tear of no particular meaning [illegible] gemmed the hard top of her cheek. Nobody could tell what went on in that little head. Waves of desire rippled there, a recent lover fell back in a swoon, hygienic doubts were raised and dismissed, contempt for everyone but herself [illegible] advertised with a flush of warmth its constant presence, here it is, cried what's her name squatting quickly my darling, <u>dushka</u> <u>moya</u> (eyebrows

[illegible]

9

Her painted eyelids were closed. A tear of no particular meaning gemmed the hard top of her cheek. Nobody could tell what went on in that little head[.] Waves of desire rippled there, a recent lover fell back in a swoon, hygienic doubts were raised and dismissed, contempt for everyone but herself advertised with a flush of warmth its constant presence, here it is, cried what's her name squatting quickly. My darling, dushka moya (eyebrows

9

她那化过妆的眼睑紧闭着。脸颊颧骨上挂着一滴并无特别含义的珍珠般的泪珠。没有人能说出她那小脑袋里在想些什么。那儿有阵阵欲望泛起的涟漪，新结识的情人在晕厥中跌落，关于卫生问题的疑虑先是产生继而消退，对除她自己之外所有人的鄙视，始终存在的一抹红晕将之彰显无遗。在这儿，哭喊着她的名字迅速地蹲下。我亲爱的，*我亲爱的*[①]（眉毛

① 原文为用拉丁字母转写的俄语。

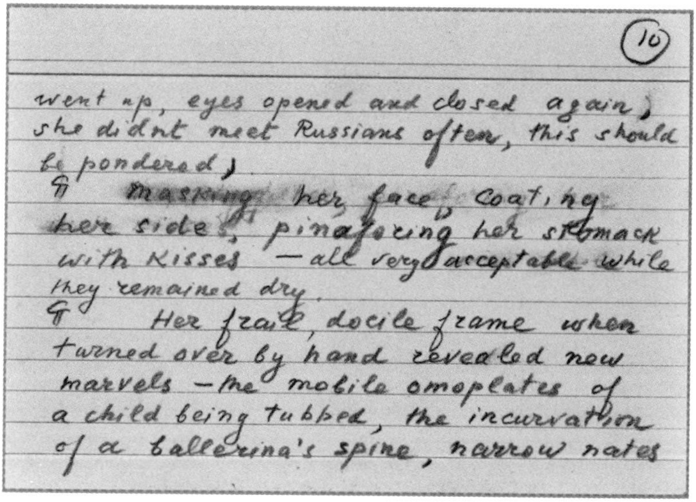
(10)

went up, eyes opened and closed again;
she didn't meet Russians often, this should
be pondered;

¶ masking her face, coating
her sides, pinaforing her stomach
with kisses — all very acceptable while
they remained dry.

¶ Her frail, docile frame when
turned over by hand revealed new
marvels — the mobile omoplates of
a child being tubbed, the incurvation
of a ballerina's spine, narrow nates

10

went up, eyes opened and closed again, she didnt meet Russians often, this should be pondered).

Masking her face, coating her side, pinaforing her stomack with kisses—all very acceptable while they remained dry.

Her frail, docile frame when turned over by hand revealed new marvels—the mobile omoplates of a child being tubbed, the incurvation of a ballerina's spine, narrow nates

10

朝上，双眼时而睁开，时而闭上，她不常见到俄罗斯人，这点应该考虑）。

遮蔽她的脸，给她的身侧盖上衣物，以亲吻护住她的腹部——当他们不动声色时，所有这一切都可接受。

用手将她那柔弱而顺从的身体转过来，又能发现新的奇迹——她有着浴盆里孩子一般灵巧的肩胛骨，脊柱的曲线如同女芭蕾舞演员一般，

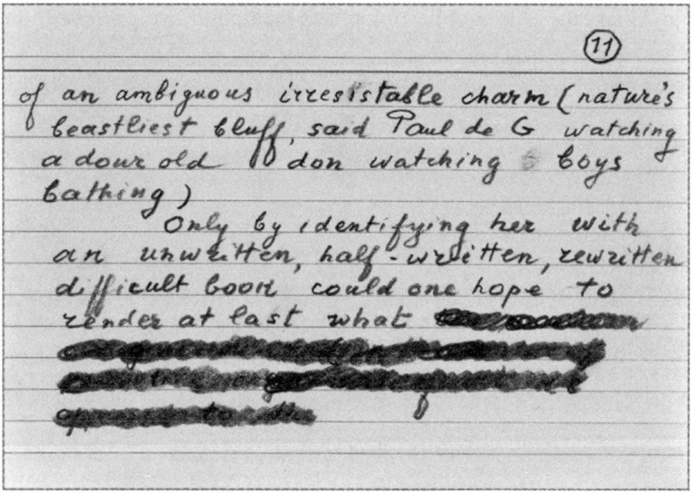
(11)

of an ambiguous irresistable charm (nature's beastliest bluff, said Paul de G watching a dour old don watching boys & bathing)

Only by identifying her with an unwritten, half-written, rewritten difficult book could one hope to render at last what [redacted]

11

of an ambiguous irresistable charm (nature's beastliest bluff, said Paul de G watching a dour old don watching boys bathing)

Only by identifying her with an unwritten, half-written, rewritten difficult book could one hope to render at last what

11

还有苗条的臀部，有一种暧昧而令人无法抵挡的魅力（大自然最令人厌恶的假象，保罗·德·G说，同时眼睛盯着那个正在看男孩子们洗澡的干瘪老头）。[①]

只有将她看作是一本还没有写、尚未写完，抑或重写的艰涩难懂的书，才有希望最终呈现出当下性爱

① dour形容人时意为“严厉的”，形容土地时意为“荒瘠的”；don在英语中意为“大学教师”，在西班牙语中则为“先生”之意。因此，原文dour old don此处可理解为双关语：“严厉的大学老师”或“干瘪的老头”。

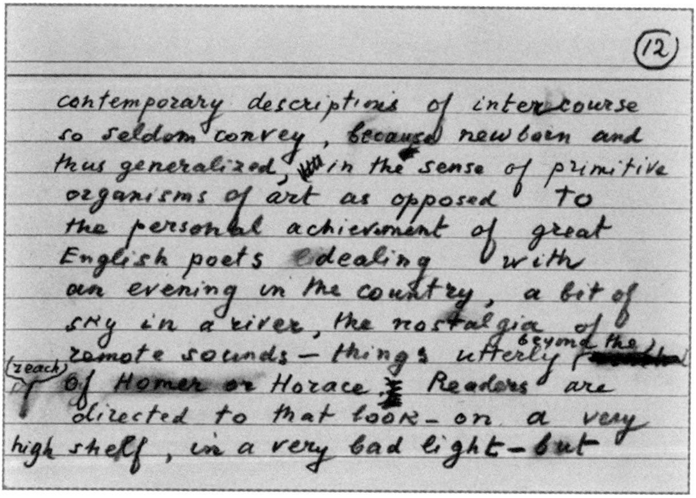

(12)

contemporary descriptions of inter-course
so seldom convey, because newborn and
thus generalized, in the sense of primitive
organisms of art as opposed to
the personal achievement of great
English poets dealing with
an evening in the country, a bit of
sky in a river, the nostalgia of
remote sounds — things utterly beyond the
(reach)
of Homer or Horace. Readers are
directed to that book — on a very
high shelf, in a very bad light — but

12

contemporary descriptions of intercourse so seldom convey, because newborn and thus generalized, in the sense of primitive organisms of art as opposed to the personal achievement of great English poets dealing with an evening in the country, a bit of sky in a river, the nostalgia of remote sounds—things utterly beyond the reach of Homer or Horace. Readers are directed to that book—on a very high shelf, in a very bad light—but

12

描写很少传达的东西，因为是新生事物，并因此被泛化，就艺术作为原始的有机体的意义而言，有别于伟大的英国诗人的个人成就，他们笔下的乡间一夜、水中的一线天际、悠远声响引发的怀旧之情——完全超出了荷马或贺拉斯的范畴。读者们被引向那本书——置于高高的书架之上，藏于幽暗的光线之中——但

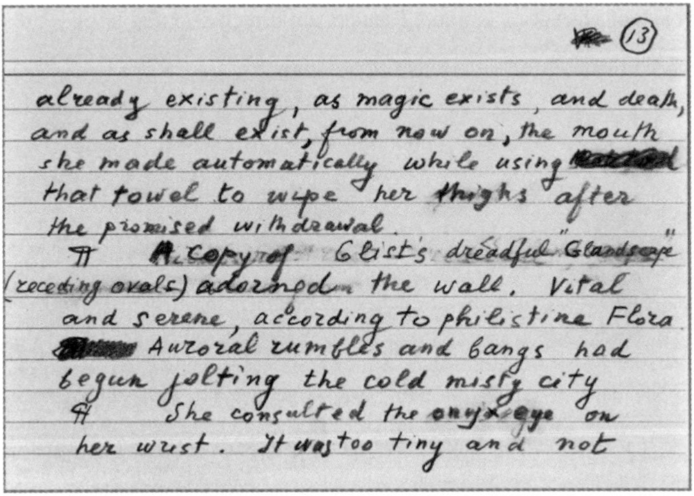

(13)

already existing, as magic exists, and death,
and as shall exist, from now on, the mouth
she made automatically while using
that towel to wipe her thighs after
the promised withdrawal.
¶ A copy of Glist's dreadful "Glandscape"
(receding ovals) adorned the wall. Vital
and serene, according to philistine Flora
Auroral rumbles and bangs had
begun jolting the cold misty city
¶ She consulted the onyx eye on
her wrist. It was too tiny and not

13

already existing, as magic exists, and death, and as shall exist, from now on, the mouth she made automatically while using that towel to wipe her thighs after the promised withdrawal.

A copy of Glist's dreadful "Glandscape" (receding ovals) adorned the wall. Vital and serene, according to philistine Flora. Auroral rumbles and bangs had begun jolting the cold misty city[.]

She consulted the onyx eye on her wrist. It was too tiny and not

13

已然存在，一如魔力的存在、死亡的存在；一如对方如约撤出后，她用毛巾擦着大腿时不由自主做出的嘴形，从今往后也将永远存在。

一幅格利斯的恐怖画作《腺茎图》（消逝中的椭圆）的复制品挂在墙上用作装饰。[①]在俗人弗洛拉眼里，这幅画既生机勃勃，又静谧安详。清晨的轰隆声开始在这个雾蒙蒙的寒冷城市沸腾开来。

她看了看自己手腕上的玛瑙眼石，实在太小了，

① 此处Glist疑为Gleizes之误。文中提到的《腺茎图》（*Glandscape*）很可能是对法国画家阿尔伯特·格莱兹（Albert Gleizes，1881—1953）的系列作品《风景》（*Landscape*）的戏仿。

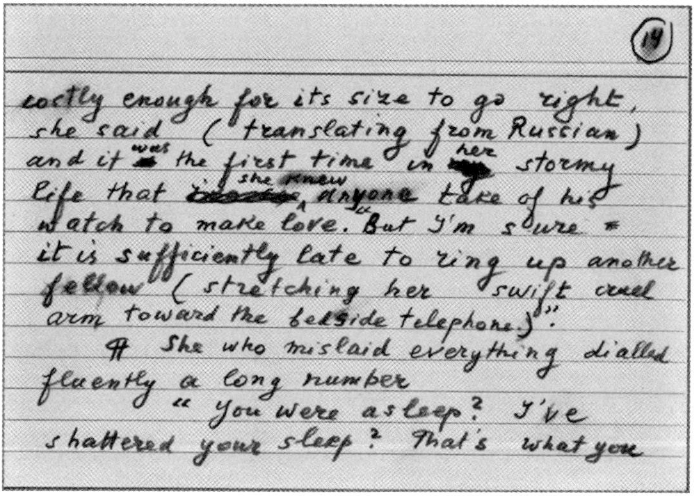
costly enough for its size to go right, she said ("translating from Russian) and it was the first time in her stormy life that she knew anyone take of his watch to make love. But I'm sure it is sufficiently late to ring up another fellow (stretching her swift cruel arm toward the bedside telephone)".

¶ She who mislaid everything dialled fluently a long number

"You were asleep? I've shattered your sleep? That's what you

14

costly enough for its size to go right, she said (translating from Russian) and it was the first time in her stormy life that she knew anyone take of[f] his watch to make love. "But I'm sure it is sufficiently late to ring up another fellow (stretching her swift cruel arm toward the bedside telephone)."

She who mislaid everything dialled fluently a long number

"You were asleep? I've shattered your sleep? That's what you

14

这种大小的不值钱，她说（是从俄语翻译过来的）在她大风大浪的一生中，他是她认识的第一个取下手表做爱的男人。"但我确信此时给另一个家伙打电话太晚了（她伸出那只敏捷而残忍的手臂去抓床边电话）。"

四处乱放东西的她流畅地拨了一个很长的号码。

"你睡了吗？我搅乱你的睡眠了吗？那是你

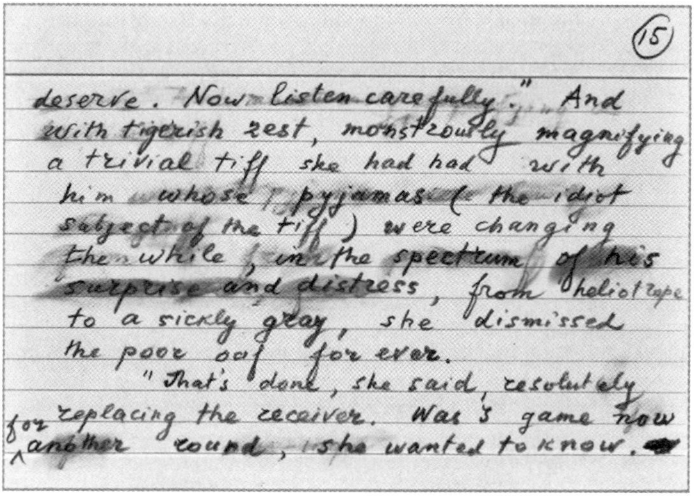

(15)

deserve. Now listen carefully." And with tigerish zest, monstrously magnifying a trivial tiff she had had with him whose pyjamas (the idiot subject of the tiff) were changing the while, in the spectrum of his surprise and distress, from heliotrope to a sickly gray, she dismissed the poor oaf for ever.

"That's done, she said, resolutely replacing the receiver. Was 's game now for another round, she wanted to know.

15

deserve. Now listen carefully." And with tigerish zest, monstrously magnifying a trivial tiff she had had with him whose pyjamas (the idiot subject of the tiff) were changing the while, in the spectrum of his surprise and distress, from heliotrope to a sickly gray, she dismissed the poor oaf for ever.

"That's done, ["] she said, resolutely replacing the receiver. Was I game now for another round, she wanted to know.

15

活该。现在给我仔细听好了。"她有如老虎发威，恶狠狠地放大着他们之间的一场小争执，其时，他的睡衣（这场争执的愚蠢主题），在他惊愕和痛苦的光谱中，由淡紫转为一种病态的灰色，她将这可怜的笨蛋永远地打发掉了。

"就这样吧。"她说着便果断地挂断了电话。她想知道，自己现在是不是该开始下一轮交战。

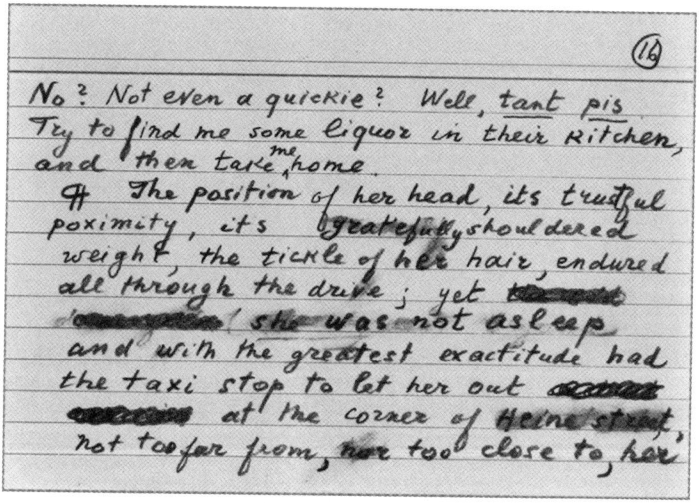

(16)

No? Not even a quickie? Well, tant pis
Try to find me some liquor in their kitchen,
and then take me home.
¶ The position of her head, its trustful
poximity, its ~~gratefully~~ shouldered
weight, the tickle of her hair, endured
all through the drive; yet [illegible]
[illegible] ~~she~~ was not asleep
and with the greatest exactitude had
the taxi stop to let her out [illegible]
[illegible] at the corner of ~~Heine street~~,
not too far from, ~~nor~~ too close to, her

16

No? Not even a quickie? Well, tant pis. Try to find me some liquor in their kitchen, and then take me home.

The position of her head, its trustful poximity, its gratefully shouldered weight, the tickle of her hair, endured all through the drive; yet she was not asleep and with the greatest exactitude had the taxi stop to let her out at the corner of Heine street, not too far from, nor too close to, her

16

不？连草草做个爱也不要吗？好吧，糟透了[①]。那到厨房给我倒点烈酒，然后送我回家吧。

驾车途中一路忍受着她脑袋的姿势，那带着信任的亲昵，肩负的令人愉快的重量，她令人发痒的头发；然而她并没有睡着，她准确无误地让出租车司机在海涅大街街角停靠，那儿离她的家既不太远，也不太近。

① 原文为法语。

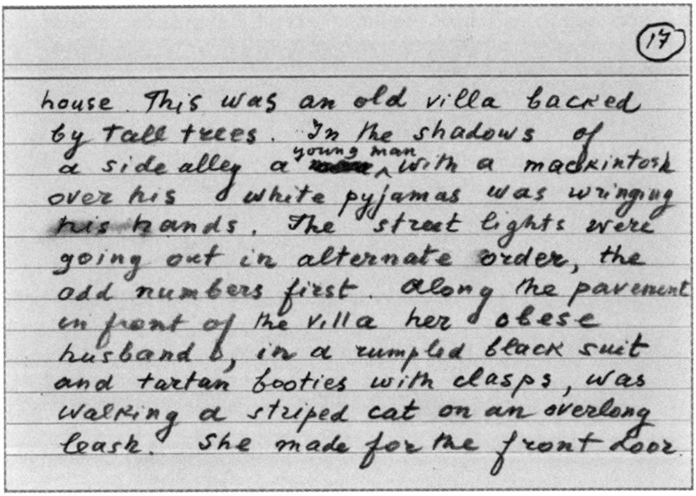

17

house. This was an old villa backed
by tall trees. In the shadows of
a side alley a ~~man~~ young man with a mackintosh
over his white pyjamas was wringing
his hands. The street lights were
going out in alternate order, the
odd numbers first. Along the pavement
in front of the villa her obese
husband, in a rumpled black suit
and tartan booties with clasps, was
walking a striped cat on an overlong
leash. She made for the front door

17

house. This was an old villa backed by tall trees. In the shadows of a side alley a young man with a mackintosh over his white pyjamas was wringing his hands. The street lights were going out in alternate order, the odd numbers first. Along the pavement in front of the villa her obese husband, in a rumpled black suit and tartan booties with clasps, was walking a striped cat on an overlong leash. She made for the front door.

17

这是一幢古老的乡间别墅，背后有茂密的参天大树。在一条僻静小巷的阴暗处，一位内穿白色睡衣、外披雨衣的年轻小伙子在不停地绞扭自己的双手。路灯交替着熄灭，奇数的在先。她肥胖的丈夫身穿一件皱巴巴的黑色西服，脚蹬一双带鞋襻的格子呢软鞋，牵着一根加长的皮带，沿着别墅前的便道在遛一只条纹猫。她朝前门走去。

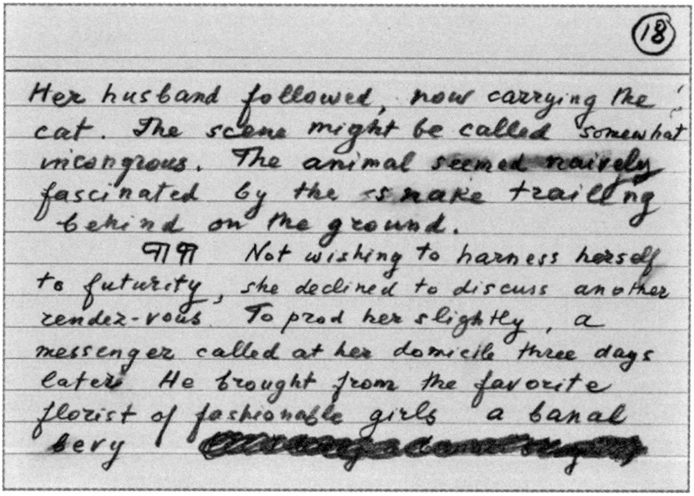

(18)

Her husband followed, now carrying the cat. The scene might be called somewhat incongruous. The animal ~~seemed naively~~ fascinated by the ~~s~~ snake trailing behind on the ground.

¶¶ Not wishing to harness herself to futurity, she declined to discuss another rendez-vous. To prod her slightly, a messenger called at her domicile three days later. He brought from the favorite florist of fashionable girls a banal bery ~~[illegible]~~

18

Her husband followed, now carrying the cat. The scene might be called somewhat incongr[u]ous. The animal seemed naively fascinated by the snake trailing behind on the ground.

Not wishing to harness herself to futurity, she declined to discuss another rendez-vous. To prod her slightly, a messenger called at her domicile three days later[.] He brought from the favorite florist of fashionable girls a banal bevy

18

她的丈夫紧随其后,这会儿他将猫抱在怀里。眼前的场景或许可以说有些不协调。这动物似乎天真地被他们身后的这条蛇迷住了。

她不希望自己将来受到约束,所以拒绝讨论下一次约会。三天后,一位信差拿着一大捆庸俗的天堂鸟来到她的住处,这是他从时髦女孩最喜欢的花店里买的,算是对她稍加提醒。

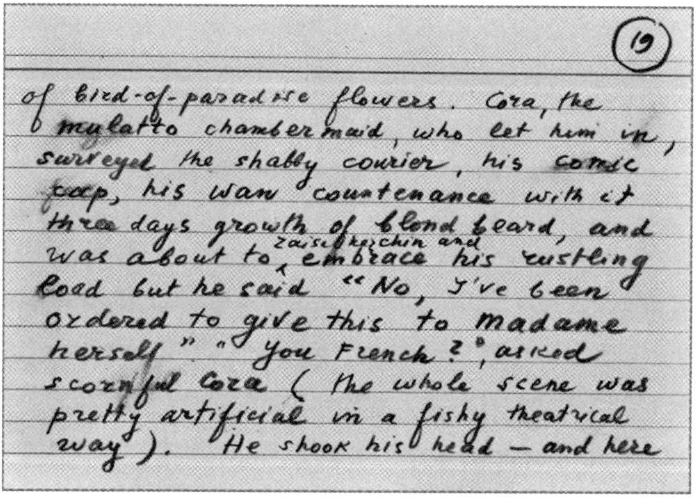

(19)

of bird-of-paradise flowers. Cora, the mulatto chambermaid, who let him in, surveyed the shabby courier, his comic cap, his wan countenance with its three days growth of blond beard, and was about to zaischerchin and embrace his rustling load but he said "No, I've been ordered to give this to madame herself". "You French?", asked scornful Cora (the whole scene was pretty artificial in a fishy theatrical way). He shook his head — and here

19

of bird-of-paradise flowers. Cora, the mulatto chambermaid, who let him in, surveyed the shabby courier, his comic cap, his wan countenance with it[s] three days growth of blond beard, and was about to raise her chin and embrace his rustling load but he said "No, I've been ordered to give this to Madame herself". "You French?" asked scornful Cora (the whole scene was pretty artificial in a fishy theatrical way). He shook his head—and here

19

女清洁工科拉是个黑白混血儿，她将他引进屋后，便从头到脚地打量这位衣衫褴褛的送花使者。他戴着一顶帽子，显得滑稽可笑，三天没有刮脸了，疲惫的脸上满是金色的胡须。女工正要抬起下巴，准备接过他手中那一大捆沙沙作响的鲜花，他却说："不，他们要求我必须把花送给太太[1]本人。""你是法国人？"科拉嘲弄地问道（整个场面有种可疑的戏剧化的氛围，显得相当造作）。他摇头否认——

① 原文为法语Madame，是对已婚妇人的尊称，故科拉后面会嘲弄地向他发问。

(20)

Madame appeared from the breakfast room. First of all she dismissed Cora with the strelitzias (hateful blooms, regalized bananas, really).

¶ "Look," she said to the beaming bum, "if you ever repeat this idiotic performance, I will never see you again. I swear I wont! In fact, I have a great mind —" He flattened her against the wall between his outstretched arms; Flora ducked, and freed herself, and showed him the door; but the telephone was already ringing [redacted] ecstatically when he reached his lodgings.

— · —

20

Madame appeared from the breakfast room. First of all she dismissed Cora with the strelitzias (hateful blooms, regalized bananas, really).

"Look," she said to the beaming bum, "if you ever repeat this idiotic performance, I will never see you again. I swear I won't! In fact, I have a great mind—" He flattened her against the wall between his outstretched arms; Flora ducked, and freed herself, and showed him the door; but the telephone was already ringing ecstatically when he reached his lodgings.

20

夫人吃完早餐从餐厅里走了出来。她首先让科拉拿走这些天堂鸟（让人生厌的花，真是华而不实的香蕉）。

"你给我听好了，"她对眼前这位满脸堆笑的乞丐说，"如果你再有这种白痴行径，我绝不会再见你。我发誓，绝不会再见你！实际上，我很想——"他把她夹紧在墙和他伸出的两只手臂间。弗洛拉猛然一低头，才挣脱出来，并赶他走。当他回到住处时，电话已在疯狂地响着。

Two (1)

Ch. Two

Her grandfather, the painter Lev Linde, emigrated in 1920 from Moscow to New York with his wife Eva and his son Adam. He also brought over a large collection of his landscapes, either unsold or loaned to him by kind friends and ~~ignorant institutions~~. ~~They~~ The pictures that were said to be the glory of Russia, ~~and~~ the pride of the people. How many times art albums had reproduced those meticulous masterpieces — clearings in pine woods, with a bear cub or two, and brown brooks between thawing snow-banks, and the vastness of ~~[illegible]~~ purple heaths!

Ch. Two

1

Her grandfather, the painter Lev Linde, emigrated in 1920 from Moscow to New York with his wife Eva and his son Adam. He also brought over a large collection of his landscapes, either unsold or loaned to him by kind friends and ignorant institutions—pictures that were said to be the glory of Russia, the pride of the people. How many times art albums had reproduced those meticulous masterpieces—clearings in pine woods, with a bear cub or two, and brown brooks between thawing snow-banks, and the vastness of purple heaths!

第二章

1

他的祖父列夫·林德是一位画家，一九二〇年他偕妻子艾娃和儿子亚当从莫斯科移民到纽约。他还带着收藏的大批风景画作，要么是没售出的，要么是一些好心的朋友和不懂行情的机构借给他的——这些画被称作俄国的光荣，是俄国人民的骄傲。艺术画册上曾多少次再现这些细节精美的杰作啊——松林中的片片空地上，一两只幼熊正在嬉戏；小溪两岸的积雪融化，棕色的溪流从中潺潺流过；还有一望无垠的紫色荒原！

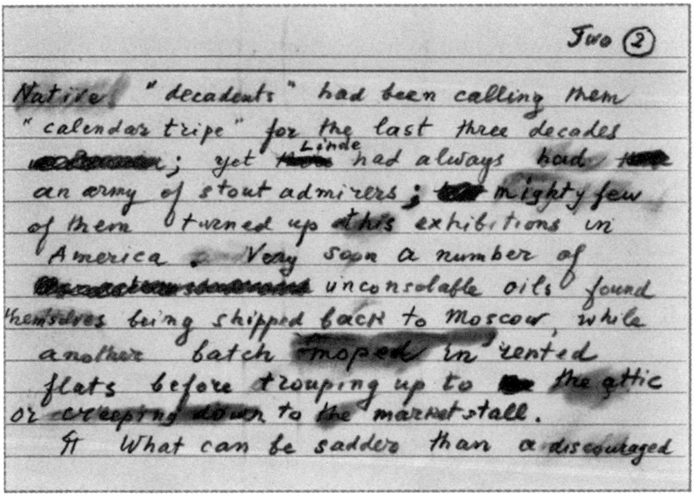
Two (2)

Native "decadents" had been calling them
"calendar tripe" for the last three decades
[illegible]; yet Linde had always had [illegible]
an army of stout admirers; [illegible] mighty few
of them turned up at his exhibitions in
America. Very soon a number of
[illegible] unconsolable oils found
themselves being shipped back to Moscow, while
another batch moped in rented
flats before trouping up to [illegible] the attic
or creeping down to the market stall.
¶ What can be sadder than a discouraged

2

Native "decadents" had been calling them "calendar tripe" for the last three decades; yet Linde had always had an army of stout admirers; mighty few of them turned up at his exhibitions in America. Very soon a number of unconsolable oils found themselves being shipped back to Moscow, while another batch moped in rented flats before trouping up to the attic or creeping down to the marketstall.

What can be sadder than a discouraged

2

在过去的三十多年里，尽管本国“颓废派艺术家”把它们称为“没有价值的挂历画”，林德还是拥有大批坚定不移的仰慕者。但在美国，前来为他的画展捧场的人却屈指可数。不久，一批极可悲的油画被运回了莫斯科，另一些则忧郁地游荡于租来的公寓里，等着在阁楼上展出，或是被偷偷运到集市上贱卖掉。

还有什么比一个失意的

Two (3)

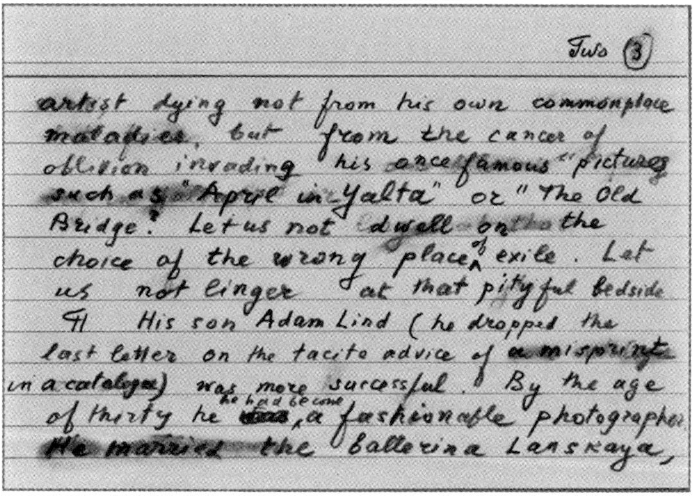
artist dying not from his own commonplace
maladies, but from the cancer of
oblivion invading his once famous "pictures
such as "April in Yalta" or "The Old
Bridge". Let us not dwell on the
choice of the wrong place of exile. Let
us not linger at that pityful bedside
¶ His son Adam Lind (he dropped the
last letter on the tacit advice of a misprint
in a catalogue) was more successful. By the age
of thirty he ~~was~~ had become a fashionable photographer.
He married the ballerina Lanskaya,

3

artist dying not from his own commonplace maladies, but from the cancer of oblivion invading his once famous pictures such as "April in Yalta" or "The Old Bridge["]? Let us not dwell on the choice of the wrong place of exile. Let us not linger at that pity-ful bedside.

His son Adam Lind (he dropped the last letter on the tacite advice of a misprint in a catalogue) was more successful. By the age of thirty he had become a fashionable photographer. He married the ballerina Lanskaya,

3

艺术家不是死于平常的疾病，而是死于他曾经名噪一时的作品被遗忘的癌症侵袭更令人悲伤的事呢？例如《雅尔塔的四月》或《古桥》。我们别再唠叨他选错了流亡地点，也不要在他那凄凉的床边徘徊停留了。

他的儿子亚当·林德比他成功（他受一本目录上印刷错误的启发，心照不宣地漏掉了姓里的最后一个字母）。三十岁时他成为一名时尚摄影师，娶了芭蕾舞演员兰斯卡雅，

Two (4)

a delightful dancer, ~~though with~~ something fragile and gauche about her that kept her teetering on a narrow ledge between benevolent recognition and the rave reviews ~~[illegible]~~ of nonentities. ~~Her first~~ lovers ~~belonged mostly~~ to the Union of Property Movers, ~~[illegible]~~ simple fellows of Polish extraction; but Flora was probably ~~[illegible]~~ Adam's daughter. Three years after her birth Adam discovered that the boy ~~he loved~~ had strangled ~~[illegible]~~ another, unattainable, boy

4

a delightful dancer, though with something fragile and gauche about her that kept her teetering on a narrow ledge between benevolent recognition and the rave reviews of nonentities. Her first lovers belonged mostly to the Union of Property Movers, simple fellows of Polish extraction; but Flora was probably Adam's daughter. Three years after her birth Adam discovered that the boy he loved had strangled another, unattainable, boy

4

一个可爱的舞者，尽管感情有些脆弱，处事也不够老练，这令她在架于善意的认可与小人物的热捧之间的狭窄平台上摇摇欲坠。她的第一批情人大多属于“财产搬运工联盟”，都是淳朴的波兰裔小伙；但弗洛拉有可能是亚当的女儿。弗洛拉出生三年后，亚当才发现自己爱恋的小伙子掐死了另一个他没有得到、

Two (5)

whom he loved even more. Adam Lind had always had an inclination for trick photography and this time, before shooting himself in a Montecarlo hotel (on the night, sad to relate, of his wife's very real success in Piker's "Narcisse et Narcette"), he geared and focussed his camera in a corner of the drawing room so as to record the event from different angles. These automatic pictures of his last moments and of a table's lion-paws did not come out to well; but his widow

5

whom he loved even more. Adam Lind had always had an inclination for trick photography and this time, before shooting himself in a Montecarlo hotel (on the night, sad to relate, of his wife's very real success in Piker's "Narcisse et Narcette"), he geared and focussed his camera in a corner of the drawing room so as to record the event from different angles. These automatic pictures of his last moments and of a table's lion-paws did not come out to[o] well; but his widow

5

却爱得更深的男孩。亚当·林德向来偏好特技摄影，这次在蒙特卡罗的一家旅馆开枪自杀之前（说起来令人伤感，那天晚上恰逢他妻子表演的派克的《那喀索斯与那喀塞特》[①]大获成功），他在客厅的一个角落安置好照相机，调好焦距，以便从不同的角度来记录这一事件。他自动拍摄的人生的最后镜头以及餐桌狮爪脚的效果并不太好；可他的遗孀

① 原文为法语。那喀索斯为希腊神话中的俊美少年，因迷恋自己在湖中的倒影而憔悴至死。之后湖畔的草丛中长出了娇黄的水仙花。故在希腊词中，此词还有水仙花、自恋者之意。那喀塞特则是与那喀索斯对应的女性人名。

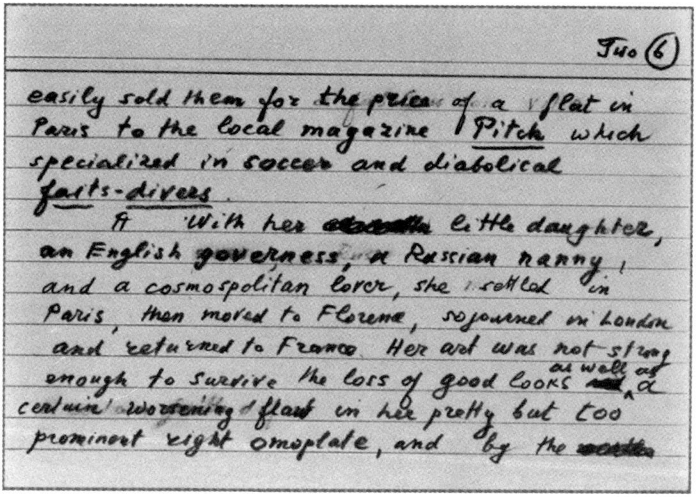
Two (6)

easily sold them for the price of a flat in
Paris to the local magazine *Pitch* which
specialized in soccer and diabolical
faits-divers.

¶ With her little daughter,
an English governess, a Russian nanny,
and a cosmopolitan lover, she settled in
Paris, then moved to Florence, sojourned in London
and returned to France. Her art was not strong
enough to survive the loss of good looks as well as a
certain worsening flaw in her pretty but too
prominent right omoplate, and by the

easily sold them for the price of a flat in Paris to the local magazine Pitch which specialized in soccer and diabolical faits-divers.

With her little daughter, an English governess, a Russian nanny, and a cosmospolitan lover, she settled in Paris, then moved to Florence, sojourned in London and returned to France. Her art was not strong enough to survive the loss of good looks as well as a certain worsening flaw in her pretty but too prominent right omoplate, and by the

轻而易举地将这些照片卖给当地一家名为“音调”的杂志，该刊物专门报道足球和骇人听闻的社会新闻[①]，交易所得够在巴黎买一套公寓。

她带着自己的小女儿、一位英语女家庭教师、一位俄国保姆，还有一个四海为家的情人，先在巴黎安顿下来，随后搬到了佛罗伦萨，在伦敦小住一段时间后，又回到法国。她的舞蹈艺术无法抵御美貌消逝的损耗，同时，她那虽然漂亮却过于突出的右肩胛骨也每况愈下，

① 原文为法语。

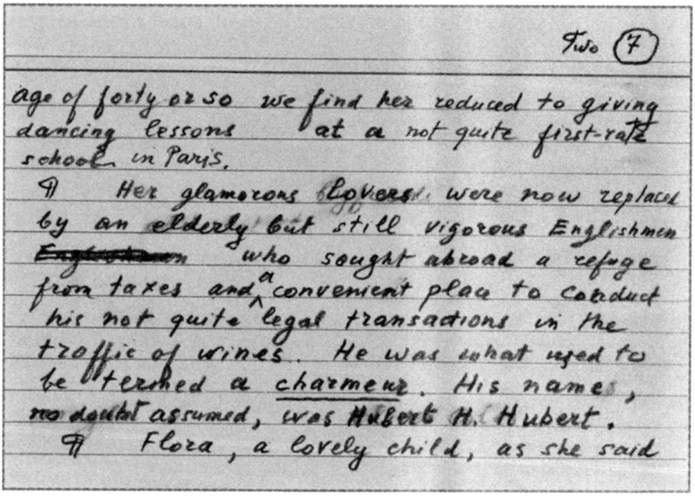

Two (7)

age of forty or so we find her reduced to giving
dancing lessons at a not quite first-rate
school in Paris.
¶ Her glamorous lovers were now replaced
by an elderly but still vigorous Englishmen
~~Englishman~~ who sought abroad a refuge
from taxes and a convenient place to conduct
his not quite legal transactions in the
traffic of wines. He was what used to
be termed a charmeur. His name,
no doubt assumed, was Hubert H. Hubert.
¶ Flora, a lovely child, as she said

7

age of forty or so we find her reduced to giving dancing lessons at a not quite first-rate school in Paris.

Her glamorous lovers were now replaced by an elderly but still vigorous Englishm[a]n who sought abroad a refuge from taxes and a convenient place to conduct his not quite legal transactions in the traffic of wines. He was what used to be termed a charmeur. His name, no doubt assumed, was Hubert H. Hubert.

Flora, a lovely child, as she said

7

在四十岁左右时，我们发现她已沦落到去巴黎一所算不上一流的学校教授舞蹈课程。

一位上了年纪、精力却还算旺盛的英国男人则取代了她以前那些风流倜傥的情人们。此人旅居巴黎是为了寻求一个既有利于避税，又便于从事一些不那么合法的红酒交易的处所。他就是过去人们口中的一个有诱惑力的人[1]。毋庸置疑，他的姓名叫休伯特·赫·休伯特。[2]

弗洛拉是个可爱的孩子，每次谈及

① 原文为法语。

② 休伯特·赫·休伯特（Hubert H. Hubert）的拼写与《洛丽塔》中的男主人公亨伯特·亨伯特（Humbert Humbert）的名字相似。

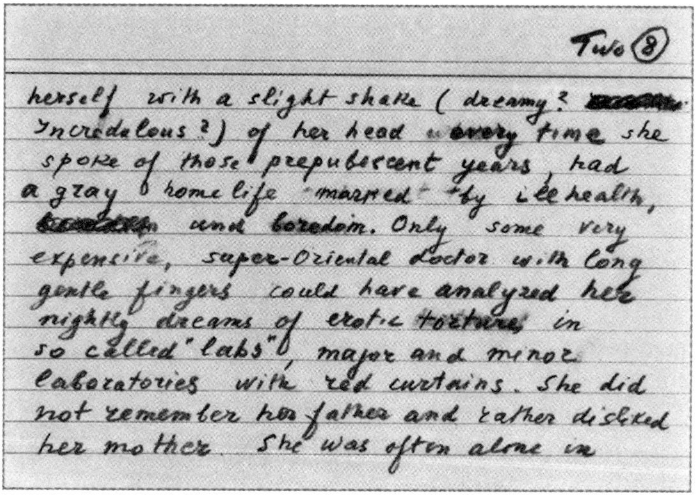

Two (8)

herself with a slight shake (dreamy? ~~[illegible]~~
Incredulous?) of her head ~~every~~ time she
spoke of those prepubescent years, had
a gray home life marred by ill health,
~~[illegible]~~ and boredom. Only some very
expensive, super-Oriental doctor with long
gentle fingers could have analyzed her
nightly dreams of erotic torture in
so called "labs", major and minor
laboratories with red curtains. She did
not remember her father and rather disliked
her mother. She was often alone in

8

herself with a slight shake (dreamy? Incredulous?) of her head every time she spoke of those prepubescent years, had a gray home life marked by ill health, and boredom. Only some very expensive, super-oriental doctor with long gentle fingers could have analyzed her nightly dreams of erotic torture in so called “labs”, major and minor laboratories with red curtains. She did not remember her father and rather disliked her mother. She was often alone in

8

那些青春期前的岁月——那段带着疾病与厌倦烙印的家庭生活——时，她总是（梦幻般？怀疑地？）轻轻摇着头。或许只有某些收费昂贵、手指温润修长、极具东方气质的医生，才能在所谓的“实验室”——挂着红色窗帘的重点或非重点实验室——里，分析她夜间做的那些性虐待的梦。她记不得自己的父亲了，更是讨厌她的母亲。她常常独自

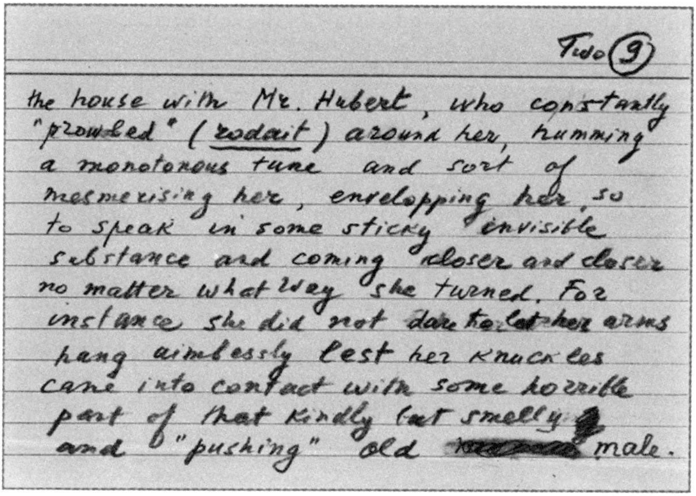
Two (9)

the house with Mr. Hubert, who constantly "prowled" (rodait) around her, humming a monotonous tune and sort of mesmerising her, enveloping her, so to speak in some sticky invisible substance and coming closer and closer no matter what way she turned. For instance she did not dare to let her arms hang aimlessly lest her knuckles came into contact with some horrible part of that kindly but smelly and "pushing" old male.

9

the house with Mr. Hubert, who constantly "prowled" (rodait) around her, humming a monotonous tune and sort of mesmerising her, envelopping her, so to speak in some sticky invisible substance and coming closer and closer no matter what way she turned. For instance she did not dare to let her arms hang aimlessly lest her knuckles came into contact with some horrible part of that kindly but smelly and "pushing" old male.

9

与休伯特先生待在屋子里,休伯特总在她身边“转悠”(rodait①),嘴里哼着单调的曲子,多多少少有些迷惑着她,可以说用某种黏糊的无形物质越来越紧地围困住她,让她无论转向哪边都躲避不开。比如,她不敢让自己的胳膊随意晃动,生怕自己的指关节会触碰到这位和蔼但却臭烘烘且“咄咄逼人”的老男人身上某个可怕部位。

① 法语rôder的第三人称未完成式,意为“不怀好意地转来转去”。

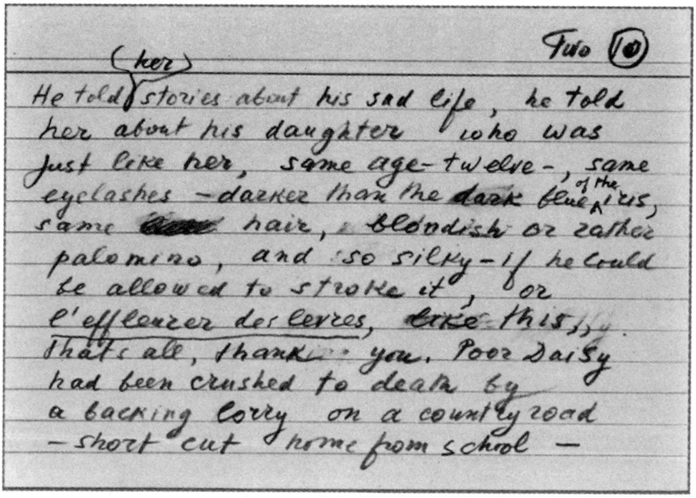

Two (10)

He told (her) stories about his sad life, he told
her about his daughter who was
just like her, same age—twelve—, same
eyelashes—darker than the ~~dark~~ blue of the iris,
same ~~[illegible]~~ hair, ~~b~~ blondish or rather
palomino, and so silky—if he could
be allowed to stroke it, or
l'effleurer des lèvres, ~~like~~ this, ~~by~~.
That's all, thank you. Poor Daisy
had been crushed to death by
a backing lorry on a country road
—short cut home from school—

10

He told her stories about his sad life, he told her about his daughter who was just like her, same age—twelve—, same eyelashes—darker than the dark blue of the iris, same hair, blondish or rather palomino, and so silky—if he could be allowed to stroke it, or l'effleurer des levres, like this, thats all, thank you. Poor Daisy had been crushed to death by a backing lorry on a country road—short cut home from school—

10

他向她讲述自己可悲的人生，说起他那个像她一样的女儿，同样的年纪——都是十二岁，同样的比深蓝色鸢尾花更蓝的眼睫毛，同样黄棕色或者说如帕洛米诺马般淡褐色光滑如丝的头发——假如能允许他抚摸一下它，或是用嘴唇轻吻一下[①]，像这样，这就足够了，谢谢。可怜的黛西是在穿越泥泞的建筑工地的乡间小路时被一辆倒车的卡车碾死的——那条路是由学校回家的捷径——

① 原文为法语。

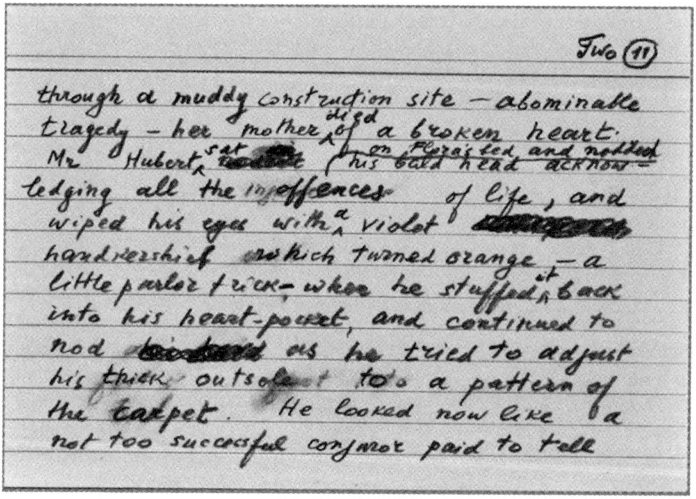

Two (11)

through a muddy construction site — abominable
tragedy — her mother died of a broken heart.
Mr Hubert sat on Flora's bed, and nodded his bald head acknow-
ledging all the offences of life, and
wiped his eyes with a violet
handkerchief which turned orange — a
little parlor trick — when he stuffed it back
into his heart-pocket, and continued to
nod as he tried to adjust
his thick outsole to a pattern of
the carpet. He looked now like a
not too successful conjuror paid to tell

11

through a muddy construction site—abominable tragedy—her mother died of a broken heart. Mr Hubert sat on Flora's bed and nodded his bald head acknowledging all the offences of life, and wiped his eyes with a violet handkerchief which turned orange—a little parlor trick—when he stuffed it back into his heart-pocket, and continued to nod as he tried to adjust his thick outsole to a pattern of the carpet. He looked now like a not too successful conjuror paid to tell

11

真是惨绝人寰的悲剧——她母亲因伤心过度而死去。休伯特先生坐在弗洛拉的床上，他那光秃秃的脑袋点了点，承认自己一生所犯的所有过错，并用一条紫色的手帕擦了擦眼睛，手帕被他塞回心形口袋时变成了橙色——不过是客厅小戏法，他在根据地毯上的图案调整自己厚厚的鞋底位置时继续点着头，此刻，他看起来就像一位不太高明的魔术师，被雇来

Two (12)

fairytales to a sleepy child at bedtime, but
he sat a little too close. Flora wore a
nightgown with short sleeves copied from
that of the Montglas de Sancerre girl,
~~[illegible]~~ a very ~~sweet and~~
depraved schoolmate, who
taught her where to kick an enterprising
gentleman.

A week or so later Flora happened
to be laid up with a chest cold. The mercury
went up to 38° in the late afternoon
and she complained of a dull buzz

12

fairytales to a sleepy child at bedtime, but he sat a little too close. Flora wore a nightgown with short sleeves copied from that of the Montglas de Sancerre girl, a very sweet and depraved schoolmate, who taught her where to kick an enterprising gentleman.

A week or so later Flora happened to be laid up with a chest cold. The mercury went up to 38° in the late afternoon and she complained of a dull buzz

12

给一个犯困的孩子讲睡前童话故事，只是他坐得太近了些。弗洛拉模仿一位桑塞尔市的蒙哥拉斯姑娘的打扮，身穿一件短袖睡袍。那姑娘是她的一个非常可爱但家境贫寒的同学。她教过弗洛拉该踢一位过分大胆的绅士哪个部位。

大约一周后的一天，弗洛拉胸口发凉，卧病在床。傍晚时水银体温计显示为三十八摄氏度，她抱怨说两边太阳穴隐约发出了嗡嗡声。

Two (13)

in the temples. Mrs Lind cursed the old
housemaid for buying asparagus instead
of Asperin and hurried to the pharmacy
herself. Mr Hubert had brought his
pet a thoughtful present: a miniature
chess set ("she knew the moves") with
tickly-looking little holes bored in the squares
to admit and grip the red and white
pieces; the pin-sized pawns penetrated
easily, but the slightly larger noblemen
had to be forced in with an enervating
joggle. The pharmacy was perhaps closer

13

in the temples. Mrs Lind cursed the old housemaid for buying asparagus instead of Asp[i]rin and hurried to the pharmacy herself. Mr Hubert had brought his pet a thoughtful present: a miniature chess set (“she knew the moves”) with tickly-looking little holes bored in the squares to admit and grip the red and white pieces; the pin-sized pawns penetrated easily, but the slightly larger noblemen had to be forced in with an ennervating joggle. The pharmacy was perhaps closed

13

林德太太责骂上了年纪的女仆买回来的是芦笋，而不是阿司匹林，[1] 自己匆忙去了药店。休伯特先生颇费心思地给自己宠爱的女孩买了件礼物：一副微型国际象棋（“她懂走棋”），棋盘上有很多看着令人发痒的小孔，红白棋子可以插入这些小孔，并被卡住。大头针般大小的卒子能轻易地从中穿过，而体型稍大一点的贵族棋则需要轻轻晃动一下才能塞进去。药店大概关门了，

---

① 在英文中，asparagus（芦笋）与Aspirin（阿司匹林）发音接近，故这里有可能是女佣听错。

Two (14)

and ~~she~~ had to go to the one ~~next to the church~~
or else she had met some friend of hers
in the street and would never return. A
fourfold smell — tobacco, sweat, rum
and bad teeth — emanated from poor
old harmless Mr Hubert, it was
all very pathetic. His fat porous nose with
red nostrils full of hair nearly touched her
bare throat as he helped to prop the
pillows behind her shoulders, and the muddy road
was again, was for ever a short cut between
here and school, between school and death,

14

and she had to go to the one next to the church or else she had met some friend of hers in the street and would never return. A fourfold smell—tobacco, sweat, rum and bad teeth—emanated from poor old harmless Mr Hubert, it was all very pathetic. His fat porous nose with red nostrils full of hair nearly touched her bare throat as he helped to prop the pillows behind her shoulders, and the muddy road was again, was for ever a short cut between her and school, between school and death,

14

她只得去了教堂旁边的那家药店，要么就是在大街上遇到了她昔日的朋友，再也不会回来。一种混合着烟草、汗渍、朗姆酒，还有坏牙的腥臭这四种味道的气息，从可怜而又无害的老休伯特身上散发出来，这一切太可悲了。他肥大的鼻子上满是粗大的汗毛孔，红红的鼻孔里长满鼻毛，在为她支起背后的枕头时，他的鼻子几乎都要碰到了她裸露的前颈了；泥泞小路又出现了，它永远是一条捷径，在她与学校之间、学校与死亡之间，

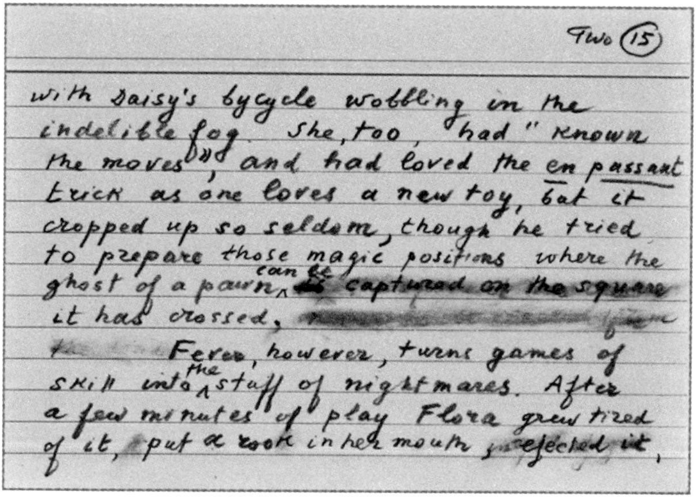
Two (15)

with Daisy's bycycle wobbling in the
indelible fog. She, too, had "known
the moves", and had loved the *en passant*
trick as one loves a new toy, but it
cropped up so seldom, though he tried
to prepare those magic positions where the
ghost of a pawn can be captured on the square
it has crossed, [illegible]
[illegible] Fever, however, turns games of
skill into the stuff of nightmares. After
a few minutes of play Flora grew tired
of it, put a rook in her mouth, ejected it,

15

with Daisy's bycycle wobbling in the indelible fog. She, too, had "known the moves", and had loved the en passant trick as one loves a new toy, but it cropped up so seldom, though he tried to prepare those magic positions where the ghost of a pawn can be captured on the square it has crossed.

Fever, however, turns games of skill into the stuff of nightmares. After a few minutes of play Flora grew tired of it, put a rook in her mouth, ejected it,

15

黛西那辆摇晃着的自行车也定格在一片无法抹去的浓雾中。弗洛拉也"懂得走棋"，曾经像喜欢一个新玩具一样对"巧行将吃"[①]这一招着迷不已，却很少有机会能使出来，尽管他努力布好局，好让那神出鬼没的卒子一越过方格便被吃掉。

然而，高烧却把这种凭借技巧取胜的游戏变成了一场噩梦。玩了几分钟后，弗洛拉就厌倦了，拿起一枚车放进嘴里又吐了出来，

① 原文为法语。

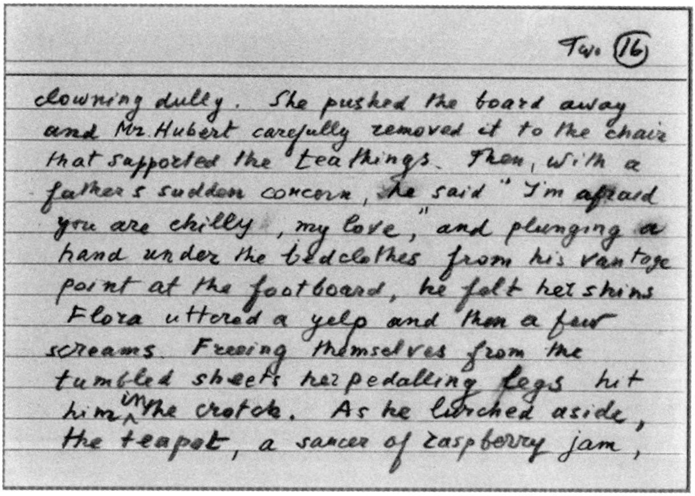
Two (16)

clowning dully. She pushed the board away
and Mr. Hubert carefully removed it to the chair
that supported the tea things. Then, with a
father's sudden concern, he said "I'm afraid
you are chilly, my love," and plunging a
hand under the bedclothes from his vantage
point at the footboard, he felt her shins.
Flora uttered a yelp and then a few
screams. Freeing themselves from the
tumbled sheets her pedalling legs hit
him in the crotch. As he lurched aside,
the teapot, a saucer of raspberry jam,

16

clowning dully. She pushed the board away and Mr. Hubert carefully removed it to the chair that supported the tea things. Then, with a father's sudden concern, he said "I'm afraid you are chilly, my love," and plunging a hand under the bedclothes from his vantage point at the footboard, he felt her shins[.] Flora uttered a yelp and then a few screams. Freeing themselves from the tumbled sheets her pedalling legs hit him in the crotch. As he lurched aside, the teapot, a saucer of raspberry jam,

16

没精打采地耍着宝。她把棋盘推开，休伯特先生小心翼翼地将它移到放茶具的椅子上。然后，他突然带着父亲般的关心说"宝贝，我担心你会冷"，就势从他所在的床尾板这个有利位置将一只手伸进被窝，摸到了她的小腿。弗洛拉大喊一声，接着又是几声尖叫，双腿挣扎着掀掉被单时一脚踢中了他的命根子。他身子一斜，茶壶、一碟覆盆子酱，

Two (17)

an several tiny chessmen joined in the silly
fray. Mrs Lind who had just returned and
was sampling some grapes she had bought,
heard the screams and the crash and
arrived at a dancer's run. She soothed
the absolutely furious, deeply insulted
Mr Hubert before scolding her daughter.
He was a dear man, and his life lay
in ruins all around him. He wanted
to marry him, saying she was the image
of the young actress who had been his wife,
and indeed to judge by the photographs

17

an[d] several tiny chessmen joined in the silly fray. Mrs Lind who had just returned and was sampling some grapes she had bought, heard the screams and the crash and arrived at a dancer's run. She soothed the absolutely furious, deeply insulted Mr Hubert before scolding her daughter. He was a dear man, and his life lay in ruins all around him. He wanted [her] to marry him, saying she was the image of the young actress who had been his wife, and indeed to judge by the photographs

17

还有几个小棋子也加入了这场可笑的打斗。林德太太刚回到家，正在品尝她买回来的葡萄，听到嘶叫声和哐啷声，她迈着舞蹈演员的步子跑了过来。她先是安慰了一番着实气坏了、也深感被侮辱的休伯特先生，然后斥责了女儿。他是个仁慈的男人，但他的生活已如同一片废墟。他想娶她为妻，因为她酷似他从前的妻子，一位年轻的女演员，而从照片上看，

she, madame Lanskaya, did resemble
poor Daisy's mother.
¶ There is little to add about the
incidental, but not unattractive
Mr Hubert H. Hubert. He lodged for another
happy year in that cosy house and
died of a stroke in a hotel lift
after a business dinner. Going up,
one would like to surmise.

—·—

18

she, Madame Lanskaya, did ressemble poor Daisy's mother.

There is little to add about the incidental, but not unattractive Mr Hubert H. Hubert. He lodged for another happy year in that cosy house and died of a stroke in a hotel lift after a business dinner. Going up, one would like to surmise.

18

兰斯卡雅夫人的确很像黛西那可怜的母亲。

对那位次要的、无趣的休伯特·赫·休伯特先生没什么可补充的了。他在那所舒适的房子里又快乐地寄居了一年，一次商务晚宴结束后，突然在酒店电梯里中风死去。死于电梯上行时，人们会这样猜测。

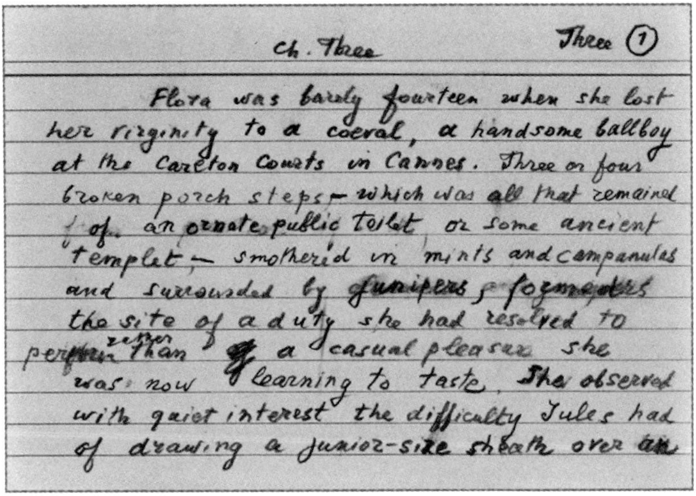

Ch. Three

Three (1)

Flora was barely fourteen when she lost her virginity to a coeval, a handsome ballboy at the Carleton Courts in Cannes. Three or four broken porch steps—which was all that remained of an ornate public toilet or some ancient templet—smothered in mints and campanulas and surrounded by junipers, the site of a duty she had resolved to perform rather than a casual pleasure she was now learning to taste. She observed with quiet interest the difficulty Jules had of drawing a junior-size sheath over an

Ch. Three

1

Flora was barely fourteen when she lost her virginity to a coeval, a handsome ballboy at the Carlton Courts in Cannes. Three or four broken porch steps—which was all that remained of an ornate public toilet or some ancient templet—smothered in mints and campanulas and surrounded by junipers, formed the site of a duty she had resolved to perform rather than a casual pleasure she was now learning to taste. She observed with quiet interest the difficulty Jules had of drawing a junior-size sheath over an

第三章

1

弗洛拉把童贞给了戛纳卡尔顿球场一个英俊的同龄球童，当时她年仅十四岁。三四级破损的门廊台阶——是一间华丽的公共厕所，或是一些古老垫木仅存的部分——笼罩在浓郁的薄荷与风铃草的气味之中，四周被刺柏环绕，这就是她决定要尽职而不是学着偷欢的场所。她饶有兴致地看着朱尔艰难地在自己的

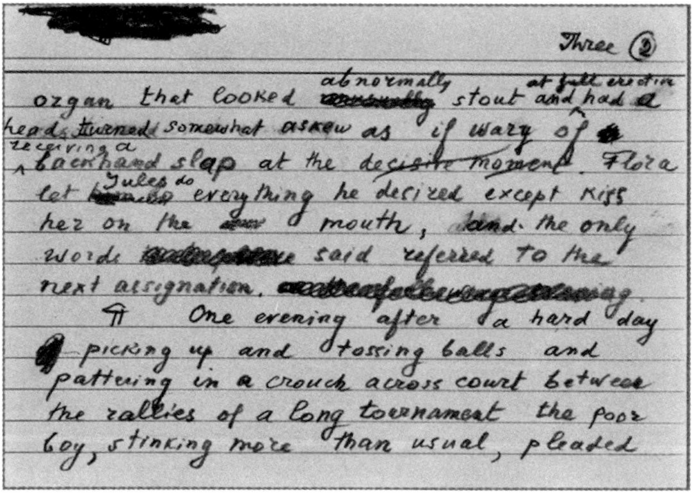

Three (2)

organ that looked abnormally stout at full erection and had a head, somewhat askew as if wary of receiving a backhand slap at the decisive moment. Flora let Jules do everything he desired except kiss her on the mouth, the only words said referred to the next assignation.

¶ One evening after a hard day picking up and tossing balls and pattering in a crouch across court between the rallies of a long tournament the poor boy, stinking more than usual, pleaded

2

organ that looked abnormally stout and at full erection had a head turned somewhat askew as if wary of receiving a backhand slap at the decisive moment. Flora let Jules do everything he desired except kiss her on the mouth, and the only words said referred to the next assignation.

One evening after a hard day picking up and tossing balls and pattering in a crouch across court between the rallies of a long tournament the poor boy, stinking more than usual, pleaded

2

生殖器上套一只小号的避孕套，这个完全勃起的阳物不同寻常地粗壮，龟头略偏向一边，仿佛在防备着关键时刻被反手一击。弗洛拉满足朱尔提出的所有要求，只不同意他亲吻她的嘴唇，他俩唯一说的话是关于下次的幽会。

有一次，朱尔经历了一场时间超长的比赛，因为一整天不停地捡球、投球，并在连续对打的球场上弯着腰急促地跑来跑去，可怜的男孩那天晚上散发着甚于平常的汗臭，

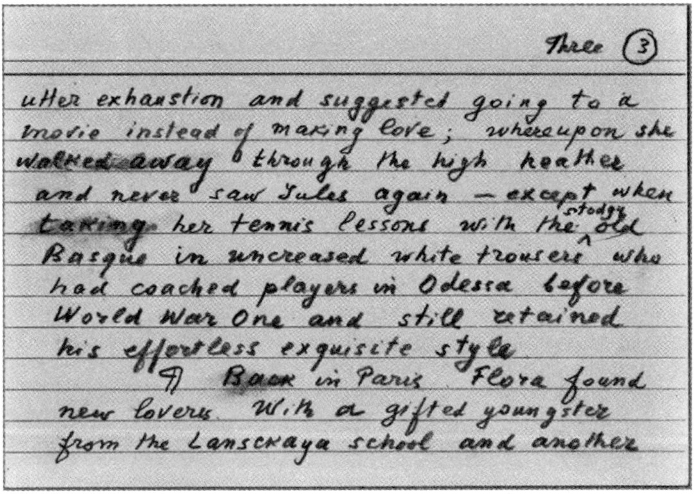

Three ③

utter exhaustion and suggested going to a movie instead of making love; whereupon she walked away through the high heather and never saw Jules again — except when taking her tennis lessons with the stodgy old Basque in uncreased white trousers who had coached players in Odessa before World War One and still retained his effortless exquisite style.

¶ Back in Paris Flora found new lovers. With a gifted youngster from the Lanskaya school and another

3

utter exhaustion and suggested going to a movie instead of making love; whereupon she walked away through the high heather and never saw Jules again—except when taking her tennis lessons with the stodgy old Basque in uncreased white trousers who had coached players in Odessa before World War One and still retained his effortless exquisite style.

Back in Paris[,] Flora found new lovers. With a gifted youngster from the [Lanskaya] school and another

3

他承认自己精疲力竭，建议那天他俩不做爱，改去看电影，于是她穿过高高的石南树丛走开了，后来再没见过他——除了在网球课上之外，给她上网球课的是一位古板的老巴斯克人[1]，穿着一条笔挺的白色裤子。一战前，他曾在敖德萨[2]当过网球教练，至今仍然保持着那种轻松而讲究的派头。

一回到巴黎，弗洛拉就有了新情人，其中一个是兰斯卡雅学院里的多才多艺的年轻人，以及一对

① 西南欧民族，分布在西班牙，法国及拉丁美洲各国。

② 乌克兰南部城市。

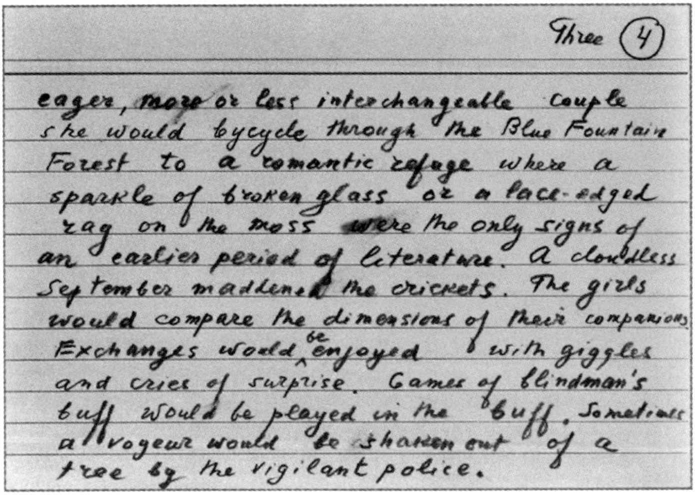
Three (4)

eager, more or less interchangeable couple
she would bycycle through the Blue Fountain
Forest to a romantic refuge where a
sparkle of broken glass or a lace-edged
rag on the moss were the only signs of
an earlier period of literature. A cloudless
September maddened the crickets. The girls
would compare the dimensions of their companions
Exchanges would be enjoyed with giggles
and cries of surprise. Games of blindman's
buff would be played in the buff. Sometimes
a voyeur would be shaken out of a
tree by the vigilant police.

4

eager, more or less interchangeable couple she would bycycle through the Blue Fountain Forest to a romantic refuge where a sparkle of broken glass or a lace-edged rag on the moss were the only signs of an earlier period of literature. A cloudless September maddened the crickets. The girls would compare the dimensions of their companions. Exchanges would be enjoyed with giggles and cries of surprise. Games of blindman's buff would be played in the buff. Sometimes a voyeur would be shaken out of a tree by the vigilant police.

4

迫切的、多少可以互换的情侣，她会骑着自行车穿过“清溪森林”，来到一个充满浪漫气息的庇护所，一块闪闪发光的玻璃碎片或青苔上一小块蕾丝花边碎布，是早期文学仅存的痕迹。九月的天空一碧如洗，蟋蟀发狂般地嘶鸣，姑娘们相互比较着各自伴侣的尺寸。交换的过程伴有阵阵窃笑和惊呼，想必十分愉快。捉迷藏的游戏得一丝不挂地玩，藏在树上的偷窥狂有时会被警觉的警察摇下来。

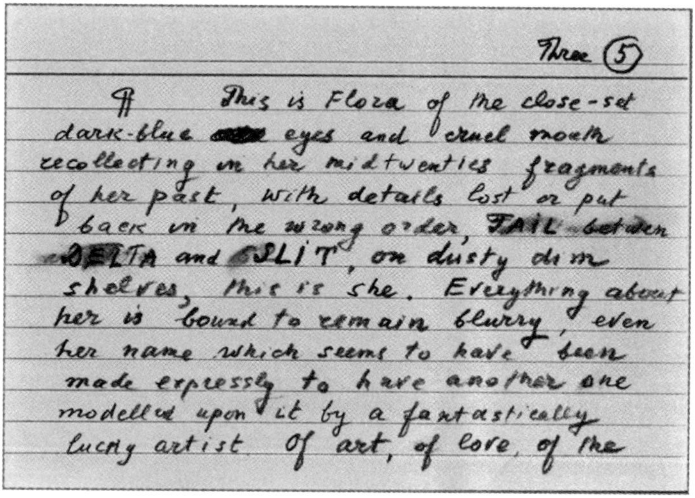

Three (5)

¶ This is Flora of the close-set
dark-blue [redacted] eyes and cruel mouth
recollecting in her midtwenties fragments
of her past, with details lost or put
back in the wrong order, FAIL between
DELTA and SLIT, on dusty dim
shelves, this is she. Everything about
her is bound to remain blurry, even
her name which seems to have been
made expressly to have another one
modelled upon it by a fantastically
lucky artist. Of art, of love, of the

5

This is Flora of the close-set dark-blue eyes and cruel mouth recollecting in her midtwenties fragments of her past, with details lost or put back in the wrong order, TAIL betwe[e]n DELTA and SLIT, on dusty dim shelves, this is she. Everything about her is bound to remain blurry, even her name which seems to have been made expressly to have another one modelled upon it by a fantastically lucky artist. Of art, of love, of the

5

这就是弗洛拉，两只深蓝色的眼睛紧挨着，嘴显得有些冷峻，在自己二十几岁时回忆着零星往事，有的细节丢失了，还有些细节顺序颠三倒四。那些鸡零狗碎的男女苟合，[1]在落满灰尘的昏暗书架上，这就是她。有关她的一切注定都是扑朔迷离的，就连她的名字也不例外，似乎有个极为幸运的艺术家明显地效仿了她。

① 原文是“TAIL betwe[e]n DELTA and SLIT”，若直译，则为“三角区与裂缝之间的尾巴”，译者采用了意译。参看第二〇七页的注释。

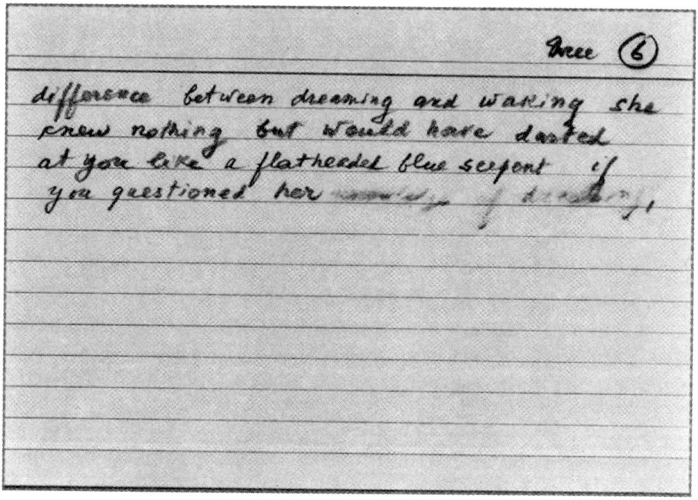
Three ⑥

difference between dreaming and waking she
knew nothing but would have darted
at you like a flatheaded blue serpent if
you questioned her [illegible],

6

difference between dreaming and waking she knew nothing but would have darted at you like a flatheaded blue serpent if you questioned her.

6

对艺术，对爱，对梦与醒之间的差别，她都一无所知，但假如你质疑她，她会像一条蓝色扁头毒蛇一样扎向你。

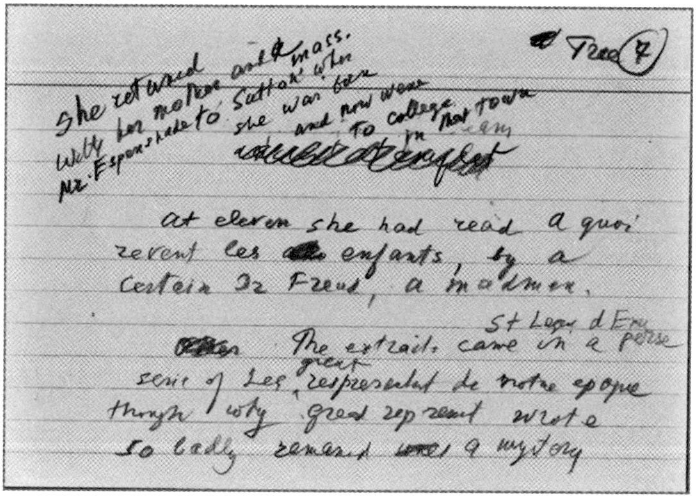

Tree (7)

She returned with her mother and to Mr. Esposhade to Sutton, Mass. where she was born and now were to college in that town

at eleven she had read A quoi revent les enfants, by a certain Dr Freud, a madman.

St Leger d Exu

The extraits came in a perse serie of Les great representant de notre epoque though why great represent wrote so badly remained a mystery

7

She returned with her mother and Mr. Espenshade to Sutton, Mass. where she was born and now went to college in that town.

At eleven she had read A quoi revent les enfants, by a certain Dr Freud, a madman.

The extracts came in a St Leger d'Exuperse series of Les great representant de notre epoque though why great represent [atives] wrote so badly remained a mystery

7

她随母亲和埃斯本谢德先生一道回到了马萨诸塞的萨顿，这是她的出生地，眼下她已在此地念大学。

十一岁时，她曾读过一本名为《什么是孩子的梦境》的书，作者是一个叫弗洛伊德的疯子医生。①

该书的摘要发表于由圣·里格公司出版的系列丛书“我们时代的伟大代表作”②，尽管为什么伟大代表作却写得如此糟糕这一问题依然是个谜。

① 《什么是孩子的梦境》（*A quoi rêvent les enfants*）的作者应为法国心理学家达尼埃尔·达洛（Danielle Dalloz）。纳博科夫可能是故意通过混淆作者与作品名来讥讽弗洛伊德的《梦的解析》。

② 原文为法语。

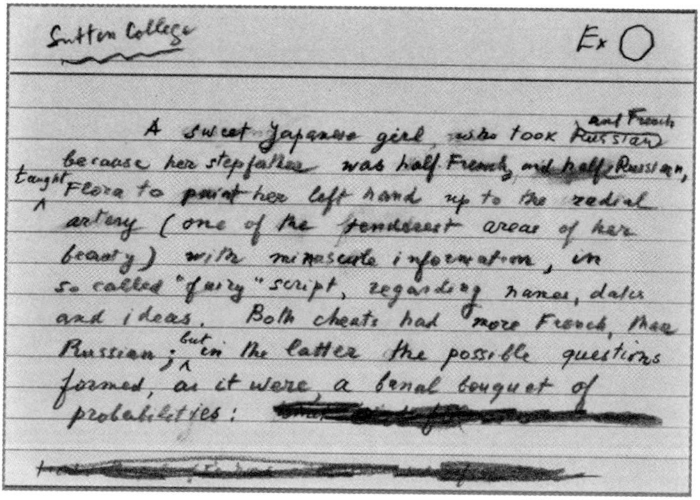

Sutton College Ex O

A sweet Japanese girl, who took Russian and French because her stepfather was half-French, ~~and half~~ Russian, taught Flora to ~~paint~~ her left hand up to the radial artery (one of the tenderest areas of her beauty) with minuscule information, in so called "fairy" script, regarding names, dates and ideas. Both cheats had more French, than Russian; but in the latter the possible questions formed, as it were, a banal bouquet of probabilities: [redacted]

[redacted]

Sutton College

Ex [0]

A sweet Japanese girl who took Russian and French because her stepfather was half French and half Russian, taught Flora to paint her left hand up to the radial artery (one of the tenderest areas of her beauty) with minuscule information, in so called "fairy" script, regarding names, dates and ideas. Both cheats had more French than Russian; but in the latter the possible questions formed, as it were, a banal bouquet of probabilities:

萨顿学院

Ex [0]

一位甜美的日本姑娘教弗洛拉如何在自己左手至桡动脉一带（这是她美丽身体最敏感的部位之一）用所谓"小精灵"文字绘上缩微信息：一些名字、日期和想法。日本姑娘的继父是法俄混血儿，因此她既学俄语也学法语。这两个作弊者上法语课比俄语课更多；但上俄语课时可能遇到的问题，某种程度上都是些陈词滥调：

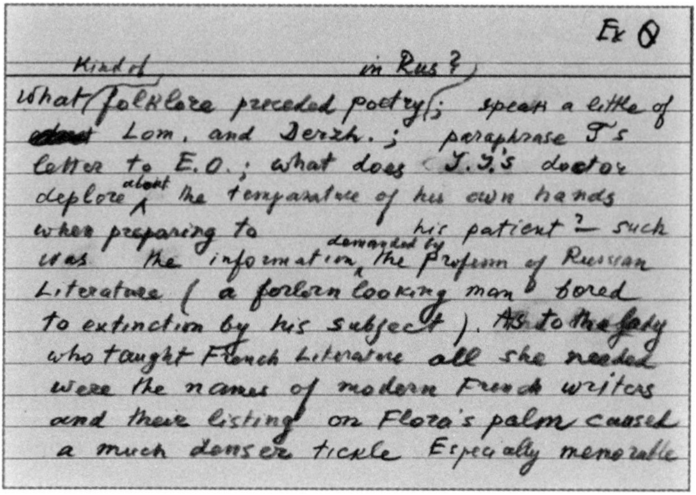
Ex Q

Kind of　　　　in Rus?
What folklore preceded poetry; speak a little of
Lom. and Derzh.; paraphrase T's
letter to E.O.; what does I.I.'s doctor
deplore about the temperature of his own hands
when preparing to　　　his patient? — such
was the information demanded by the Professor of Russian
Literature (a forlorn looking man bored
to extinction by his subject). As to the lady
who taught French Literature all she needed
were the names of modern French writers
and their listing on Flora's palm caused
a much denser tickle Especially memorable

---

* 上文中的姓名缩写指的是罗蒙诺索夫和杰尔查文，达吉雅娜和叶甫盖尼·奥涅金，还有托尔斯泰笔下的伊凡·伊里奇；符号[　]为作者有意留下的空格。——德米特里·纳博科夫

① 米哈伊尔·罗蒙诺索夫(Mikhail Lomonosov, 1711—1765)，俄罗斯著名科学家，也是俄罗斯现代语言的创始人。加甫里尔·杰尔查文(Gavrila Derzhavin, 1743—1816)，俄罗斯著名古典主义诗人。

② 《叶甫盖尼·奥涅金》是普希金创作的诗体小说，达吉雅娜是该作品的女主人公。纳博科夫将它译成英文，在长达两千页的译稿中，译文只占十分之一，其他全是注释。

③ 《伊凡·伊里奇之死》是托尔斯泰晚年(一八八六年)的重要代表作，讲述生命与死亡的故事。第八节中有这样的情景：医生在为即将咽气的病人伊凡·伊里奇测量体温前，不停地搓着手说："啊，真冷，可把我冻坏了。"托尔斯泰要表达的是，医生潜意识里在为自己双手冰冷是因寒冷气候、而非疾病所致感到庆幸，因为他知道病人逐渐冷却的尸体不能再恢复往日的温度了。

Ex [1]

What kind of folklore preceded poetry in Rus?; speak a little of Lom. and Derzh.; paraphrase T's letter to E. O.; what does I.I.'s doctor deplore about the temperature of his own hands when preparing to [ ] his patient?—such was the information demanded by the professor of Russian Literature (a forlorn looking man bored to extinction by his subject).* As to the lady who taught French Literature[,] all she needed were the names of modern French writers and their listing on Flora's palm caused a much denser tickle[.] Especially memorable

Ex [1]

俄罗斯的何种民间文学先于诗歌；简述罗蒙诺索夫和杰尔查文；① 解读达吉雅娜给叶甫盖尼·奥涅金② 的信；在伊凡·伊里奇的医生准备为他的病人［ ］时，何以会为自己冰冷的双手而慨叹③——这就是俄罗斯文学教授（一位满面愁容、被自己的研究课题折磨得要死的男人）所需要的信息。*至于那位教授法国文学的女士，她所需要的全部，只是现代法国作家的姓名而已；这些人名被抄列在弗洛拉的手掌上，弄得她一阵奇痒。尤为令人难忘的

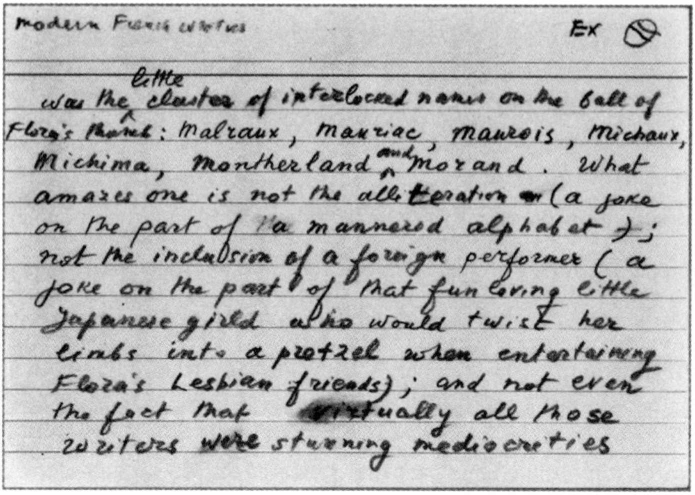
modern French writers　Ex

was the little cluster of interlocked names on the ball of Flora's thumb: Malraux, Mauriac, Maurois, Michaux, Michima, Montherland and Morand. What amazes one is not the alliteration (a joke on the part of a mannered alphabet); not the inclusion of a foreign performer (a joke on the part of that fun loving little Japanese girl who would twist her limbs into a pretzel when entertaining Flora's Lesbian friends); and not even the fact that virtually all those writers were stunning mediocrities

---

① 安德烈·马尔罗（Andre Malraux，1901—1975），法国小说家、文艺理论家和政治家。弗朗索瓦·莫里亚克（François Mauriac，1885—1970），法国小说家，一九五二年诺贝尔文学奖获得者。安德烈·莫洛亚（Andre Maurois，1885—1967），法国文学院院士，著名传记作家。亨利·米肖（Henri Michaux，1899—1984），原籍比利时，后移居法国，一九二七年出版第一部诗集《我曾是谁》，第二次世界大战后，他与夏尔、蓬热一起，被称为法国当代诗坛的“三剑客”，他还是一位出色的画家。三岛由纪夫（Yukio Mishima，1925—1970），日本小说家、剧作家、记者、电影制作人、电影演员，是日本战后文学大师之一，曾两度入围诺贝尔文学奖，此处纳博科夫将Mishima写成了Michima。亨利·德·蒙泰朗（Henry de Montherlant，1895—1972），法国当代著名小说家、杰出剧作家、法兰西学院院士，纳博科夫将Montherlant的最后一个字母写成了d。保罗·莫朗（Paul Morand，1888—1976），法国外交家、小说家、剧作家、诗人，早期现代主义作家，法兰西学院院士。

Ex［2］

Modern French writers

....

was the little cluster of interlocked names on the ball of Flora's thumb: Malraux, Mauriac, Maurois, Michaux, Michima, Montherland and Morand. What amazes one is not the alliteration (a joke on the part of a mannered alphabet); not the inclusion of a foreign performer (a joke on the part of that fun loving little Japanese [girl] who would twist her limbs into a pretzel when entertaining Flora's Lesbian friends); and not even the fact that virtually all those writers were stunning mediocrities

Ex［2］

现代法国作家

....

是弗洛拉拇指指头上那一小簇交汇重叠的名字：马尔罗，莫里亚克，莫洛亚，米肖，三岛由纪夫，蒙泰朗和莫朗。[①]令人感到惊奇的不是这些名字的头韵（一个由造作的字母制造的笑话）；不是因为列入了一位外国演员（一个由那位爱玩乐的日本小［女孩］制造的笑话，她将自己的四肢拧成一个椒盐卷饼的形状，以逗弗洛拉的女同性恋朋友们开心）；甚至也不是那些作家实际上都平庸得令人震惊这一事实

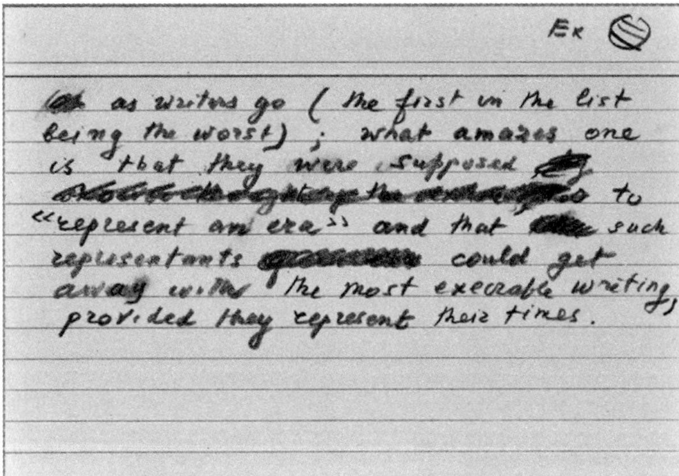

Ex

as writers go (the first in the list
being the worst); what amazes one
is that they were supposed
to
"represent an era" and that such
representants could get
away with the most execrable writing,
provided they represent their times.

Ex [3]

as writers go (the first in the list being the worst) ; what amazes one is that they were supposed to "represent an era" and that such representants could get away with the most execrable writing, provided they represent their times.

Ex [3]

(排名第一的作家是最糟糕的)；令人感到惊奇的，是这些人竟被认为应该"代表了一个时代"，并且假如他们的作品代表了他们的时代，那么即便写得极差也可以免遭指责。

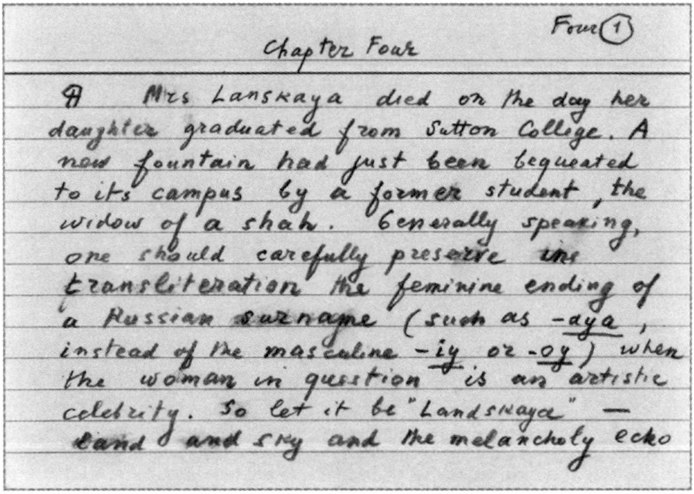

Four (1)

Chapter Four

¶ Mrs Lanskaya died on the day her daughter graduated from Sutton College. A new fountain had just been bequeated to its campus by a former student, the widow of a shah. Generally speaking, one should carefully preserve in transliteration the feminine ending of a Russian surname (such as -aya, instead of the masculine -iy or -oy) when the woman in question is an artistic celebrity. So let it be "Landskaya" — land and sky and the melancholy echo

Chapter Four

1

Mrs Lanskaya died on the day her daughter graduated from Sutton College. A new fountain had just been bequeat[h]ed to its campus by a former student, the widow of a shah. Generally speaking, one should carefully preserve in transliteration the feminine ending of a Russian surname (such as -aya, instead of the masculine -iy or -oy) when the woman in question is an artistic celebrity. So let it be "Landskaya"—land and sky and the melancholy echo

第四章

1

兰斯卡雅夫人是在女儿从萨顿学院毕业那天去世的。一位校友,伊朗国王的遗孀,刚刚资助学院新建了一个喷泉。一般说来,如果被谈论的女士是一位艺术名流,在音译其俄文姓氏时,一定要谨慎地保留其阴性后缀(比如要用"阿雅",而不是阳性后缀"奥伊"或"欧伊")。那么,就叫"兰德斯卡雅"吧——大地(land)、天空(sky),以及她舞者名字的忧郁回声。

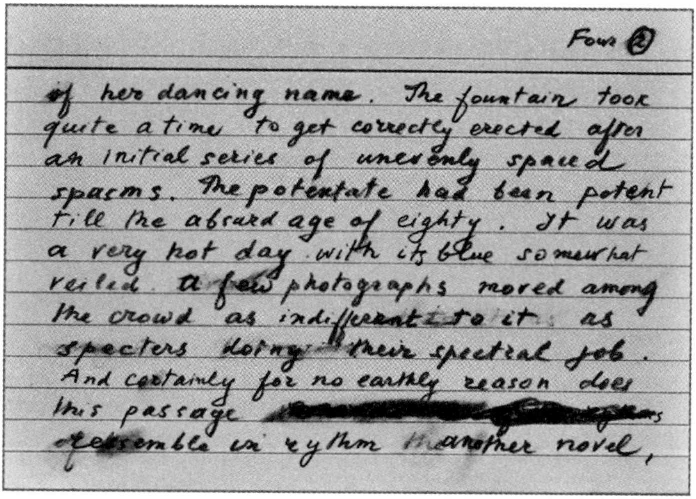

Four ②

of her dancing name. The fountain took
quite a time to get correctly erected after
an initial series of unevenly spaced
spasms. The potentate had been potent
till the absurd age of eighty. It was
a very hot day with its blue somewhat
veiled. A few photographs moved among
the crowd as indifferent to it as
specters doing their spectral job.
And certainly for no earthly reason does
this passage [illegible]
resemble in rythm another novel,

2

of her dancing name. The fountain took quite a time to get correctly erected after an initial series of unevenly spaced spasms. The potentate had been potent till the absurd age of eighty. It was a very hot day with its blue somewhat veiled. A few photograph[er]s moved among the crowd as indifferent to it as specters doing their spectral job. And certainly for no earthly reason does this passage ressemble in r[h]ythm another novel,

2

刚开始时喷泉的水柱间隔不匀称，过了好一阵子才喷涌得挺直稳当了。这一王者风度持续到了八十这一荒谬的年岁。那天天气十分炎热，天空中有些许浮云。几位摄影师在人群中游走，如同幽灵履行幽灵职责般漠然。当然没有任何理由让这段情节与另一本小说《我的劳拉》节奏近似。

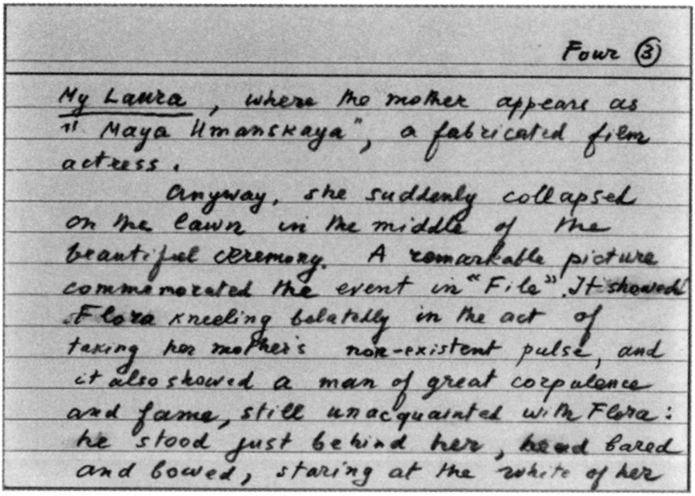

Four (3)

My Laura, where the mother appears as "Maya Umanskaya", a fabricated film actress.

Anyway, she suddenly collapsed on the lawn in the middle of the beautiful ceremony. A remarkable picture commemorated the event in "File". It showed Flora kneeling belatedly in the act of taking her mother's non-existent pulse, and it also showed a man of great corpulence and fame, still unacquainted with Flora: he stood just behind her, head bared and bowed, staring at the white of her

My Laura, where the mother appears as “Maya Umanskaya”, a fabricated film actress.

Anyway, she suddenly collapsed on the lawn in the middle of the beautiful ceremony. A remarkable picture commemorated the event in “File”. It showed Flora kneeling belatedly in the act of taking her mother’s non-existent pulse, and it also showed a man of great corpulence and fame, still unacquainted with Flora: he stood just behind her, head bared and bowed, staring at the white of her

那部书中的母亲名叫“玛雅·乌曼斯卡娅”，是一位虚构的女电影演员。

总之，在华美的毕业典礼进行过程中，她突然昏倒在草坪上。一张引人注目的“存档”照片留下了对这一事件的纪念。照片上，反应迟了些的弗洛拉跪在她母亲身旁，摸着母亲不再跳动的脉搏，还有一位身体极其肥胖的名人就站在她的身后，此人当时还不认识弗洛拉；他秃着头，弯着腰，眼睛盯着她

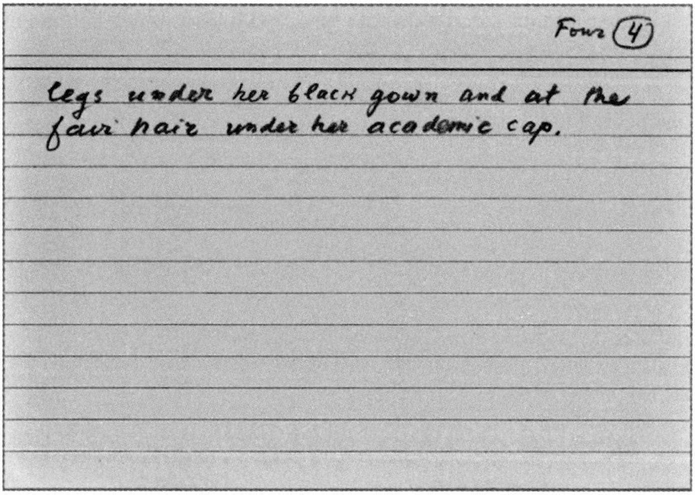
Four (4)

legs under her black gown and at the
fair hair under her academic cap.

4

legs under her black gown and at the fair hair under her academic cap.

4

黑色长袍下白皙的大腿和学士帽下的金发。

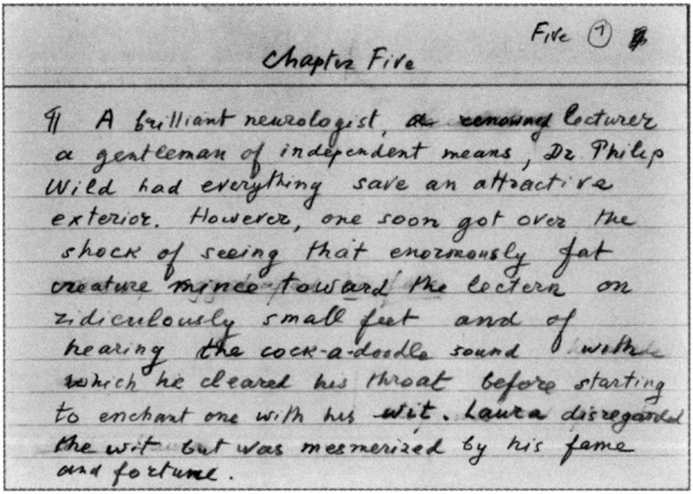

Five (1)

Chapter Five

¶ A brilliant neurologist, a renowned lecturer
a gentleman of independent means, Dr Philip
Wild had everything save an attractive
exterior. However, one soon got over the
shock of seeing that enormously fat
creature mince toward the lectern on
ridiculously small feet and of
hearing the cock-a-doodle sound with
which he cleared his throat before starting
to enchant one with his wit. Laura disregarded
the wit but was mesmerized by his fame
and fortune.

Chapter Five

1

A brilliant neurologist, a renowned lecturer [and] a gentleman of independent means, Dr Philip Wild had everything save an attractive exterior. However, one soon got over the shock of seeing that enormously fat creature mince toward the lectern on ridiculously small feet and of hearing the cock-a-doodle sound with which he cleared his throat before starting to enchant one with his wit. Laura disregarded the wit but was mesmerized by his fame and fortune.

第五章

1

作为一名出色的神经病学家，一个颇负盛名的演讲者，一位拥有足够财产可以生活优渥的绅士，菲利普·王尔德医生可谓应有尽有，就是长相寒碜了点儿。然而，在看着这一庞然大物用小得可笑的双脚碎步走向讲台，听着他如公鸡打鸣般清了清嗓子，开始用他的机智风趣蛊惑听众时，人们会很快从最初的震惊中恢复过来。劳拉对这种机智毫无兴趣，蛊惑她的是他的名望和财富。

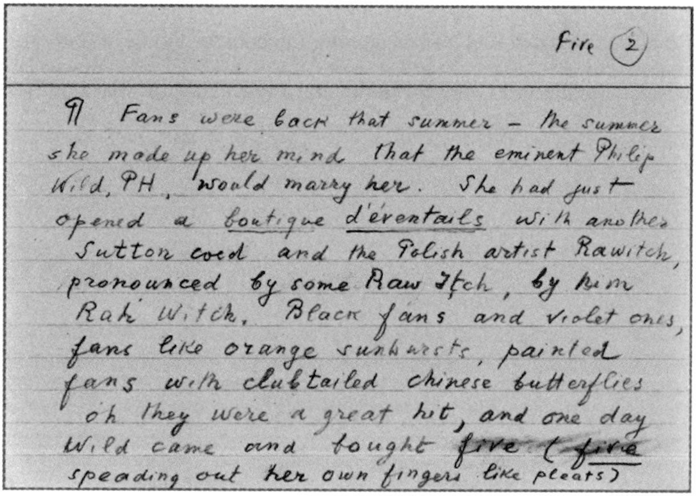

Fire (2)

¶ Fans were back that summer – the summer she made up her mind that the eminent Philip Wild, PH, would marry her. She had just opened a boutique d'éventails with another Sutton coed and the Polish artist Rawitch, pronounced by some Raw Itch, by him Rah Witch. Black fans and violet ones, fans like orange sunbursts, painted fans with clubtailed chinese butterflies oh they were a great hit, and one day Wild came and bought ~~five (five~~ speading out her own fingers like pleats)

2

Fans were back that summer—the summer she made up her mind that the eminent Philip Wild, PH, would marry her. She had just opened a boutique d'éventails with another Sutton coed and the Polish artist Rawitch, pronounced by some Raw Itch, by him Rah Witch. Black fans and violet ones, fans like orange sunbursts, painted fans with clubtailed Chinese butterflies[,] oh they were a great hit, and one day Wild came and bought five (five spreading out her own fingers like pleats)

2

那年夏天扇子又开始流行，就是在这个夏天，她打定主意要让大名鼎鼎的菲利普·王尔德医生娶她。她和萨顿学院的女同学，还有一个名叫拉维奇的波兰艺术家一道开了家精品扇子店[①]。有人管这位波兰艺术家叫“诺伊奇”，而他自称为“莱维奇”。[②]有黑色和紫罗兰色的扇子，呈旭日般橘色的扇子，绘有锤尾凤蝶的扇子，哦，它们风靡一时。有一天，王尔德到店里买了五把扇子（“五”张开她自己的手指，有如衣服上的褶皱），

① 原文为法语。

② 拉维奇（Rawitch）、诺伊奇（Raw Itch）和莱维奇（Rah Witch）这三个人名的英文中分别含有“没有经验的巫婆”、“痒得发痛”和“喝彩的巫婆”之意。

Fire (3)

for "two aunts and three nieces" who did not really exist, but never mind, it was an unusual extravagance on his part His shyness suprized and amused Flaura.

¶ Less amusing suprises awaited her. To day after three years of marriage she had enough of his fortune and fame. He was a domestic miser. His New Jersey house was absurdly understaffed. The ranchito in Arizona had not been redecorated for years. The villa on the

3

for "two aunts and three nieces" who did not really exist, but nevermind, it was an unusual extravagance on his part[.] His shyness suprized and amused Flaura.

Less amusing surprises awaited her. To day after three years of marriage she had enough of his fortune and fame. He was a domestic miser. His New Jersey house was absurdly understaffed. The ranchito in Arizona had not been redecorated for years. The villa on the

3

送给他的并不存在的“两个姑姑和三个侄女”，但没有关系，他难得这么奢侈一回。他的腼腆让弗洛拉又惊又喜。

但让弗洛拉惊喜的事儿后来就很少了。结婚三年后的如今，她可是受够了他的所谓财富和名望。他在家里简直是个吝啬鬼。他在新泽西的住宅用人少得可怜。亚利桑那州的墨西哥餐厅已经多年没有重新装修了。

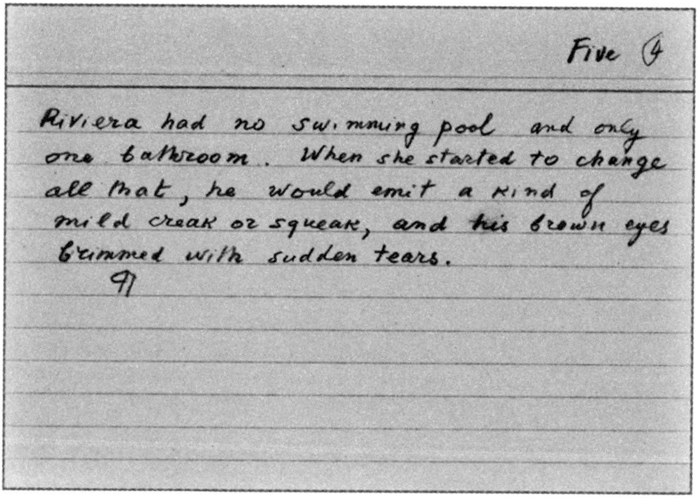

Five (4)

Riviera had no swimming pool and only one bathroom. When she started to change all that, he would emit a kind of mild creak or squeak, and his brown eyes brimmed with sudden tears.

¶

4

Riviera had no swimming pool and only one bathroom. When she started to change all that, he would emit a kind of mild creak or squeak, and his brown eyes brimmed with sudden tears.

4

里维埃拉的别墅连个游泳池也没有，而且只有一个卫生间。当弗洛拉想要改变一下时，她丈夫就会哼哼唧唧的，那双褐色的眼睛里还会突然噙满泪水。

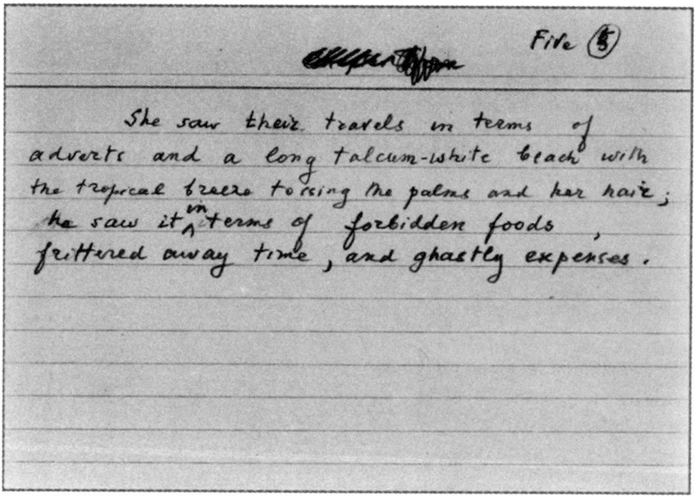

Five (5)

She saw their travels in terms of adverts and a long talcum-white beach with the tropical breeze tossing the palms and her hair; he saw it in terms of forbidden foods, frittered away time, and ghastly expenses.

5

She saw their travels in terms of adverts and a long talcum-white beach with the tropical breeze tossing the palms and her hair; he saw it in terms of forbidden foods, frittered away time, and ghastly expenses.

5

她把他们的旅行视为某种广告，一片长长的、白净如洗的沙滩，热带的微风轻拂过棕榈叶和她的秀发；而他则将出游视为某种禁果，完全是虚掷光阴，还有可怕的开支。

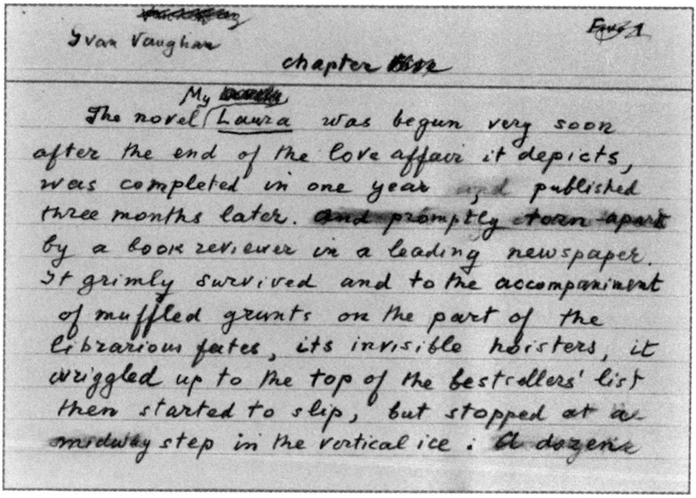

Ivan Vaughan

chapter ~~[illegible]~~

~~[illegible]~~ 1

My ~~[illegible]~~

The novel Laura was begun very soon after the end of the love affair it depicts, was completed in one year ~~and~~, published three months later. ~~and promptly torn apart~~ by a book reviewer in a leading newspaper. It grimly survived and to the accompaniment of muffled grunts on the part of the librarious fates, its invisible hoisters, it wriggled up to the top of the bestsellers' list then started to slip, but stopped at ~~a midway~~ step in the vertical ice : ~~A dozen~~

Chapter [Five]*

1

Ivan Vaughan

The novel My Laura was begun very soon after the end of the love affair it depicts, was completed in one year, published three months later[,] and promptly torn apart by a book reviewer in a leading newspaper. It grimly survived and to the accompaniment of muffled grunts on the part of the librarious fates, its invisible hoisters, it wriggled up to the top of the bestsellers' list then started to slip, but stopped at a midway step in the vertical ice. A dozen

第五章*

1

伊凡·沃恩

小说《我的劳拉》的创作开始于恋情刚结束不久，完成于一年以后，脱稿三个月后出版，很快就有一位书评人在某家权威报纸上将它批得体无完肤。它勉强存活下来，有关其命运的含混的嘀咕成了它无形的提升机，它艰难地爬升到畅销书排行榜榜首，接着排名开始下滑，但停在了垂直冰山的半道中。

---

* 本章原本被标为第五章，但作者似乎打算改掉其章节序号。

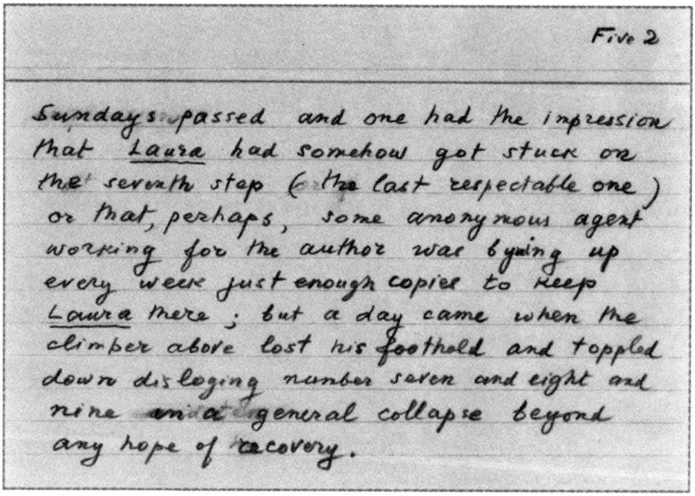

Five 2

Sundays passed and one had the impression
that *Laura* had somehow got stuck on
the seventh step (the last respectable one)
or that, perhaps, some anonymous agent
working for the author was buying up
every week just enough copies to keep
Laura there; but a day came when the
climber above lost his foothold and toppled
down dislodging number seven and eight and
nine in a general collapse beyond
any hope of recovery.

2

sundays passed and one had the impression that Laura had somehow got stuck on the seventh step (the last respectable one) or that, perhaps, some anonymous agent working for the author was [buying] up every week just enough copies to keep Laura there; but a day came when the climber above lost his foothold and toppled down [dislodging] number seven and eight and nine in a general collapse beyond any hope of recovery.

2

十来周过后，《我的劳拉》似乎固定在了第七名（属于体面之列的最后一名）；或许，有某个为作者服务的匿名经纪人每周购买足够数量的书，以保持其在排行榜上的位置；但那一天到来了，排在前一位的攀登者失足摔了出去，引发了一场全面的崩塌，排名第七、第八和第九的作品也统统跌落，毫无扭转颓势的希望。

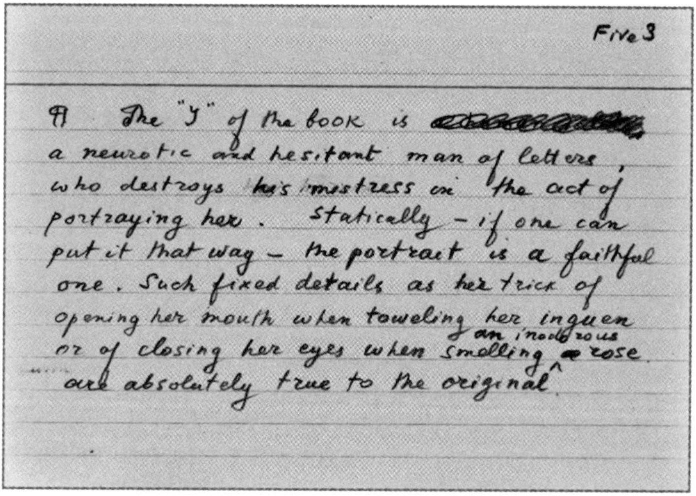

Five 3

¶ The "I" of the book is [redacted]
a neurotic and hesitant man of letters,
who destroys his mistress in the act of
portraying her. Statically – if one can
put it that way – the portrait is a faithful
one. Such fixed details as her trick of
opening her mouth when toweling her inguen
or of closing her eyes when smelling an inodorous rose
are absolutely true to the original.

3

The "I" of the book is a neurotic and hesitant man of letters, who destroys his mistress in the act of portraying her. Statically—if one can put it that way—the portrait is a faithful one. Such fixed details as her trick of opening her mouth when toweling her inguen or of closing her eyes when smelling an inodorous rose are absolutely true to the original.

3

书中的"我"是一位神经过敏、优柔寡断的作家，他对他的情人的刻画足以毁灭她。静态观之——如果可以这么表述的话——他的刻画是忠实可靠的。用毛巾擦腹股沟时，她有意将嘴巴张开；用鼻子闻一朵没有香味的玫瑰时，她刻意闭上双眼；她这些惯常的小把戏被他刻画得绝对忠实于原型。

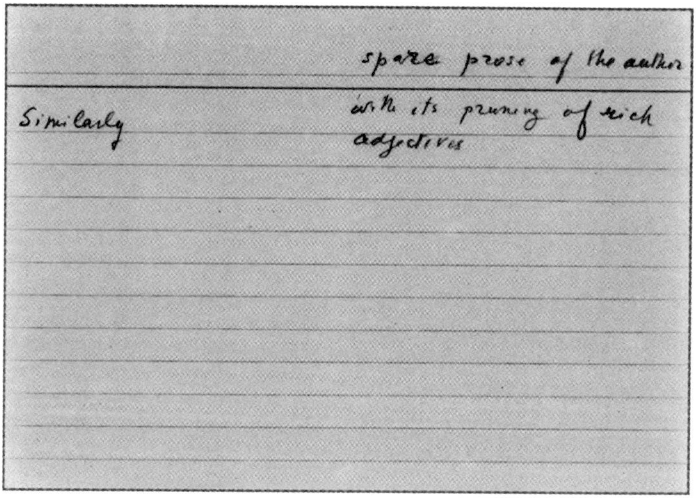
spare prose of the author
Similarly with its pruning of rich adjectives

Similarly [the] spare prose of the author with its pruning of rich adjectives

就像作者那惜字如金的散文体，丰富的形容词被修剪得十分精炼

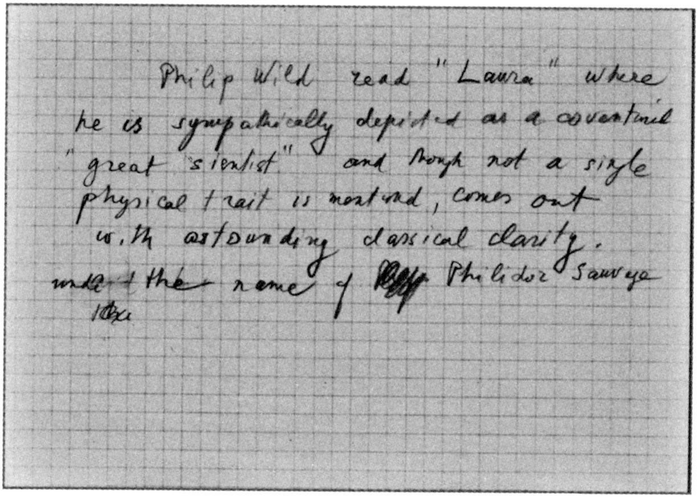

Philip Wild read "Laura" where he is sympathetically depicted as a conventional "great scientist" and though not a single physical trait is mentioned, comes out with astounding classical clarity.
under the name of Philidor Sauvage
Idea

Philip Wild read "Laura" where he is sympath[et]ically depicted as a co[n]ventional "great s[c]ientist" and though not a single physical trait is mentioned, comes out with astounding classical clarity, under the name of Philidor Sauvage

菲利普·王尔德读了《我的劳拉》,他在书中被悲悯地描写为一个传统的"伟大科学家",尽管没有提及任何他个人的身体特征,但被命名为"菲里多·索瓦吉"的这一形象却有着惊人的权威般的清晰。

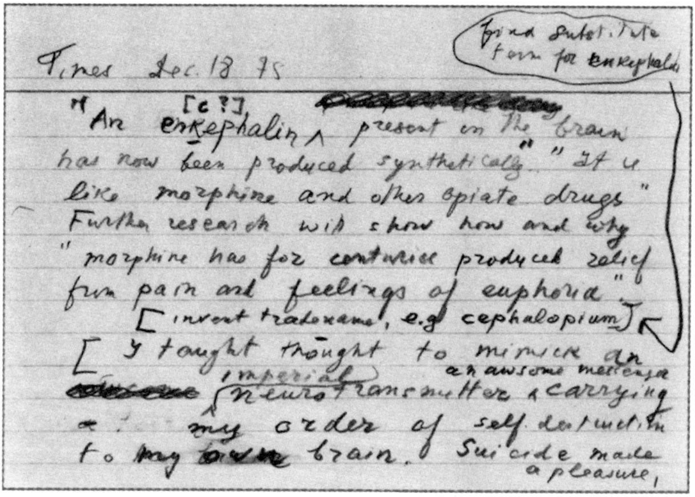
Times Dec. 18 75

Find substitute term for enkephalin

"An enkephalin [c?] present in the brain has now been produced synthetically." "It is like morphine and other opiate drugs" Further research will show how and why "morphine has for centuries produced relief from pain and feelings of euphoria".

[invent tradename, e.g. cephalopium]

[I taught thought to mimick an imperial neurotransmitter an awsome message carrying my order of self destruction to my own brain. Suicide made a pleasure,

① "cephalopium" 是纳博科夫造的词，该词由 "cephalon"（头）和 "opium"（鸦片）两部分组成。

[Chapter Six]

Times Dec. 18,75

"An enk(c?) ephalin present in the brain has now been produced synthetically" "It is like morphine and other opiate drugs" Further research will show how and why "morphine has for centuries produced relief from pain and feelings of euphoria".

(invent tradename, e.g. cephalopium[;] find substitute term for enkephalin)

I taught thought to mimick an imperial neurotransmitter an aw [e]some messenger carrying my order of self destruction to my own brain. Suicide made a pleasure,

[第六章]

《时报》七五年十二月十八日

"存在于大脑中的脑啡肽如今已可用合成技术生产。""它就像吗啡和其他鸦片毒品。"进一步的研究会证明为什么以及通过怎样的方式"数百年来吗啡可以止痛并令人产生安乐感"。

（编造商标名，比如脑鸦片 [cephalopium] ①；给脑啡肽找个替代术语）

我让自己的想法模仿一台特级神经信号发射器，让这个了不起的信使将自我毁灭命令传到大脑。自杀引发了一种愉悦，

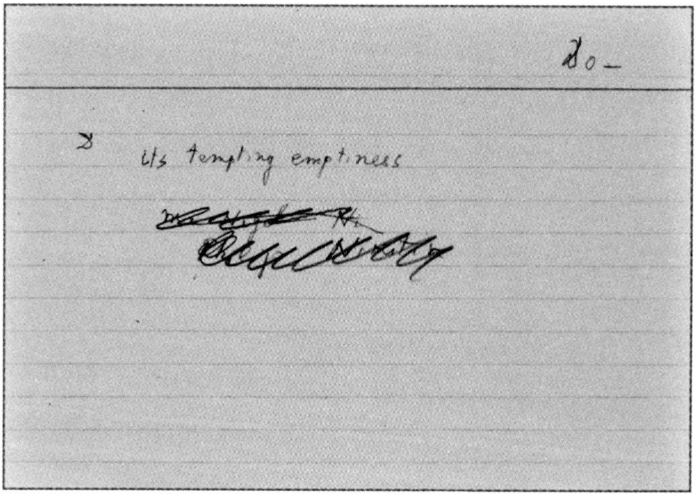
80–

8 its tempting emptiness

D0

D

its tempting emptiness

D0

D

它诱人的空虚

Settling for a "simple" like

D1

The student who desires to die should learn first of all to project a mental image of himself upon his inner blackboard. This surface which at its virgin best has a dark-plum, rather than black, depth of opacity is none other than the underside of one's closed eyelids.

¶ To ensure a complete smoothness of background, care must be taken to eliminate the hypnagogic gargoyles and entoptic swarms which plague tired

D1

Settling for a single line

The student who desires to die should learn first of all to project a mental image of himself upon his inner blackboard. This surface which at its virgin best has a dark-plum, rather than black, depth of opacity is none other than the underside of one's closed eyelids.

To ensure a complete smoothness of background, care must be taken to eliminate the hypnagogic gargoyles and entoptic swarms which plague tired

D1

足以造就一行诗句。

渴望死去的学生首先要学会在内心的黑板上勾勒出自己精神的影像。这个表面正是一个人闭合的眼睑之底部,其上最好原本有一块暗紫红色,而不是一片不透明而又深不见底的纯黑。

要确保背景表面完整光滑,必须小心地赶走催眠滴水兽,还有

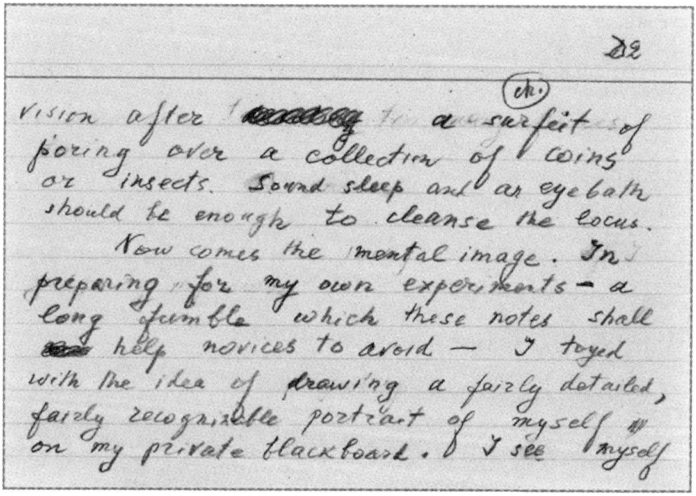
D2

(ch.)

vision after a surfeit of
poring over a collection of coins
or insects. Sound sleep and an eyebath
should be enough to cleanse the locus.
Now comes the mental image. In
preparing for my own experiments — a
long fumble which these notes shall
help novices to avoid — I toyed
with the idea of drawing a fairly detailed,
fairly recognizable portrait of myself
on my private blackboard. I see myself

D2

vision after a surfeit of poring over a collection of coins or insects. Sound sleep and an eyebath should be enough to cleanse the locus.

Now comes the mental image. In preparing for my own experiments—a long fumble which these notes shall help novices to avoid—I toyed with the idea of drawing a fairly detailed, fairly recognizable portrait of myself on my private blackboard. I see myself

D2

在凝视硬币或昆虫收藏品过久之后因视觉疲劳而出现的眼内蜂群。饱睡一觉,外加一杯洗眼液应该足以将这些痕迹清洁干净。

接下来便是精神的影像。在准备我自己的实验时——这些笔记将帮助新手们省略掉这一漫长的摸索过程——我漫不经心地考虑过,在自己的私人黑板上勾勒一幅细致入微、清晰可辨的自画像。我看到了壁橱镜子里

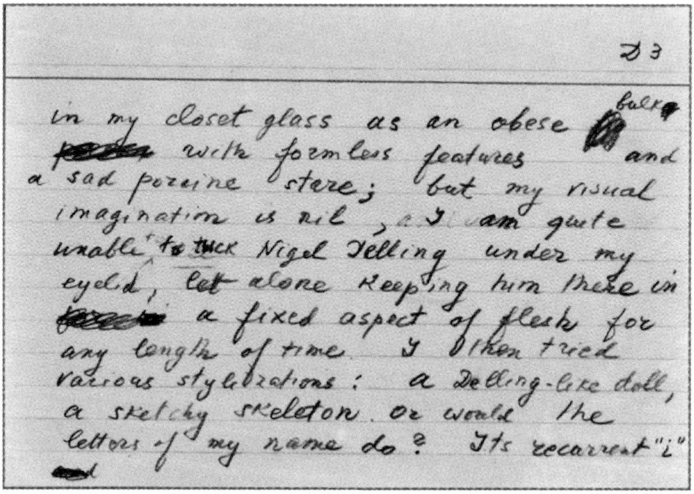

D3

in my closet glass as an obese bulk with formless features and a sad porcine stare; but my visual imagination is nil, I am quite unable to tuck Nigel Dalling under my eyelid, let alone keeping him there in a fixed aspect of flesh for any length of time. I then tried various stylizations: a Dalling-like doll, a sketchy skeleton. Or would the letters of my name do? Its recurrent "i"

D3

in my closet glass as an obese bulk with formless features and a sad porcine stare; but my visual imagination is nil, I am quite unable to tuck Nigel D[a]lling under my eyelid, let alone keeping him there in a fixed aspect of flesh for any length of time. I then tried various stylizations: a D[a]lling-like doll, a sketchy skeleton. Or would the letters of my name do? Its recurrent "i"

D3

自己那肥胖的身体，模糊的面容，猪一般可悲的目光；但我的视觉想象一片空白。我的眼皮下根本容不下奈吉尔·达林，更不用说让他保持稳定的形态在那儿停留一段时间了。于是，我尝试着仿效各种风格，一个达林样貌的布娃娃，一幅草草勾勒的骨架，或许由我姓名的字母构成？反复出现的字母"i"

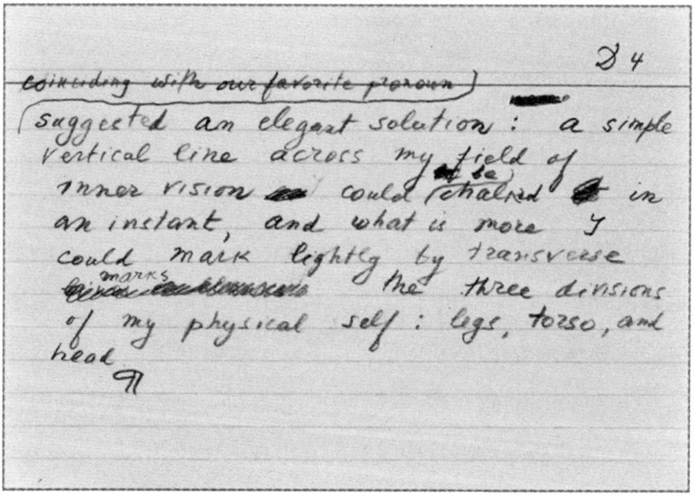
D4

~~coinciding with our favorite pronoun)~~

(suggested an elegant solution: a simple vertical line across my field of inner vision could be chalked in an instant, and what is more I could mark lightly by transverse marks the three divisions of my physical self: legs, torso, and head ¶

D4

coinciding with our favorite pronoun suggested an elegant solution: a simple vertical line across my field of inner vision could be chalked in an instant, and what is more I could mark lightly by transverse marks the three divisions of my physical self: legs, torso, and head

D4

恰好是我们最喜欢的人称代词“我”，它暗示了一种文雅的解决方案：我可以瞬间用粉笔画就径直穿越我脑海中整个视野的一根简单的垂直线，我还能用横线轻轻标出我自己身体的三个要件：双腿、躯干和头部。

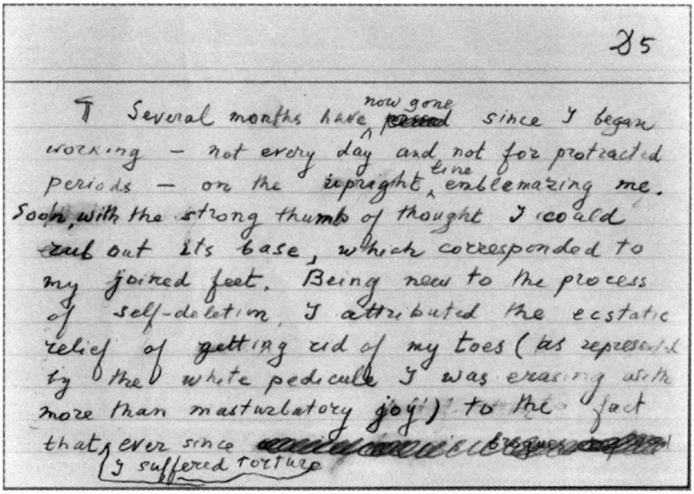

85

¶ Several months have ~~passed~~ now gone since I began working — not every day and not for protracted periods — on the ~~upright~~ line emblemazing me. Soon, with the strong thumb of thought I could rub out its base, which corresponded to my joined feet. Being new to the process of self-deletion, I attributed the ecstatic relief of ~~getting~~ rid of my toes (as represented by the white pedicule I was erasing with more than masturbatory joy) to the fact that I suffered torture ever since [illegible]

D5

Several months have now gone since I began working—not every day and not for protracted periods—on the upright line emblemazing me. Soon, with the strong thumb of thought I could rub out its base, which corresponded to my joined feet. Being new to the process of self-deletion, I attributed the ecstatic relief of getting rid of my toes (as represented by the white pedicule I was erasing with more than masturbatory joy) to the fact that I suffered torture ever since

D5

我开始研究这条象征我自己的垂直线至今已有数月——不过并未每天或长时间地耗在这里头。很快，用我意念中的大拇指，我可以抹掉“I”的底部，就是对应我连着的双脚的部分。在自我删除这一全新的过程中，我将去除我的脚趾所获得的莫大快慰（我擦掉表示脚趾的白色残端时感觉比手淫还要爽）归因于一个事实，

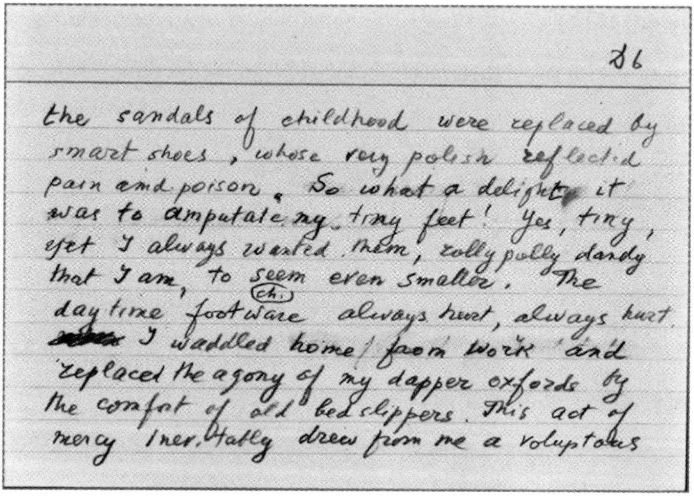
26

the sandals of childhood were replaced by smart shoes, whose rosy polish reflected pain and poison. So what a delight it was to amputate my tiny feet! Yes, tiny, yet I always wanted them, rolly polly dandy that I am, to seem even smaller. The daytime footware (chi) always hurt, always hurt. I waddled home from work and replaced the agony of my dapper oxfords by the comfort of old bedslippers. This act of mercy inevitably drew from me a voluptuous

D6

the sandals of childhood were replaced by smart shoes, whose very polish reflected pain and poison. So what a delight it was to amputate my tiny feet! Yes, tiny, yet I always wanted them, rolly polly dandy that I am, to seem even smaller. The daytime footware always hurt, always hurt. I waddled home from work and replaced the agony of my dapper oxfords by the comfort of old bed slippers. This act of mercy inevitably drew from me a volupt[u]ous

D6

那就是自从孩提时穿的凉鞋被时髦漂亮、折射出痛苦与毒害的亮闪闪的鞋取代后，我的脚趾就一直受折磨。因此，切断我那小小的双脚是一件多么令人愉快的事啊！是的，小小的，然而过去的我，圆滚滚的花花公子，总希望它们显得更小些。白天穿的鞋子总是伤脚，总是伤脚。我下班后一瘸一拐地回到家，用床边的旧拖鞋换下光鲜亮丽的牛津鞋，疼痛这才消除。这一幸事常常让我情不自禁地发出舒服的叹息，而如果一不留神

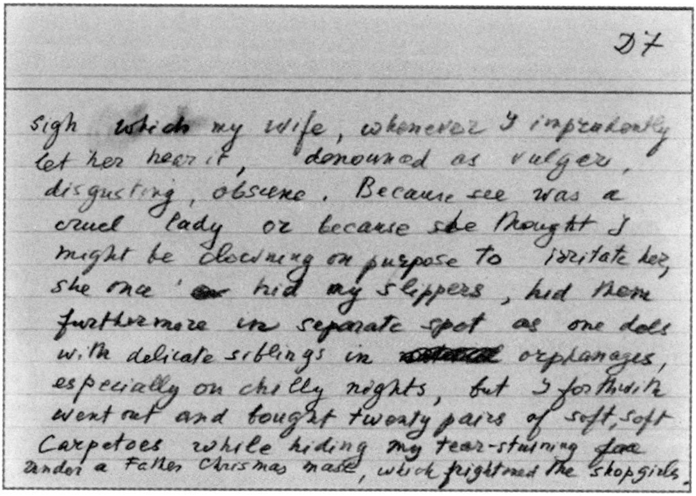
D7

sigh which my wife, whenever I imprudently
let her hear it, denounced as vulgar,
disgusting, obscene. Because she was a
cruel lady or because she thought I
might be clowning on purpose to irritate her,
she once hid my slippers, hid them
furthermore in separate spot as one does
with delicate siblings in orphanages,
especially on chilly nights, but I forthwith
went out and bought twenty pairs of soft, soft
Carpetoes while hiding my tear-stained face
under a Father Christmas mask, which frightened the shopgirls.

D7

sigh which my wife, whenever I imprudently let her hear it, denounced as vulgar, disgusting, obscene. Because [she] was a cruel lady or because she thought I might be clowning on purpose to irritate her, she once hid my slippers, hid them furthermore in separate spot[s] as one does with delicate siblings in orphanages, especially on chilly nights, but I forthwith went out and bought twenty pairs of soft, soft Carpetoes while hiding my tear-staining face under a Father Chris[t]mas mask, which frightened the shopgirls.

D7

被我的妻子听到，她便会斥责我低俗、恶心、下流。因为她生性冷酷，也或许是因为她认为我可能是在开玩笑蓄意惹她生气。她有一次竟把我的拖鞋藏了起来，而且还将两只鞋藏在不同的地方，就像对待孤儿院里无助的兄弟俩，尤其还是在异常寒冷的夜晚。但我立即去买了二十双极软极软的“毛毯趾”牌拖鞋，我把泪迹斑斑的脸藏在圣诞老人的面具之下，着实把女售货员吓了一跳。

the orange awnings of southern summers.

28

¶ For a moment I wondered with some apprehension if the deletion of my procreative system might produce nothing much more than a magnified orgasm. I was relieved to discover that the process continued sweet death's ineffable sensation which had nothing in common with ejaculations or sneezes. The three or four times that I reached that stage I forced myself to restore the lower half of my white "I" on my mental blackboard and thus wriggle out of my perilous trance. ¶

D8

The orange awnings of southern summers.

For a moment I wondered with some app[r]ehension if the deletion of my procreative system might produce nothing much more than a magnified orgasm. I was relieved to discover that the process continued sweet death's ineffable sensation which had nothing in common with ejaculations or sneezes. The three or four times that I reached that stage I forced myself to restore the lower half of my white "I" on my mental blackboard and thus wriggle out of my perilous trance.

D8

南方夏日里的橙色遮雨篷。

一时间，我会有些担心抹去生殖系统能带来的不过是一次被夸大其词的性高潮。我很欣慰地发现，这一过程延续了如同甜美的死亡般妙不可言的感觉，与射精和打喷嚏完全不可同日而语。有那么三四次我达到了那种状态，每次又强迫自己在脑海里的黑板上恢复我白色"I"里的下半身，这才得以从危险的昏睡中挣脱出来。

I, Philip Wild D9

Lecturer in Experimental Psychology, University of Ganglia

suffered for the last seventeen years from a humiliating stomach ailment which severely limited the jollities of companionship in small dining rooms

D9

I, Philip Wild[,] [l]ecturer in Experimental Psychology, University of Ganglia[, have] suffered for the last seventeen years from a humiliating stomach ailment which severely limited the jollities of companionship in small diningrooms

D9

我，菲利普·王尔德，神经中枢大学的实验心理学讲师，在人生最后的十七年里，因为患有不光彩的胃疾而吃尽了苦头，在小餐厅里与他人共同进餐的乐趣受到了极大的限制。

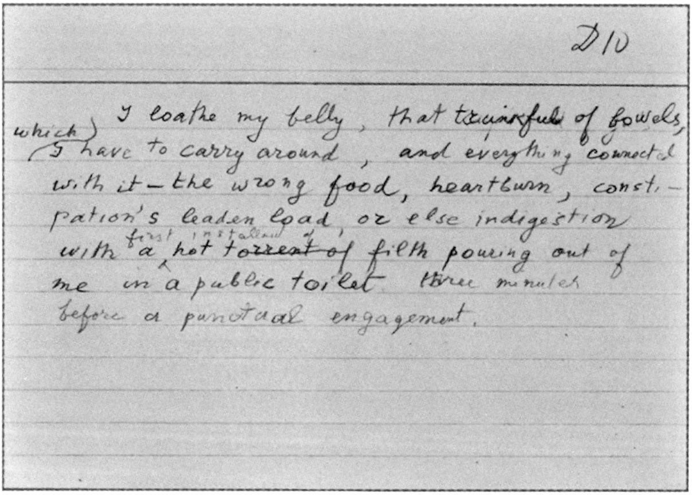

D10

I loathe my belly, that trunkful of bowels, which I have to carry around, and everything connected with it—the wrong food, heartburn, constipation's leaden load, or else indigestion with a first installment of hot ~~torrent of~~ filth pouring out of me in a public toilet three minutes before a punctual engagement.

D10

I loathe my belly, that trunkful of bowels, which I have to carry around, and everything connected with it—the wrong food, heartburn, constipation's leaden load, or else indigestion with a first installment of hot filth pouring out of me in a public toilet three minutes before a punctual engagement.

D10

我讨厌我的肚子，那塞满腑脏的肚子，我走到哪里都不得不随身带着它。我也讨厌与肚子相关的一切——吃错的食物、胃灼热、便秘引起的肠胃重负，还有消化不良，连同我准时赴约之前三分钟在公共厕所里排出的第一批热乎乎的秽物。

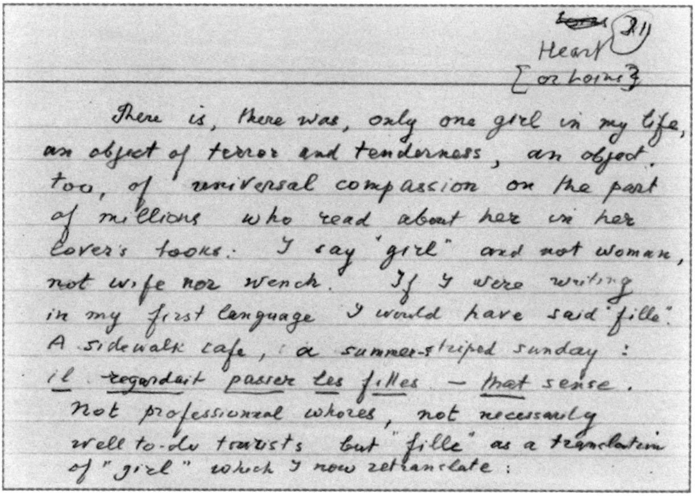
211
Heart
[or Loins]

There is, there was, only one girl in my life, an object of terror and tenderness, an object, too, of universal compassion on the part of millions who read about her in her lover's books. I say "girl" and not woman, not wife nor wench. If I were writing in my first language I would have said "fille". A sidewalk cafe, a summer-striped sunday: *il regardait passer les filles* — *that* sense. Not professional whores, not necessarily well to-do tourists but "fille" as a translation of "girl" which I now retranslate:

① 法语，意为“女儿、女孩”，通常相当于英语的daughter或girl。
② 原文为法语。

D11

Heart (or Loins?)

There is, there was, only one girl in my life, an object of terror and tenderness, an object too, of universal compassion on the part of millions who read about her in her lover's books. I say "girl" and not woman, not wife nor wench. If I were writing in my first language I would have said "fille" . A sidewalk cafe, a summer-striped sunday: il regardait passer les filles—that sense. Not professional whores, not necessarily well to-do tourists but "fille" as a translation of "girl" which I now retranslate:

D11

心脏（或生殖器官？）

无论现在还是过去，我的生命中只出现过一个姑娘，一个既可怕又温柔的实体，也是一个获得了数百万读者普遍同情的实体，那些读者从她情人撰写的小说中读到了她的故事。我称她为"姑娘"，而非"女人"或"妻子"或"少妇"。如果我用我的本国语写作，我会使用"fille"[①]一词。在街头咖啡店，身着夏日条纹衫的星期天：他眼睁睁地看着那些姑娘[②]——正是那种感觉。不是职业妓女，也未必是富有的游客，而是"fille"，这是此刻我重译"姑娘"时所用的词：

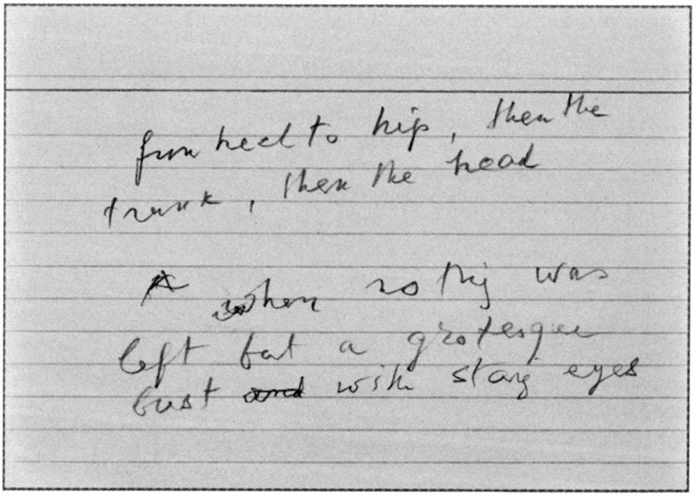
from heel to hip, then the
trunk, then the head

when nothing was
left but a grotesque
bust ~~and~~ with staring eyes

from heel to hip, then the trunk, then the head when nothing was left but a grotesque bust with staring eyes

从脚跟到臀部，再到躯体，再到头部，此时除了一个奇形怪状的上半身和目不转睛的双眼之外，什么都没有了。

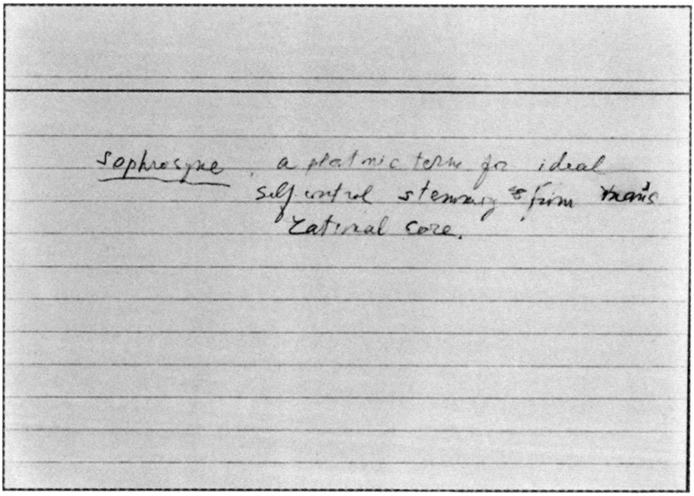
Sophrosyne, a platonic term for ideal
self control stemming from man's
rational core.

Sophrosyne, a platonic term for ideal self-control stemming from man's rational core.

节制，一个柏拉图术语，表示源自人类理性的内核的完美的自我控制。

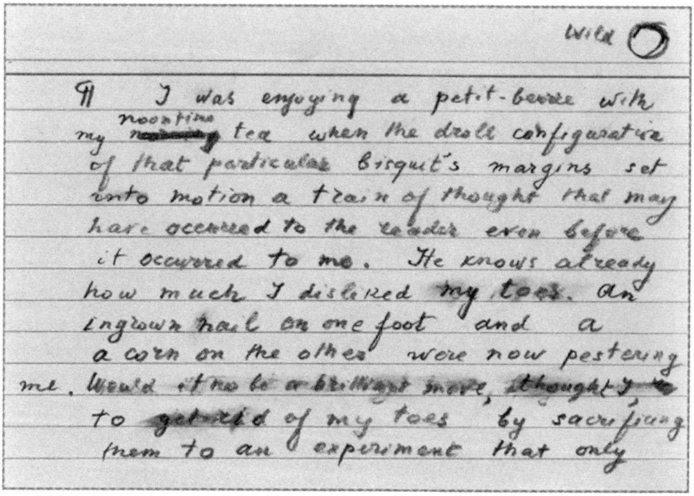

Wild ○

¶ I was enjoying a petit-beurre with
my ~~[illegible]~~ noontime tea when the droll configuration
of that particular biscuit's margins set
into motion a train of thought that may
have occurred to the reader even before
it occurred to me. He knows already
how much I disliked my toes. An
ingrown nail on one foot and a
a corn on the other were now pestering
me. ~~Would it no be a brilliant move, thought I, to~~
to get rid of my toes by sacrificing
them to an experiment that only

[Chapter Seven]

Wild [0]

I was enjoying a petit-beurre with my noontime tea when the droll configuration of that particular bisquit's margins set into motion a train of thought that may have occurred to the reader even before it occurred to me. He knows already how much I disliked my toes. An ingrown nail on one foot and a corn on the other were now pestering me. Would it no[t] be a brilliant move, thought I, to get rid of my toes by sacrificing them to an experiment that only

第七章

王尔德［0］

我正在享用午茶和黄油小脆饼时，饼干边缘的滑稽形状突然让我产生了一系列联想，也许会有位读者还先于我产生这种联想。他已经知道我对自己的脚趾深恶痛绝。一只脚上的某个趾甲长进了肉里，另一只脚上长了一个鸡眼，让我此刻深受其害。我在想着，去掉脚趾，将之捐献给一场仅仅因为胆怯而延迟的实验，岂不是一个明智之举？

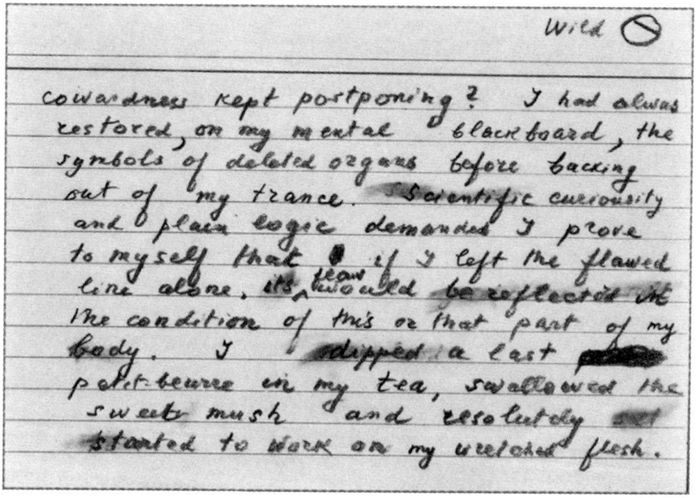

Wild ⊘

cowardness kept postponing? I had alwas restored, on my mental blackboard, the symbols of deleted organs before backing out of my trance. Scientific curiosity and plain logic demanded I prove to myself that if I left the flawed line alone, its flaw would be reflected in the condition of this or that part of my body. I dipped a last petit-beurre in my tea, swallowed the sweet mush and resolutely started to work on my wretched flesh.

Wild [1]

cowardness kept postponing? I had alwa[y]s restored, on my mental blackboard, the symbols of deleted organs before backing out of my trance. Scientific curiousity and plain logic demanded I prove to myself that if I left the flawed line alone, its flaw would be reflected in the condition of this or that part of my body. I dipped a last petitbeurre in my tea, swallowed the sweet mush and resolutely started to work on my wretched flesh.

王尔德 [1]

我总在脱离昏睡状态之前，让代表被删除器官的符号在脑海里的黑板上恢复原状。科学的好奇心和普通逻辑要求我向自己证明，如果对这条有缺陷的垂直线采取不理不睬的态度，其缺陷就会在我身体的这个或那个部位反映出来。我把最后一块黄油小脆饼在茶水中蘸了蘸，咽下这甜腻黏糊的玩意，[①]决心开始对我不幸的肉身下手。

① 原文为mush，意为“糊状物，脆弱的感情、伤感的文字”。

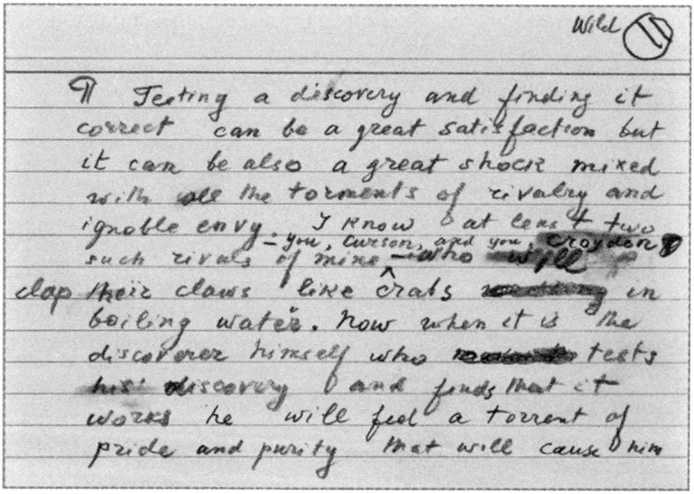
Wild (11)

¶ Testing a discovery and finding it correct can be a great satisfaction but it can be also a great shock mixed with the torments of rivalry and ignoble envy. I know at least two such rivals of mine – you, Curson, and you, Croydon – who clap their claws like crabs in the boiling water. Now when it is the discoverer himself who tests his discovery and finds that it works he will feel a torrent of pride and purity that will cause him

Wild [2]

Testing a discovery and finding it correct can be a great satisfaction but it can be also a great shock mixed with all the torments of rivalry and ignoble envy. I know at least two such rivals of mine—you, Curson, and you, Croydon—who will clap their claws like crabs in boiling water. Now when it is the discoverer himself who tests his discovery and finds that it works he will feel a torrent of pride and purity that will cause him

王尔德 [2]

测试一项发现时，如果得知其结果是正确的，这会给人带来莫大的满足感，但也可能引起极大的震惊，并与由竞争和卑鄙的妒忌带来的折磨交织在一起。我至少认识两个这样的竞争对手——你，科尔森，还有你，科罗尔登——他们会像沸水里的螃蟹一样张牙舞爪。现在，正是发现者本人在测试自己的发现并验证其正确性，此人将产生巨大的自豪与纯洁的情感，这种纯洁的情感令他竟然

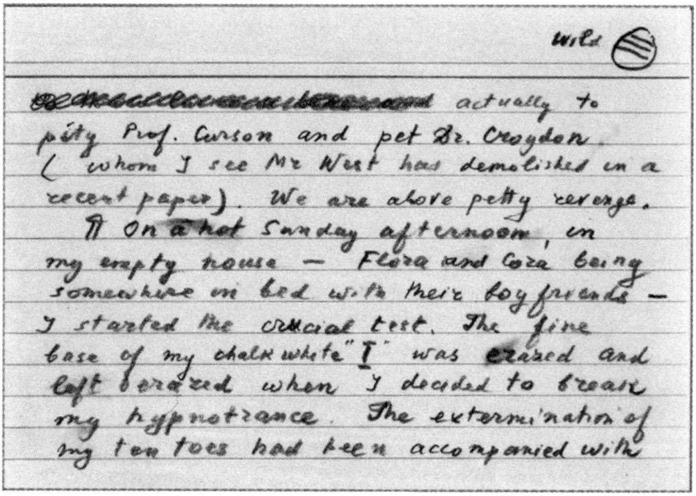

Wild

actually to
pity Prof. Carson and pet Dr. Croydon.
(whom I see Mr West has demolished in a
recent paper). We are above petty revenge.
¶ On a hot Sunday afternoon, in
my empty house — Flora and Cora being
somewhere in bed with their boyfriends —
I started the crucial test. The fine
base of my chalk white "I" was erased and
left erased when I decided to break
my hypnotrance. The extermination of
my ten toes had been accompanied with

Wild [3]

actually to pity Prof. Curson and pet Dr. Croydon (whom I see Mr West has demolished in a recent paper). We are above petty revenge.

On a hot Sunday afternoon, in my empty house—Flora and Cora being somewhere in bed with their boyfriends—I started the crucial test. The fine base of my chalk white "I" was erazed and left erazed when I decided to break my hypnotrance. The extermination of my ten toes had been accompanied with

王尔德 [3]

怜悯起科尔森教授，抚慰起科罗尔登博士来（我看到韦斯特先生在最近的一篇论文中诋毁了他）。我们不屑于睚眦必报。

一个炎热的周日下午，在我空荡荡的寓所里——弗洛拉和科拉正与她们的男朋友们躺在不知何处的床上鬼混——我开始了这个至关重要的实验。用白色粉笔画出的"I"的美妙底座被擦掉了，当我决定摆脱恍惚昏睡的状态时，它还是被抹去的样子。根除十个脚趾的过程伴随着

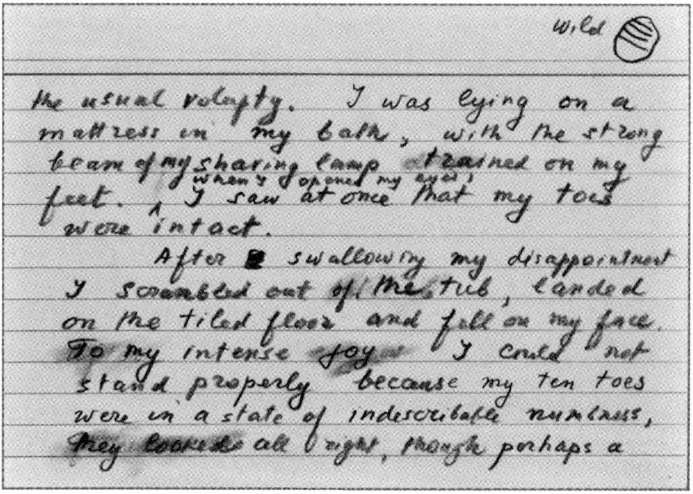

Wild

the usual volupty. I was lying on a mattress in my bath, with the strong beam of my shaving lamp trained on my feet. when I opened my eyes, I saw at once that my toes were intact.

After swallowing my disappointment I scrambled out of the tub, landed on the tiled floor and fell on my face. To my intense joy I could not stand properly because my ten toes were in a state of indescribable numbness, they looked all right, though perhaps a

Wild [4]

the usual volupty. I was lying on a mattress in my bath, with the strong beam of my shaving lamp trained on my feet. When I opened my eyes, I saw at once that my toes were intact.

After swallowing my disappointment I scrambled out of the tub, landed on the tiled floor and fell on my face. To my intense joy I could not stand properly because my ten toes were in a state of indescribable numbness. They looked all right, though perhaps a

王尔德 [4]

一贯的舒适感。我躺在浴缸垫上，剃须灯的强光瞄准我的双脚。我睁开眼时，立刻发现脚趾依然完好无损。

强忍着内心的失望，我吃力地从浴缸里爬了出来，双脚刚踩到瓷砖铺砌的地板，就脸冲下栽倒在地。我欣喜若狂地发现，我站不稳是因为我的十个脚趾有一种难以名状的麻木感。它们看上去完好无损，也许比

Wild

a little paler than usual, but all sensation had been slashed away by a razor of ice. I palpated warily the hallux and the four other digits of my right foot, then of my left one and all was rubber and rot. The immediate setting-in of decay was especially sensationally. I crept on all fours into the adjacent bedroom and with infinite effort into my bed.

The rest was mere cleaning-up. In the course of the night I teased off the shrivelled white flesh and contemplated with utmost delight

before

Wild [5]

a little paler than usual, but all sensation had been slashed away by a razor of ice. I palpated warily the hallux and the four other digits of my right foot, then of my left one and all was rubber and rot. The immediate setting in of decay was especially sensationally. I crept on all fours into the adjacent bedroom and with infinite effort into my bed.

The rest was mere cleaning-up. In the course of the night I teased off the shrivelled white flesh and contemplated with utmost delight[.]

[before his bath]

王尔德 [5]

平常看上去略显苍白，但如冰一般的剃须刀已经将所有知觉切割殆尽。我先是小心翼翼地触诊我右脚的大拇指和其他四个脚趾，然后又查看我的左脚，它们都软如橡胶，腐如朽木。这么快就开始腐烂实在太妙了。我手脚并用地爬到邻近的卧室，费了九牛二虎之力才爬到床上。

剩下的只是清理工作。整个通宵我一边剔除干瘪苍白的死肉，一边欣喜若狂地沉思。

[在他洗澡之前]

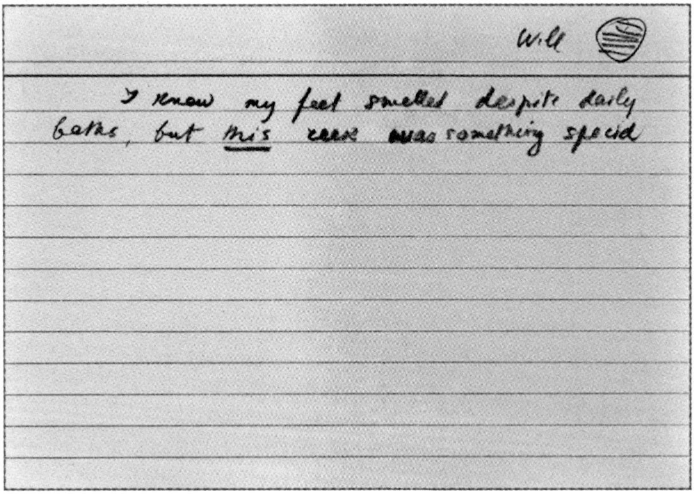
Will

I know my feet smelled despite daily baths, but this was something special

Wild［6］

I know my feet smelled despite daily baths, but this reek was something special

王尔德［6］

我知道，尽管每天洗澡，我的两脚依然有气味，但这种臭味非常特别。

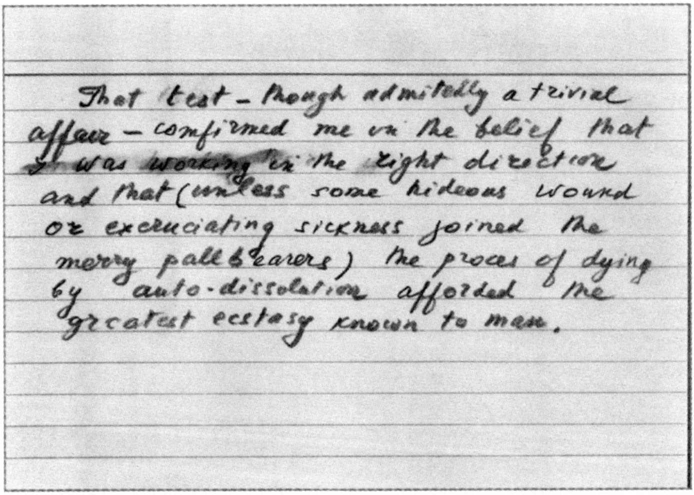
That test – though admittedly a trivial
affair – confirmed me in the belief that
I was working in the right direction
and that (unless some hideous wound
or excruciating sickness joined the
merry pallbearers) the process of dying
by auto-dissolution afforded the
greatest ecstasy known to man.

That test—though admit[t]edly a trivial affair—confirmed me in the belief that I was working in the right direction and that (unless some hideous wound or excruciating sickness joined the merry pallbearers) the proces[s] of dying by auto-dissolution afforded the greatest ecstasy known to man.

那次测试——尽管我承认那并非什么惊人之举——坚定了我的信念，让我确信自己的思路是正确的，也确信自动消解的死亡方式能给人类带来已知的最大的快乐（除非一些可怕的伤口或疼痛的疾病也来凑热闹加入快乐的护柩者行列）。

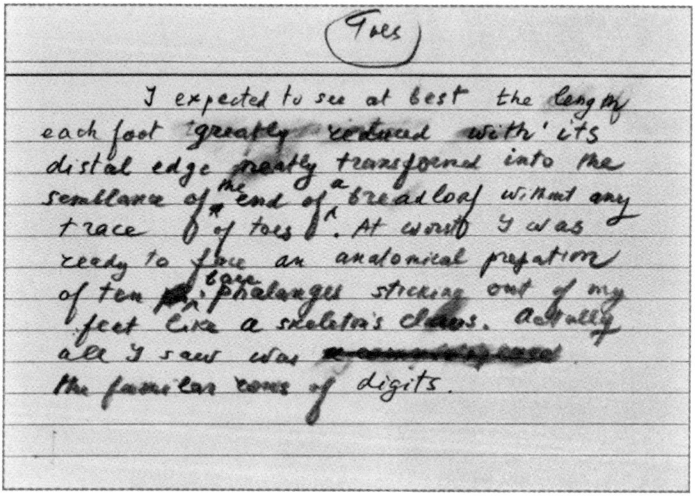
Toes

I expected to see at best the length of each foot greatly reduced with its distal edge neatly transformed into the semblance of the end of a breadloaf without any trace of toes. At worst I was ready to face an anatomical preparation of ten bare phalanges sticking out of my feet like a skeleton's claws. Actually all I saw was ~~[illegible]~~ the familiar rows of digits.

Toes

I expected to see at best the length [of] each foot greatly reduced with its distal edge neatly transformed into the semblance of the end of a breadloaf without any trace of toes. At worst I was ready to face an anatomical prep[ar]ation of ten bare phalanges sticking out of my feet like a skeleton's claws. Actually all I saw was the famil[i]ar rows of digits.

脚　趾

我期待看到的最好情况是，每只脚的长度都有大幅度的缩减，同时其末端的边缘变得如一整块面包般干净利落，没有任何脚趾的痕迹。而我打算面对的最坏的情况是一个解剖手术的准备，十个光秃秃的趾骨如同骷髅的爪子一般从我的脚上伸出来。而事实上出现在我眼前的依然是两排熟悉的脚趾。

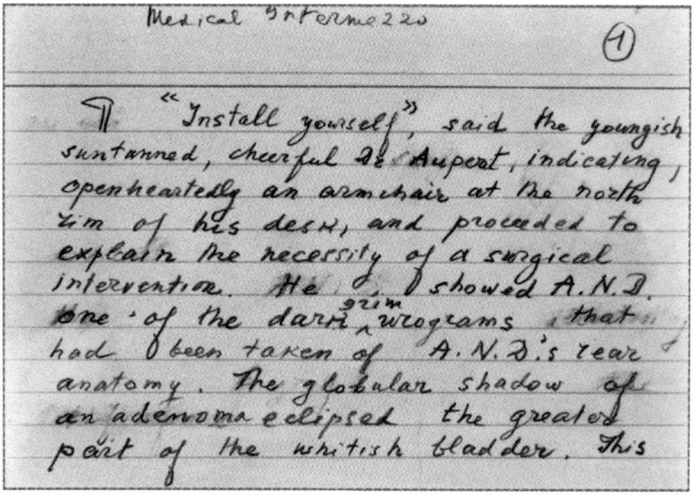
Medical Intermezzo

(1)

¶ "Install yourself", said the youngish
suntanned, cheerful Dr Aupert, indicating,
openheartedly an armchair at the north
rim of his desk, and proceeded to
explain the necessity of a surgical
intervention. He showed A.N.D.
one of the dark grim urograms that
had been taken of A.N.D.'s rear
anatomy. The globular shadow of
an adenoma eclipsed the greater
part of the whitish bladder. This

Medical Intermezzo

1

"Install yourself," said the youngish suntanned, cheerful Dr Aupert, indicating openheartedly an armchair at the north rim of his desk, and proceeded to explain the necessity of a surgical intervention. He showed A. N. D. one of the dark grim urograms that had been taken of A. N. D.'s rear anatomy. The globular shadow of an adenoma eclipsed the greater part of the whitish bladder. This

医学间奏曲

1

尚算年轻的奥佩尔医生晒得黝黑，显得十分愉快，他指着他办公桌北侧的一把扶手椅，豪爽地说："请坐。"接着他解释了外科手术治疗的必要性，从好些呈病态的黑色的尿路造影照片中拿了一张给A. N. D.看，那是在给A. N. D.作背部解剖时拍的。一个球形的腺瘤阴影遮蔽了比发白的膀胱更大的一块。这个

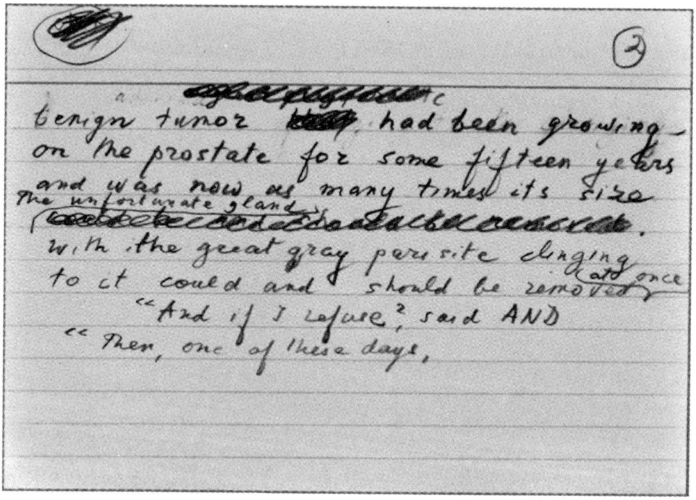

(2)

benign tumor had been growing
on the prostate for some fifteen years
and was now as many times its size.
The unfortunate gland,
with the great gray parasite clinging
to it could and should be removed at once.
"And if I refuse?" said AND
"Then, one of these days,

2

benign tumor had been growing on the prostate for some fifteen years and was now as many times its size. The unfortunate gland with the great gray par[a]site clinging to it could and should be removed at once

"And if I refuse?["] said A[.]N[.]D.

"Then, one of these days,

2

良性肿瘤在前列腺上已长了大约十五年，现在比前列腺还要大好几倍。不幸的前列腺连同依附于它的这个巨大的灰色寄生虫可以而且应当立即切除掉。

"如果我不同意呢？" A. N. D.说。

"那么，总有一天，

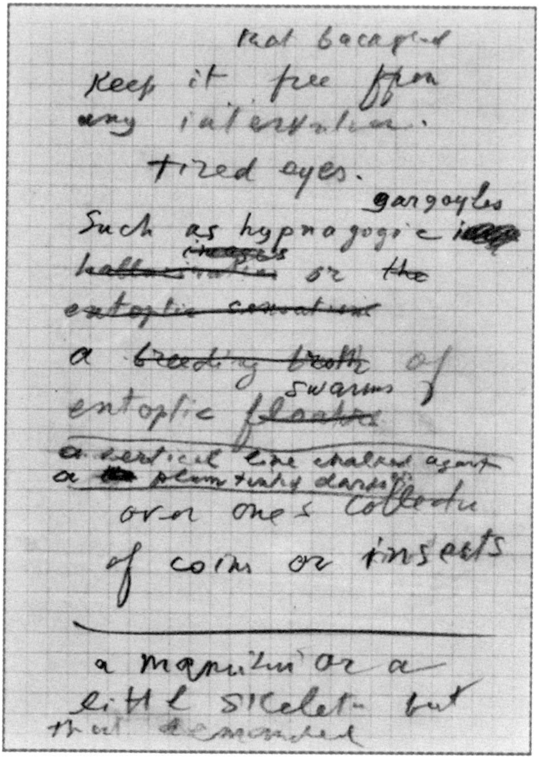
not escaped
Keep it free from
any interpolation.
tired eyes.
gargoyles
Such as hypnagogic ~~i…~~ images
~~hallucinations~~ or ~~the~~
~~entoptic sensations~~
a ~~breeding broth~~ of
swarms
entoptic ~~floaters~~
~~a vertical line chalked against~~
~~a plum tinted darkness~~
over one's collection
of coins or insects

a mannikin or a
little skeleton but
that demanded

---

that back[grd] keep it free from any intervention. tired eyes.

Such as hypnagogic gargoyles* or entoptic swarms*

a vertical line chalked against a plum* tinted darkness

over one's collection of coins or insects

a manikin or a little skeleton but that demanded

这个背景会令任何治疗都无济于事。疲惫的眼睛。

比如催眠滴水兽*或眼内蜂群*

一根垂直的粉笔线条迎面划过一块暗紫红色*

在某人的硬币或昆虫收藏之上,

一个假人或一具小小的骨架,但要求

---

* 这些词组也在第一三三页和一三五页出现过,可能表明此卡片是相关素材的草稿。

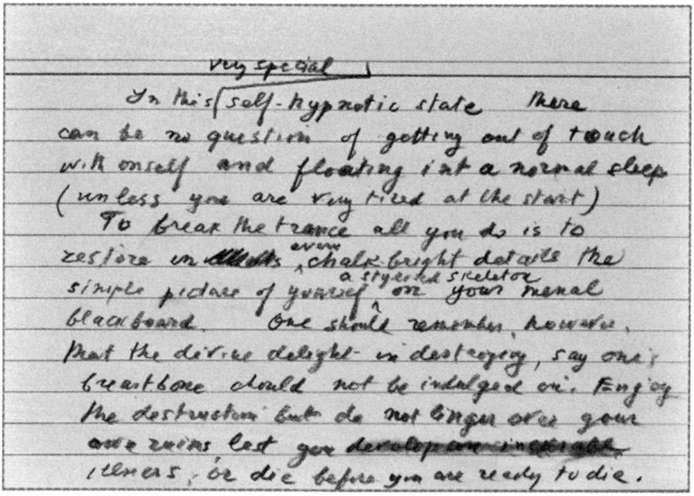

very special

In this [self-hypnotic state there can be no question of getting out of touch with oneself and floating into a normal sleep (unless you are very tired at the start)

To break the trance all you do is to restore in ~~[illegible]~~ even chalk-bright details the simple picture of yourself a stylized skeleton on your mental blackboard. One should remember, however, that the divine delight in destroying, say one's breastbone should not be indulged in. Enjoy the destruction but do not linger over your own ruins, lest you ~~develop an incurable~~ illness, or die before you are ready to die.

In this very special self-hypnotic state there can be no question of getting out of touch with on[e]self and floating int[o] a normal sleep (unless you are very tired at the start)[.]

To break the trance all you do is to restore in every chalkbright details the simple picture of yourself a stylized skeleton on your men[t]al blackboard. One should remember, however, that the divine delight in destroying, say[,] one's breastbone should not be indulged in. Enjoy the destruction but do not linger over your own ruins lest you develop an incurable illness, or die before you are ready to die.

在这种非同寻常的自我催眠的状态中，要做到物我两忘，并逐渐沉入正常的睡眠之中毫无问题（除非你一开始就异常疲惫）。

要想摆脱这种昏睡状态，你只需要用鲜亮的粉笔线条恢复你自己简单画像的细节，在你脑海中那块黑板上勾勒格式固定的骨架。但要切记，无论如何，都不可沉溺于摧残胸骨时产生的极致愉悦中。享受毁灭，但不要在自身的废墟上流连，以免患上不治之症，或在准备好去死之前死去。

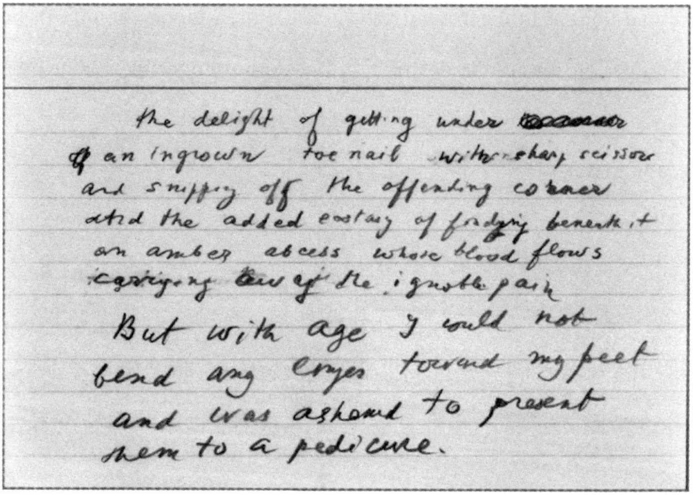

the delight of getting under [illegible]
of an ingrown toenail with sharp scissors
and snipping off the offending corner
and the added ecstasy of finding beneath it
an amber abcess whose blood flows
carrying away of the ignoble pain
But with age I could not
bend any longer toward my feet
and was ashamed to present
them to a pedicure.

the delight of getting under an ingrown toenail with sharp scissors and snipping off the offending corner and the added ecstasy of finding beneath it an amber ab[s]cess whose blood flows[,] carrying away the ignoble pain[.]

But with age I could not bend any longer toward my feet and was ashamed to present them to a pedicure.

将锋利的剪刀伸入一个向内生长的趾甲下剪掉那个令人不适的角而产生的愉悦，加上因为发现其下还有一个琥珀色的脓肿流着脓血带走了可恶的疼痛而额外生出的惊喜。

然而年龄渐长，我已不能弯下腰去够到双脚了，又羞于将它们交给足疗师。

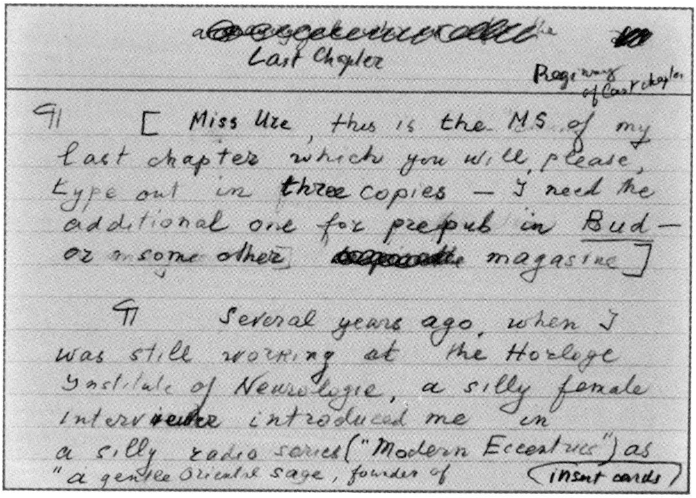

Last Chapter

Beginning of last chapter

¶ [Miss Ure, this is the MS of my last chapter which you will, please, type out in three copies — I need the additional one for prepub in Bud— or some other magazine]

¶ Several years ago, when I was still working at the Horloge Institute of Neurologie, a silly female interviewer introduced me in a silly radio series ("Modern Eccentrics") as "a gentle Oriental sage, founder of (insert cards)

Last Chapter

Beginning of last chapter

[Miss Ure, this is the MS of my last chapter which you will, please, type out in three copies—I need the additional one for prepub in Bud—or some other maga[z]ine.]*

Several years ago, when I was still working at the Horloge Institute of Neurologie, a silly female interviewer introduced me in a silly radio series ("Modern Eccentrics") as "a gentle oriental sage", founder of

最后一章

最后一章的开始部分

[尤尔小姐，这是我的小说最后一章的手稿，请打印三份，我还需要另外打一份，提前发表在《萌芽》或其他杂志上。]*

几年前，我还在"钟塔神经病学院"工作时，一个愚蠢的女性采访者在一档傻乎乎的广播系列节目（"现代怪人"）中介绍我时，称我为"温文尔雅的东方圣人"，……的创立者

---

* 第一段的方括号也许是提示将此段设为摘录。

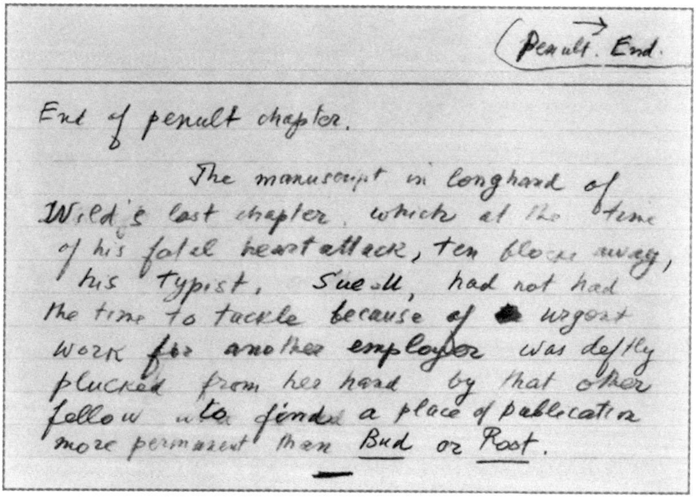
(Penult. End

End of penult chapter.

The manuscript in longhand of Wild's last chapter, which at the time of his fatal heartattack, ten blocks away, his typist, Sue ll, had not had the time to tackle because of urgent work for another employer was deftly plucked from her hand by that other fellow to find a place of publication more permanent than Bud or Root.

—

Penult. End.

End of penult chapter.

The manuscript in longhand of Wild's last chapter, which at the time of his fatal heart attack, ten blocks away, his typist, Sue U, had not had the time to tackle because of urgent work for another employer[,] was deftly plucked from her hand by that other fellow to find a place of publication more permanent than Bud or Root.

倒数第二部分结尾

倒数第二章的结尾。

当王尔德的致命心脏病发作时，他的打字员苏·尤尔距离他有十个街区之遥，当时因为忙着处理另一位雇主的紧急事务而无暇顾及王尔德手稿的最后一章，另一个家伙机灵地从苏的手中掠走了手稿，找了家比《萌芽》和《根》更长久的刊物发表了。

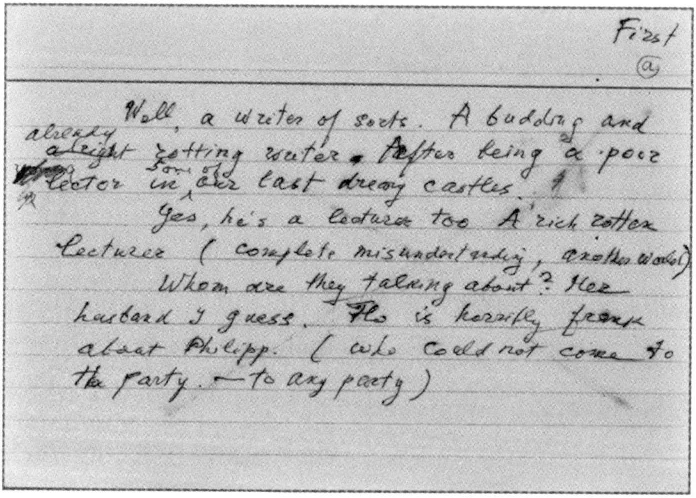

First

(a)

Well, a writer of sorts. A budding and ~~alright~~ already rotting writer. After being a poor lector in some of our last dreary castles.

Yes, he's a lecturer too. A rich rotten lecturer (complete misunderstanding, another world)

Whom are they talking about? Her husband I guess. Flo is horribly frank about Philipp. (who could not come to the party — to any party)

First a

Well, a writer of sorts. A budding and already rotting writer. After being a poor lector in some of our last dreary castles.

Yes, he's a lecturer too[.] A rich rotten lecturer (complete misunderstanding, another world).

Whom are they talking about? Her husband I guess. Flo is horribly frank about Philipp (who could not come to the party—to any party)*.

第一部分 a

是啊，勉强称得上是一位作家。一位刚刚崭露头角就已日渐腐烂的作家。此前，他曾是某些我们最后的凄凉城堡里一位可怜的诵经员。

是的，他也是一位讲师。一位富有而又腐朽的讲师（完全是误会，是另一个世界）。

他们在议论谁呢？我猜，是她的丈夫吧。弗洛拉谈及菲利普时口无遮拦得可怕（菲利普不可能来参加这个聚会——他任何聚会都不参加）。*

* 这些资料与第一章中的对话吻合。

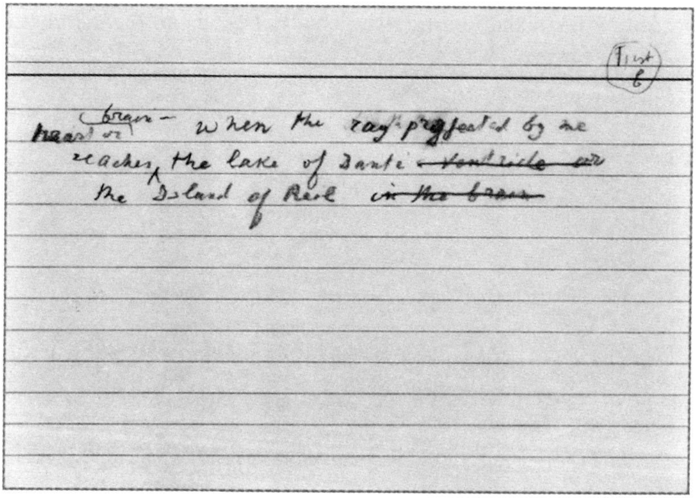

First
6

~~heart~~ or brain — when the ray projected by me reaches the lake of Dante ~~ventricle~~ or the Island of Rest ~~in the brain~~

First b

heart or brain—When the ray projected by me reaches the lake of Dante [or] the Island of Reil

第一部分 b

心脏或大脑——当我发出的射线抵达但丁湖或赖尔岛时

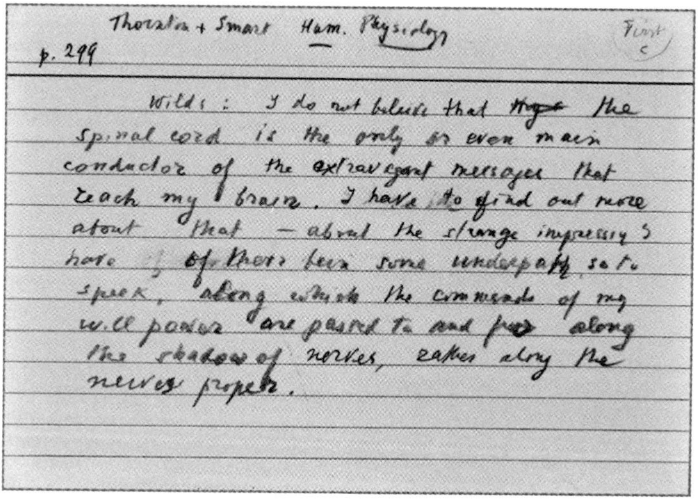
Thurston + Smart Hum. Physiology

p. 299

First
c

Wild: I do not believe that ~~the~~ the spinal cord is the only or even main conductor of the extravagant messages that reach my brain. I have to find out more about that — about the strange impression I have of there being some underpath, so to speak, along which the commands of my will power are passed to and fro along the shadow of nerves, rather along the nerves proper.

First c

Thornton+Smart Hum. Physiology

p.299

Wild's [ms.]: I do not believe that the spinal cord is the only or even main conductor of the extravagant messages that reach my brain. I have to find out more about that—about the strange impression I have of there being some underpath, so to speak, along which the commands of my will power are passed to and fro along the shadow of nerves, rather [than] along the nerves proper.

第一部分 c

桑顿研究机构+聪明的人类。《生理学》

第二九九页

王尔德的［手稿］：我不相信脊髓是将大量信息传送至我大脑的唯一或主要导体。我有一种奇怪的感觉：还存在某种秘密的信息传送渠道，也就是说，意志力发出的指令是沿着神经的虚影，而不是严格意义上的神经来回传送的。对此我还得作进一步研究。

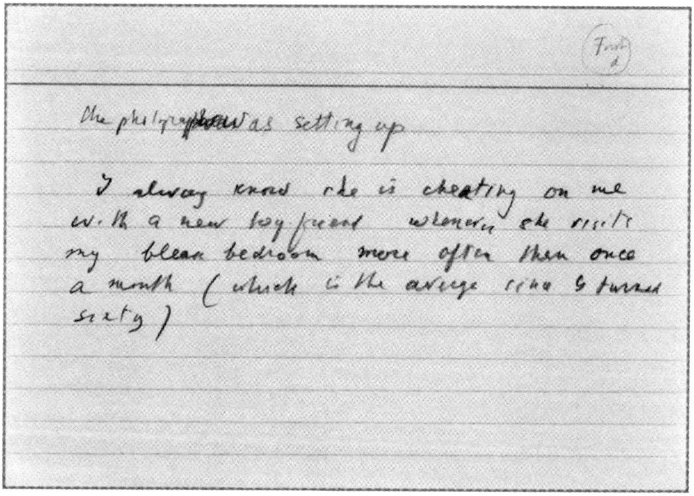
the philosopher was setting up

I always knew she is cheating on me with a new boyfriend whenever she visits my bleak bedroom more often than once a month (which is the average since I turned sixty)

First d

The photograph[er] was setting up

I alway[s] know she is cheating on me with a new boyfriend whenever she visits my bleak bedroom more often than once a month (which is the average since I turned sixty)[.]

第一部分 d

摄影师已经准备就绪。

她到我灰暗的房间里来的次数超出每个月一次时(这是自我步入六十岁后她光顾我房间的平均频率),我就知道她在欺骗我,她又交上了新男友。

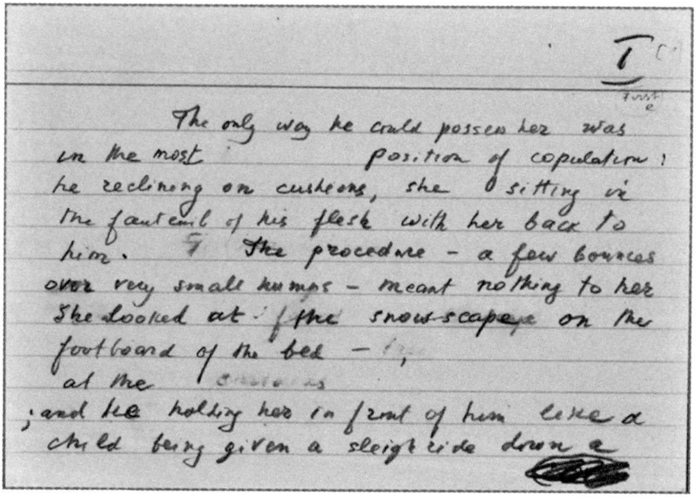
I

The only way he could possess her was in the most position of copulation: he reclining on cushions, she sitting in the fauteuil of his flesh with her back to him. ¶ The procedure - a few bounces over very small humps - meant nothing to her She looked at the snow-scape on the footboard of the bed -
at the
; and he holding her in front of him like a child being given a sleigh ride down a

I

The only way he could possess her was in the most [   ] position of copulation: he reclining on cushions: she sitting in the fauteuil of his flesh with her back to him. The procedure—a few bounces over very small humps—meant nothing to her[.] She looked at the snow-scape on the footboard of the bed—at the [curtains]; and he holding her in front of him like a child being given a sleighride down a

I

只有在交媾时居于最 [   ] 的位置，他才得以占有她：他斜躺在垫子上，她坐在他的肉体扶手椅上，背对着他。整个过程——在隆起的小小肉丘上弹跳几下——对她来说毫无意义。她看着床尾板上的雪景，看着窗帘。他搂抱着坐在前面的她，她如同一个孩子坐在友善的陌生人给她的雪橇里，

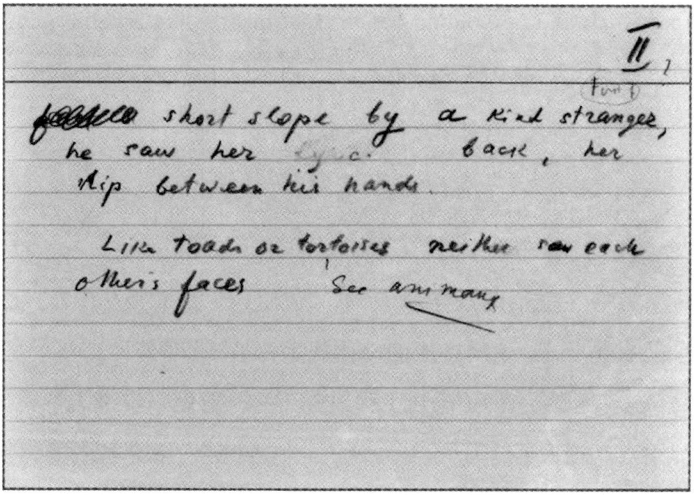
II 7

(cont.)

short slope by a kind stranger, he saw her back, her hip between his hands.

Like toads or tortoises neither saw each other's faces. See animals

II

short slope by a kind stranger, he saw her back, her hip[s] between his hands.

Like toads or tortoises neither saw each other's faces See animaux

II

沿着一条短短的斜坡往下滑。他看着她的后背，双手捧着她的臀部。

如同蟾蜍或乌龟般看不到彼此的脸

看动物抱对[1]

① 原文为animaux，法语“动物”的复数形式，此处译为“动物抱对”。

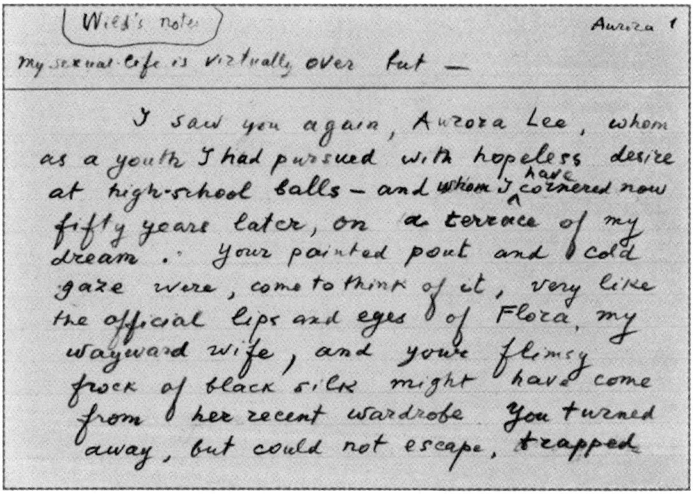
Wild's notes

Aurora 1

my sexual life is virtually over but —

I saw you again, Aurora Lee, whom as a youth I had pursued with hopeless desire at high-school balls — and whom I have cornered now fifty years later, on a terrace of my dream. Your painted pout and cold gaze were, come to think of it, very like the official lips and eyes of Flora, my wayward wife, and your flimsy frock of black silk might have come from her recent wardrobe. You turned away, but could not escape, trapped

---

① Aurora Lee，本书中王尔德的初恋情人，其姓名可能是对勃朗宁夫人著名长诗《奥罗拉・莉》（*Aurora Leigh*）的戏仿。

Wild's notes

Aurora 1

My sexual life is virtually over but—

I saw you again, Aurora Lee, whom as a youth I had pursued with hopeless desire at high-school balls—and whom I have cornered now fifty years later, on a terrace of my dream. Your painted pout and cold gaze were, come to think of it, very like the official lips and eyes of Flora, my wayward wife, and your flimsy frock of black silk might have come from her recent wardrobe. You turned away, but could not escape, trapped.

王尔德的笔记

奥罗拉 1

我的性生活几乎结束了,然而——

我又见到了你,奥罗拉·李,[①]我年轻时在高中舞会上怀着无望的渴慕追求过的人,五十年后的今天,在我梦的露台上,你无路可退。你涂满口红的小嘴、冷峻的目光,细想起来,酷似我任性的妻子弗洛拉那公认的嘴巴和眼睛。你身上穿的这件又轻又薄的黑色丝绸连衣裙或许就出自她最近的衣橱。你轻身离去,却无法逃脱,被困在了

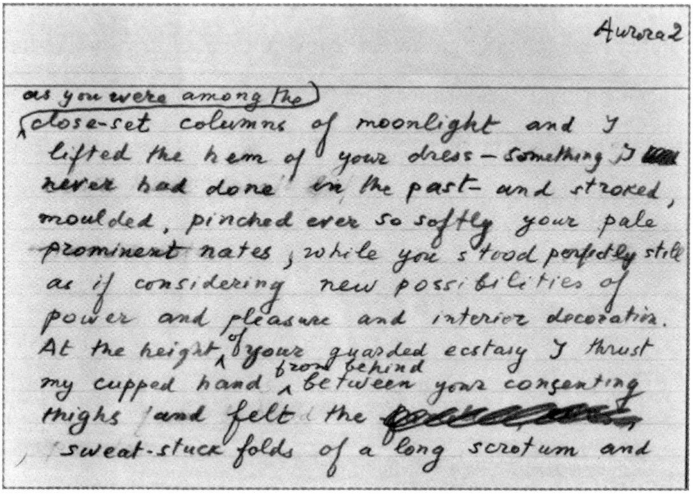

Aurora 2

as you were among the
close-set columns of moonlight and I
lifted the hem of your dress — something I
never had done ~~in~~ the past — and stroked,
moulded, pinched ever so softly your pale
~~prominent~~ nates, while you stood perfectly still
as if considering new possibilities of
power and pleasure and interior decoration.
At the height of your guarded ecstasy I thrust
my cupped hand from behind between your consenting
thighs and felt the
sweat-stuck folds of a long scrotum and

Aurora 2

as you were among the close-set columns of moonlight and I lifted the hem of your dress—something I never had done in the past—and stroked, moulded, pinched ever so softly your pale prominent nates, while you stood perfectly still as if considering new possibilities of power and pleasure and interior decoration. At the height of your guarded ecstasy I thrust my cupped hand from behind between your consenting thighs and felt the sweat-stuck folds of a long scrotum and

奥罗拉 2

两道紧挨着的月光柱之间。我撩起你的裙子——这是我以前从未做过的事——如此温存地抚摸、搂抱、揉捏着你苍白的翘臀。而你则纹丝不动，安静地站在那里，似乎在思量着种种新的可能：力量、愉悦和内心的掩饰。在你那矜持的狂喜达到高潮时，我从后面将窝成杯状的手伸入你顺从的大腿之间，触摸到浸透了汗液的长长的阴囊，接着，再往前些，是

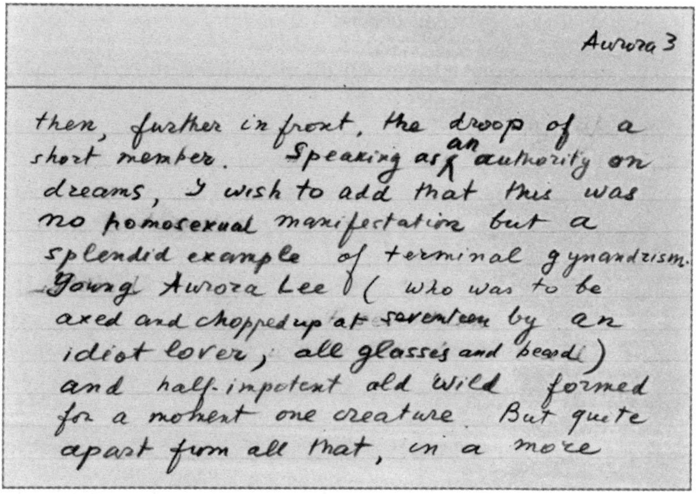
Aurora 3

then, further in front, the droop of a
short member. Speaking as an authority on
dreams, I wish to add that this was
no homosexual manifestation but a
splendid example of terminal gynandrism.
Young Aurora Lee (who was to be
axed and chopped up at seventeen by an
idiot lover, all glasses and beard)
and half-impotent old Wild formed
for a moment one creature. But quite
apart from all that, in a more

Aurora 3

then, further in front, the droop of a short member. Speaking as an authority on dreams, I wish to add that this was no homosexual manifestation but a splendid example of terminal gynandrism. Young Aurora Lee (who was to be axed and chopped up at seventeen by an idiot lover, all glasses and beard) and half-impotent old Wild formed for a moment one creature. But quite apart from all that, in a more

奥罗拉 3

耷拉在阴囊前面的短体，[①] 作为一个解梦的权威人士，我想补充两句，这并非同性恋的表现，而是一个末端的雌雄同体的杰出范例。年轻的奥罗拉·李（十七岁时就被一个戴眼镜且长着一脸大胡子的白痴情人摧残得支离破碎）和半阳痿的老王尔德一时间合二为一。但撇开这一切，就某种

① 此处的“短体”（a short member）和第八十七页中的“三角区”（delta）分别指男女生殖器，这便是典型的纳博科夫富有原创性的隐喻语言。

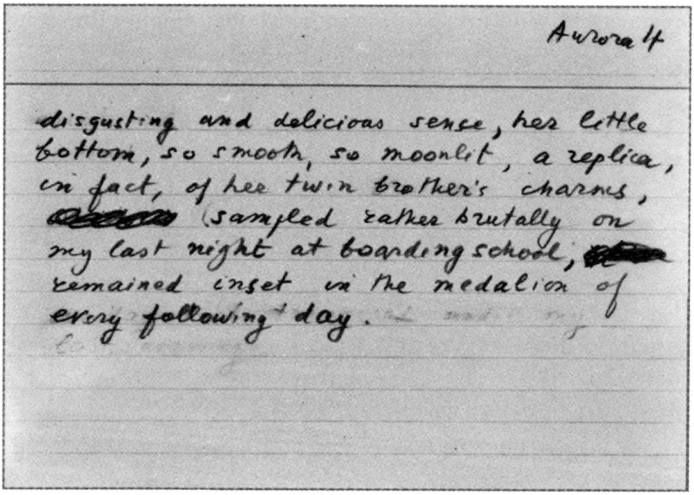

Aurora 4

disgusting and delicious sense, her little
bottom, so smooth, so moonlit, a replica,
in fact, of her twin brother's charms,
[redacted] (sampled rather brutally on
my last night at boarding school, [redacted]
remained inset in the medalion of
every following day.

Aurora 4

disgusting and delicious sense, her little bottom, so smooth, so moonlit, a replica, in fact, of her twin brother's charms, sampled rather brutally on my last night at boarding school, remained inset in the medal[l]ion of every following day.

奥罗拉 4

更为恶心、更为可口的层面而言，她小小的屁股是那么光滑，有如一轮新月般白净，简直就是她孪生兄弟的护身符的复制品，我在寄宿学校的最后一个晚上曾相当粗鲁地取过样，样本依然嵌在每个翌日的徽章里。

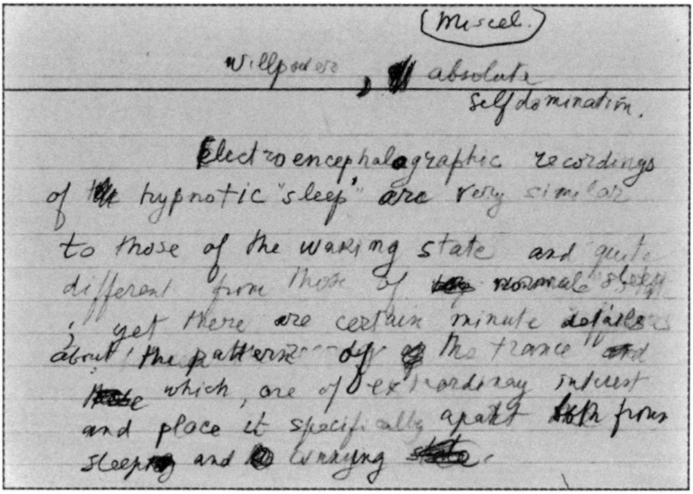

(Miscel.)

Willpower, absolute selfdomination.

Electroencephalographic recordings of the hypnotic "sleep" are very similar to those of the waking state and quite different from those of normal sleep, yet there are certain minute details about the patterns of the trance which are of extraordinary interest and place it specifically apart from sleep and waking.

Miscel.

Willpower, absolute self domination.

Electroencephalographic recordings of hypnotic “sleep” are very similar to those of the waking state and quite different from those of normal sleep; yet there are certain minute details about the pattern of the trance which are of extraordina[r]y interest and pl[a]ce it specifically apart both from sleep and [waking].

其他疾病

意志力,绝对自控力。

脑电图显示,催眠中的大脑状态与苏醒时的大脑状态很相似,但与正常睡眠时的状态完全不同;然而,这种恍惚昏睡的模式中有许多微妙的细节很有意思,也令它与睡眠和清醒这两种状态都明显地区别开来。

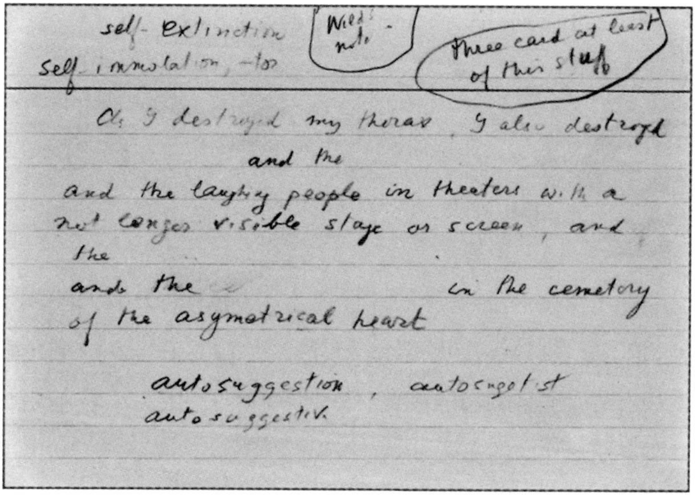
self-extinction
Self-immolation, —too

Wild! note –

Three card at least of this stuff

As I destroyed my thorax, I also destroyed
and the
and the laughing people in theaters with a
no longer visible stage or screen, and
the
and the in the cemetery
of the asymetrical heart

autosuggestion, autosuggestist
autosuggestive

Wild's note

self-extinction

self-immolation, -tor

As I destroyed my thorax, I also destroyed [ ] and the [ ] and the laughing people in theaters with a not longer visible stage or screen, and the [ ] and the [ ] in the cemetery of the asym[m]-etrical heart

autosuggestion, autosug[g]etist

autosuggestive

王尔德的笔记

自我毁灭

自我牺牲，自我牺牲者

当我毁灭我的胸膛时，我同时毁灭了［ ］，还有［ ］，以及剧院里发出大笑的人们，有形的舞台和屏幕不复存在；同时毁灭［ ］，还有失衡的心底坟墓中的［ ］

自我暗示，自我暗示者

自我暗示的

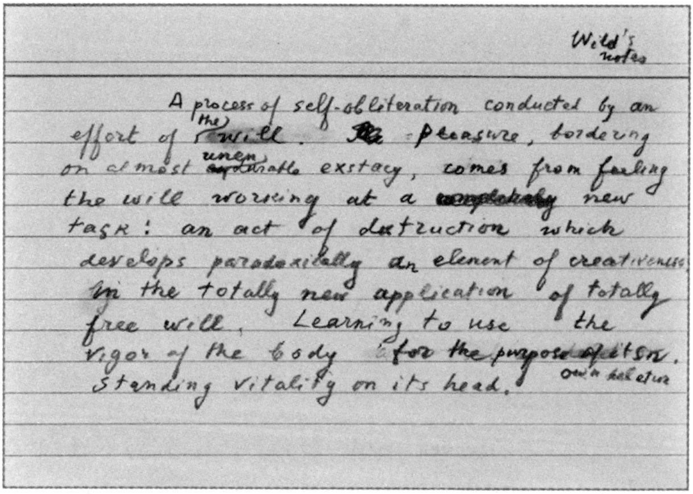
Wild's notes

A process of self-obliteration conducted by an effort of the will. Pleasure, bordering on almost uneniurable exstacy, comes from feeling the will working at a new task: an act of destruction which develops paradoxically an element of creativeness in the totally new application of totally free will. Learning to use the vigor of the body for the purpose of its own deletion. Standing vitality on its head.

Wild's notes

A process of self-obliteration conducted by an effort of the will. Pleasure, bordering on almost unendurable exstacy, comes from feeling the will working at a new task: an act of destruction which develops paradoxically an element of creativeness in the totally new application of totally free will. Learning to use the vigor of the body for the purpose of its own deletion[,] standing vitality on its head.

王尔德的笔记

自我泯灭的过程由意志力引导。快感近乎一种几乎无法承受的狂喜，它源自对于着手一项新任务的意愿的感知：一项荒谬地衍生出了一点点创意的毁灭行为，这种创意体现在对绝对自由意志的全新的应用。学会使用自身的元气达到自我删除的目的，将元气倒过来使用。

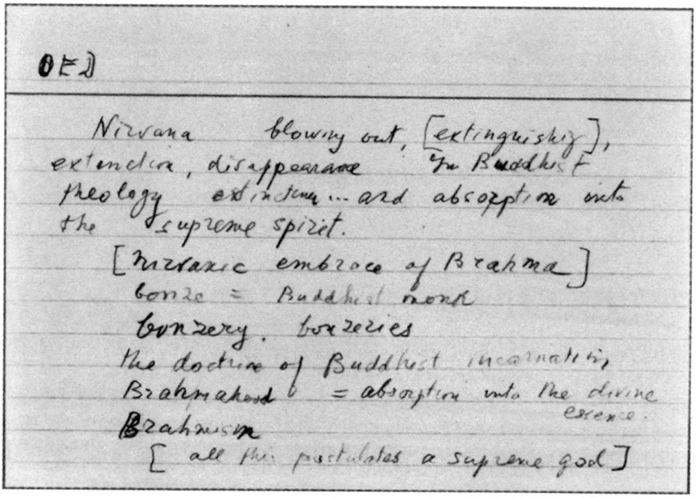

OED

Nirvana blowing out, [extinguishing], extinction, disappearance In Buddhist theology extinction... and absorption into the supreme spirit.

[nirvanic embrace of Brahma]

bonze = Buddhist monk

bonzery, bonzeries

the doctrine of Buddhist incarnation,

Brahmahood = absorption into the divine essence.

Brahmism

[all this postulates a supreme god]

OED

Nirvana [ ] blowing out (extinguishing), extinction, disappearance. In Buddhist theology extinction ... and absorption into the supreme spirit.

(nirvanic embrace of Brahma)

bonze=Buddhist monk

bonzery, bonzeries

the doctrine of Buddhist incarnation

Brahmahood=absorption into the divine essence.

Brahmism

(all this postulates a supreme god)

牛津英语词典

涅槃[ ]吹熄(熄灭),灭绝,消失。佛教观念中指消亡……并升华为至高的灵魂。

(涅槃是梵天的拥抱)

僧人=和尚

僧人,和尚

佛教转世的教义

梵天的境界=融入神的精髓

婆罗门教

(这一切都假定存在一位至高无上的神)

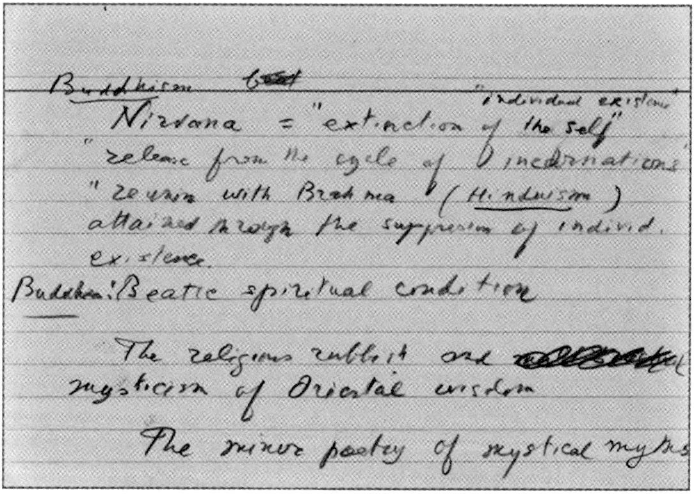

Buddhism ~~[struck out]~~

Nirvana = "extinction of the self" ["individual existence" written above "the self"]
"release from the cycle of incarnations"
"reunion with Brahma (Hinduism)
attained through the suppression of individ. existence.

Buddhism: Beatic spiritual condition

The religious rubbish and ~~[struck out]~~
mysticism of Oriental wisdom

The minor poetry of mystical myths

Buddhism

Nirvana= "extinction of the self" "individual existence"

"release from the cycle of incarnations"

"reunion with Brahma (Hinduism)["]

attained through the suppression of individ[ual] existence.

Buddhism: Beatic spiritual condition

The religious rubbish and mysticism of oriental wisdom

The minor poetry of mystical myths

佛教

涅槃 = "自我毁灭""个体存在"

"从轮回转世中解脱"

"与梵（印度教）结合"

通过抑制个体生存得以实现

佛教：令人心动的精神状态

宗教垃圾和东方智慧的玄想

关于神秘传说的二流诗歌

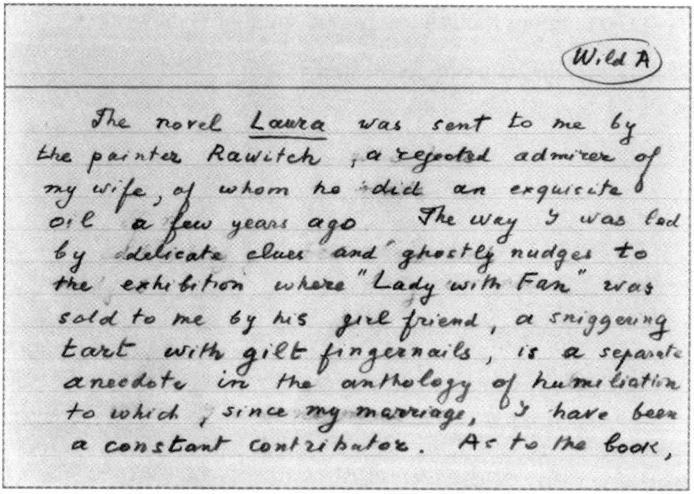

Wild A

The novel *Laura* was sent to me by the painter Rawitch, a rejected admirer of my wife, of whom he did an exquisite oil a few years ago. The way I was led by delicate clues and ghostly nudges to the exhibition where "Lady with Fan" was sold to me by his girl friend, a sniggering tart with gilt fingernails, is a separate anecdote in the anthology of humiliation to which, since my marriage, I have been a constant contributor. As to the book,

Wild A

The novel *Laura* was sent to me by the painter Rawitch, a rejected admirer of my wife, of whom he did an exquisite oil a few years ago. The way I was led by delicate clues and ghostly nudges to the exhibition where "Lady with Fan" was sold to me by his girlfriend, a sniggering tart with gilt fingernails, is a separate anecdote in the anthology of humiliation to which, since my marriage, I have been a constant contributor. As to the book,

王尔德 A

画家拉维奇将小说《劳拉》邮寄给了我，他是一位遭到我妻子拒绝的仰慕者。几年前他为我妻子画了一幅精致的油画。我受微妙线索的引导，鬼使神差地去了那个画展，他的女友把那幅《持扇女》卖给了我。这个指甲上涂着金彩的轻佻女人一直窃笑着。自结婚以来，我就一直在为耻辱故事集源源不断地贡献素材，这次经历只不过是故事集中单独的一篇。至于这本书，

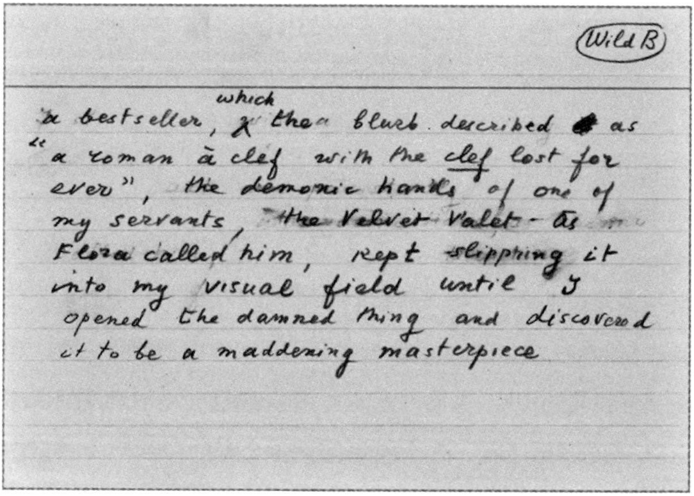

(Wild B)

a bestseller, which the blurb described as "a roman à clef with the clef lost for ever", the demonic hands of one of my servants, the Velvet Valet – as Flora called him, kept slipping it into my visual field until I opened the damned thing and discovered it to be a maddening masterpiece

Wild B

a bestseller, which the blurb described as "a roman à clef with the clef lost for ever" , the demonic hands of one of my servants, the Velvet Valet as Flora called him, kept slipping it into my visual field until I opened the damned thing and discovered it to be a maddening masterpiece

王尔德 B

可是一部畅销之作，书上的简介将它描述为"一本永远无原型可考的真人真事小说[①]"。我的一个仆人，弗洛拉管他叫"天鹅绒般温柔的贴身男仆"，老用他那双魔鬼般的手把《劳拉》塞入我的视野中。我翻开那本该死的书，发现它是一本让人气得发疯的杰作。

① 原文为法语。

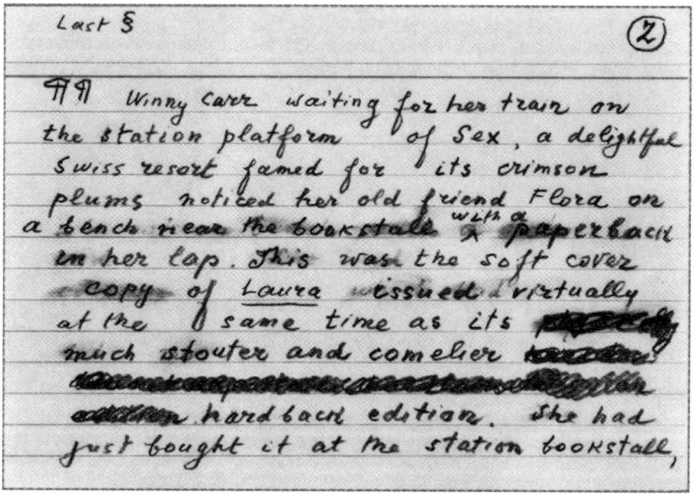

Last §

②

¶¶ Winny Carr waiting for her train on
the station platform of Sex, a delightful
Swiss resort famed for its crimson
plums noticed her old friend Flora on
a bench ~~near the bookstall~~ with a paperback
in her lap. This was the soft cover
copy of Laura issued virtually
at the same time as its [redacted]
much stouter and comelier [redacted] hardback edition. She had
just bought it at the station bookstall,

Last §

Z

Winny Carr waiting for her train on the station platform of Sex, a delightful Swiss resort famed for its crimson plums[,] noticed her old friend Flora on a bench near the bookstall with a paperback in the lap. This was the soft cover copy of Laura issued virtually at the same time as its much stouter and comelier hardback edition. She had just bought it at the station bookstall,

最　后

Z

温妮·卡尔在赛克斯火车站站台上等火车，赛克斯是瑞士一个风景宜人的度假胜地，以深红色的梅子闻名。她注意到老朋友弗洛拉正坐在书亭旁的一张长凳上，腿上放着一本平装书。这是《劳拉》的平装版，它与更为厚实考究的精装版其实是同步发行的。她刚刚在车站的书亭里买到，

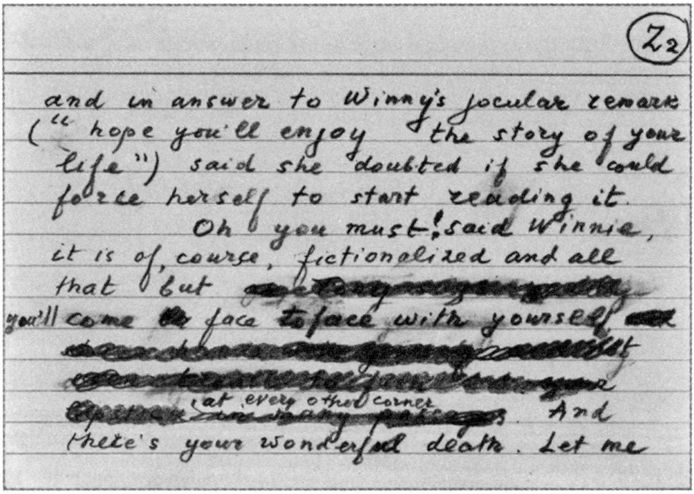

Z2

and in answer to Winny's jocular remark
("hope you'll enjoy the story of your
life") said she doubted if she could
force herself to start reading it.
Oh you must! said Winnie,
it is of, course, fictionalized and all
that but
you'll come face to face with yourself
at every other corner. And
there's your wonderful death. Let me

Z2

and in answer to Winny's jocular remark ("hope you'll enjoy the story of your life") said she doubted if she could force herself to start reading it.

Oh you must! said Winnie, it is, of course, fictionalized and all that but you'll come face to face with yourself at every other corner. And there's your wonderful death. Let me

Z2

面对温妮的戏谑（"希望你会享受你自己的人生故事"），弗洛拉回答说，她怀疑能否强迫自己开始读这本书。

哦，你一定要读！温妮说，当然，它是虚构的，基本上纯属虚构，你会在每一个转角处直面你自己。还有你精彩的死亡。让我

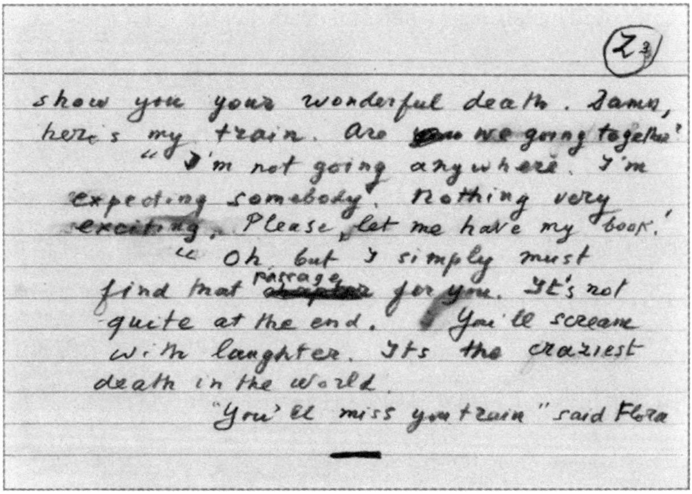
Z3

show you your wonderful death. Damn,
here's my train. Are ~~you~~ we going together?"
"I'm not going anywhere. I'm
expecting somebody. Nothing very
exciting. Please, let me have my book."
"Oh, but I simply must
find that ~~chapter~~ passage for you. It's not
quite at the end. You'll scream
with laughter. Its the craziest
death in the world."
"You'll miss your train" said Flora

Z3

show you your wonderful death. Damn, here's my train. Are we going together?

"I'm not going anywhere. I'm expecting somebody. Nothing very exciting. Please, let me have my book. "

"Oh, but I simply must find that passage for you. It's not quite at the end. You'll scream with laughter. It's the craziest death in the world. ["]

"You'll miss your train[.]" said Flora[.]

Z3

把你精彩死去的那一页翻给你看。见鬼，我的火车到站了。我们一起走吗？

“我哪里也不去，我在这里等人。没有什么特别令人兴奋的，请把我的书还给我。”

“哦，但我只是必须把那个段落给你找出来，不在很后面，你会笑得发疯的。那是尘世间最疯狂的死亡。”

“你会错过火车的。”弗洛拉说。

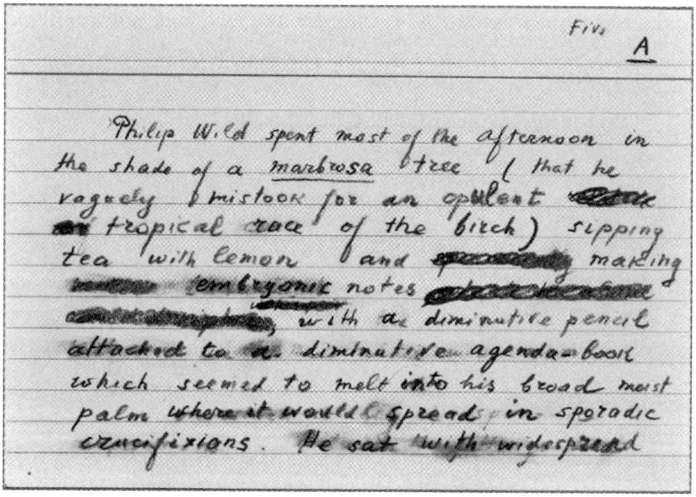

Five

A

Philip Wild spent most of the afternoon in the shade of a marbrosa tree (that he vaguely mistook for an opulent [redacted] tropical race of the birch) sipping tea with lemon and [redacted] making [redacted] embryonic notes [redacted], with a diminutive pencil attached to a diminutive agenda-book which seemed to melt into his broad moist palm where it would spread in sporadic crucifixions. He sat with widespread

Five A

Philip Wild spent most of the afternoon in the shade of a marbrosa tree (that he vaguely mistook for an opulent tropical race of the birch) sipping tea with lemon and making embryonic notes with a diminutive pencil attached to a diminutive agenda-book which seemed to melt into his broad moist palm where it would spread in sporadic crucifixions. He sat with widespread

（五）A

菲利普·王尔德在一棵马波萨树的树荫下度过了几乎整个下午（他依稀把这种树误当成了一种茂密的热带桦木）。他一边啜着柠檬茶，一边用拴在一个极小的日程记事本上的一支极小的铅笔记录下自己刚萌生的想法，日程记事本似乎与他那只湿乎乎的宽大手掌融为一体，化为零落的耶稣受难像。他双腿大张地坐

Five

B

legs to accomodate his enormous stomack and
now and then checked or made in midthought
half a movement to check the fly buttons of his
old fashioned white trousers. There was also
the recurrent search for his pencil sharpener,
which he absently put into a different pocket
every time after use. Otherwise, between all
those small movements, he sat perfectly
still, like a meditative idol. Flora would
be often present lolling in a deckchair,

Five B

legs to accom[m]odate his enormous stomack and now and then checked or made in midthought half a movement to check the fly buttons of his old fashioned white trousers. There was also the recurrent search for his pencil sharpener, which he absently put into a different pocket every time after use. Otherwise, between all those small movements, he sat perfectly still, like a meditative idol. Flora would be often present lolling in a deckchair,

（五）B

着，好给他那巨大的肚子留出空间。他时不时检查一下他那条老式白长裤的裆部纽扣，有时因想起什么而停下动作；或隔不多久就找找他每次用过后都心不在焉地放进不同口袋里的削铅笔刀。此外，没做这些小动作时，他就纹丝不动地坐在那儿，像一尊沉思的神像。弗洛拉则常常懒洋洋地出现在一张帆布躺椅上，

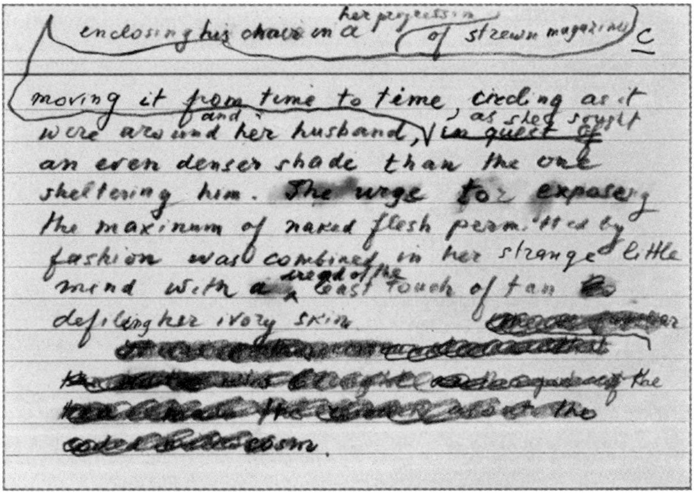

enclosing his chair in a her procession of strewn magazines C

moving it from time to time, circling as it were around her husband, and as she sought in quest of an even denser shade than the one sheltering him. The urge to expose the maximum of naked flesh permitted by fashion was combined in her strange little mind with a dread of the least touch of tan defiling her ivory skin [illegible]

[illegible] the [illegible] the [illegible]

C

moving it from time to time, circling as it were around her husband, and enclosing his chair in her progression of strewn magazines as she sought an even denser shade than the one sheltering him. The urge to expose the maximum of naked flesh permitted by fashion was combined in her strange little mind with a dread of the least touch of tan clefiling her ivory skin.

C

她不时挪动躺椅，在她丈夫周围转悠；她正寻找一处比遮蔽她丈夫的那块更浓密的树荫时，陆续散落的杂志将她丈夫的椅子包围起来。她那奇怪的小脑瓜一方面渴望依据时尚的尺度，最大限度地裸露自己的身体，另一方面又担心她那象牙白的肌肤会被染上一丁点褐黄。

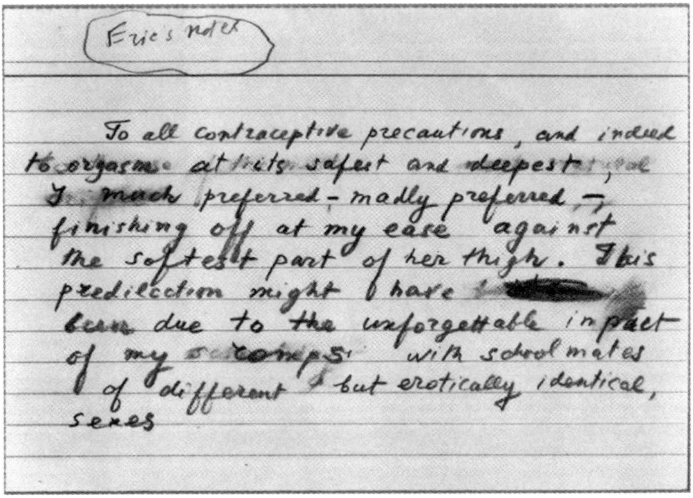
Eric's notes

To all contraceptive precautions, and indeed
to orgasm at its safest and deepest,
I much preferred – madly preferred –
finishing off at my ease against
the softest part of her thigh. This
predilection might have
been due to the unforgettable impact
of my comps with schoolmates
of different but erotically identical,
sexes

Eric's notes

To all contraceptive precautions, and indeed to orgasm at its safest and deepest, I much preferred—madly preferred—finishing off at my ease against the softest part of her thigh. This predilection might have been due to the unforgettable impact of my romps with schoolmates of different but erotically identical, sexes

埃里克的笔记

与所有的避孕措施相比，甚至是与最安全最深入的性高潮相比，我更喜欢——狂热地喜欢——无拘无束地抵住她大腿最柔软的部分完成性爱之旅。这一偏好可能要归因于学生时代的风流韵事给我留下的难以抹去的影响，跟那些风格各异却同样具有性吸引力的男女同学们

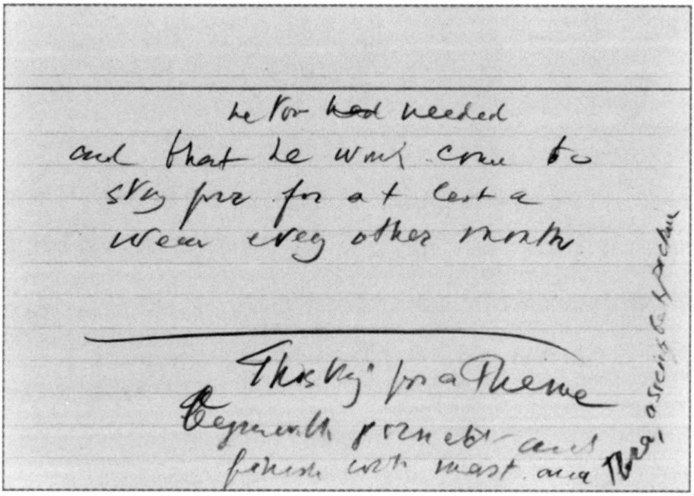
he too needed
and that he would come to
stay here for at least a
week every other month
Thinking for a Theme

he too needed

and that he would come to stay here for at least a week every other month

This [key] for a Theme

Begin with [poem] etc and

finish with mast and Flora, ascribe to picture

他也需要

每隔一个月，他会来待上至少一周。

这个 [关键] 作为主题

以 [诗] 等作为开篇

以桅杆和弗洛拉作为结尾。归因于图片

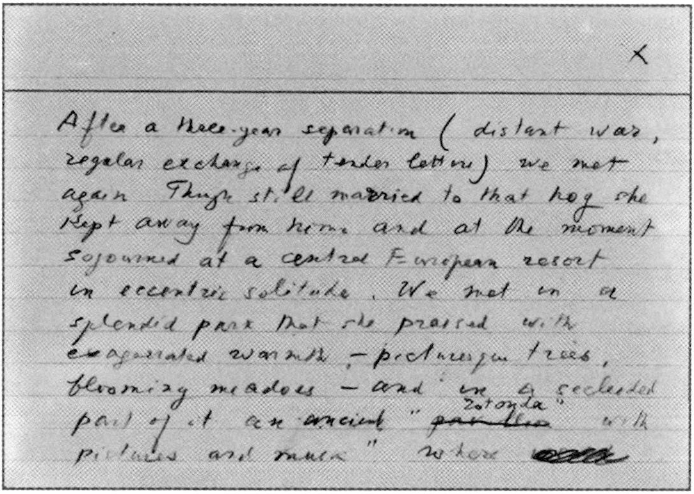

X

After a three-year separation (distant war, regular exchange of tender letters) we met again. Though still married to that hog she kept away from him and at the moment sojourned at a central European resort in eccentric solitude. We met in a splendid park that she praised with exaggerated warmth, — picturesque trees, blooming meadows — and in a secluded part of it an ~~ancient~~ "~~pavilion~~ rotonda" with pictures and music" where

X

After a three-year separation (distant war, regular exchange of tender letters) we met again. Though still married to that hog she kept away from him and at the moment sojourned at a central European resort in eccentric solitude. We met in a splendid park that she praised with [exaggerated] warmth—picturesque trees, blooming meado[w]s—and in a secluded part of it an ancient "rotonda" with pictures and music where

X

分开三年后（遥远的战争，定期温柔的信件往来），我们再次相遇。尽管她与那头猪的婚姻还维系着，但她远远地躲开他，眼下正逗留在欧洲中部一个度假胜地，离群索居。我们在一个风景优美的公园相遇了，她用夸张的热情称赞公园的漂亮——如诗似画的树木，郁郁葱葱的草场——公园僻静处有一幢绘有图画、飘着音乐的古老"圆形建筑"，

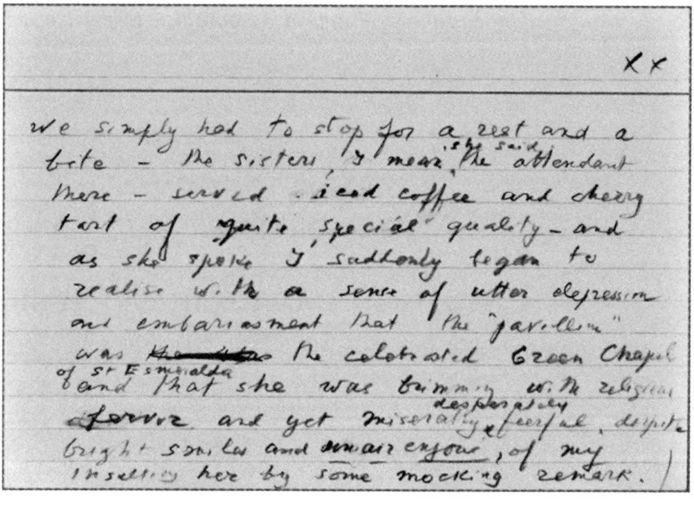

XX

we simply had to stop for a rest and a
bite – the sisters, I mean, she said, the attendant
there – served iced coffee and cherry
tart of quite special quality – and
as she spoke I suddenly began to
realise with a sense of utter depression
and embarrassment that the "pavilion"
was ~~the~~ the celebrated Green Chapel
of St Esmeralda and that she was brimming with religious
~~fervor~~ and yet miserably, desperately fearful, despite
bright smiles and ~~amour~~ enjoue, of my
insulting her by some mocking remark. /

XX

we simply had to stop for a rest and a bite—the sisters, I mean, she said, the attendant[s] there—served iced coffee and cherry tart of quite special quality—and as she spoke I suddenly began to realise with a sense of utter depression and embarrassment that the "pavilion" was the celebrated Green Chapel of St Esmeralda and that she was brimming with religious fervor and yet miserably, desperately fearful, despite bright smiles and un air enjoué, of my insulting her by some mocking remark.

XX

我们只是得停下来休息片刻，吃点东西——修女们，她说，我的意思是，那里的服务员——提供冰咖啡和一种特殊风味的樱桃馅饼——她说着这些时，我突然极其沮丧而尴尬地意识到，这个"亭子"就是著名的圣·埃斯梅拉达绿色小教堂；而她满怀宗教的狂热，尽管笑容明朗、神情愉悦[①]，却痛苦且绝望地惧怕我用冷嘲热讽羞辱她。

① 原文为法语。

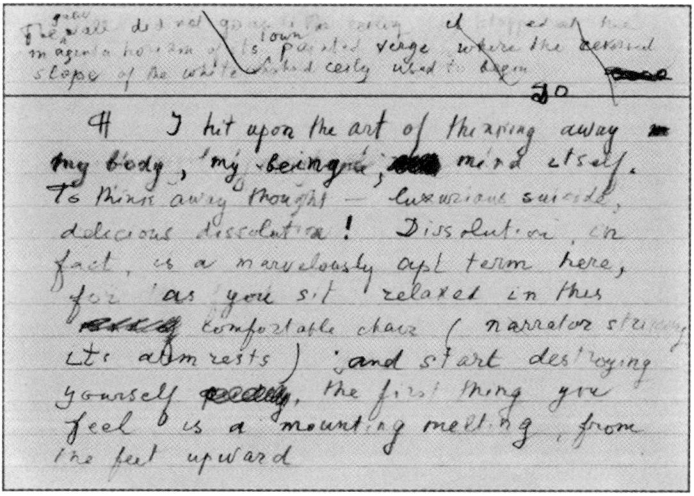
The gray wall did not go up to the ceiling: it stopped at the magenta horizon of its town painted verge where the reversed slope of the whitewashed ceiling used to begin

20

¶ I hit upon the art of thinking away my body, my being, mind itself. To think away thought — luxurious suicide, delicious dissolution! Dissolution, in fact, is a marvelously apt term here, for as you sit relaxed in this comfortable chair (narrator stroking its armrests) and start destroying yourself, the first thing you feel is a mounting melting, from the feet upward

D0

I hit upon the art of thinking away my body, my being, mind itself. To think away thought—luxurious suicide, delicious dissolution! Dissolution, in fact, is a marvelously apt term here, for as you sit relaxed in this comfortable chair (narrator striking its armrests) and start destroying yourself, the first thing you feel is a mounting melting, from the feet upward

D0

我偶然发现了这种忘却我的身体、我的存在以及思维本身的艺术。忘掉思想——奢侈的自杀，怡人的自我消亡！事实上，“自我消亡”这个措词用在这里恰如其分，因为，当你全身放松地坐在这张舒适的椅子上（叙述者敲打着扶手），并着手毁灭自己时，你首先体验到的便是自足部升腾而上的一种消融的感觉

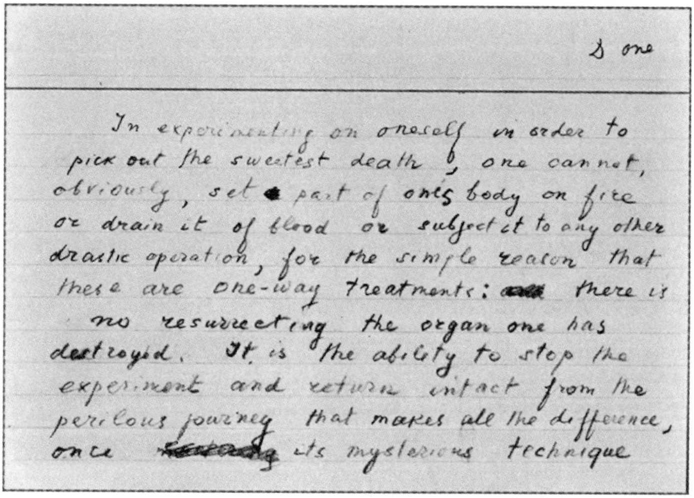

S one

In experimenting on oneself in order to
pick out the sweetest death, one cannot,
obviously, set part of ones body on fire
or drain it of blood or subject it to any other
drastic operation, for the simple reason that
these are one-way treatments: ~~[illegible]~~ there is
no resurrecting the organ one has
destroyed. It is the ability to stop the
experiment and return intact from the
perilous journey that makes all the difference,
once ~~[illegible]~~ its mysterious technique

D one

In experimenting on oneself in order to pick out the sweetest death, one cannot, obviously, set part of one's body on fire or drain it of blood or subject it to any other drastic operation, for the simple reason that these are one-way treatments: there is no resurrecting the organ one has destroyed. It is the ability to stop the experiment and return intact from the perilous journey that makes all the difference, once its mysterious technique

D 一

一个人在自己身上做实验，以求找到一种最痛快的死亡方式时，显然不能将自己的身体付之一炬，也不能抽干体内血液，或采取其他极端手段。原因很简单，这些方式都是单向治疗：毁坏的器官再无复生的可能。学习自我毁灭的学生，一旦掌握了神秘的实验技巧，能够中止实验并从险境中全身而退才是至关重要的。

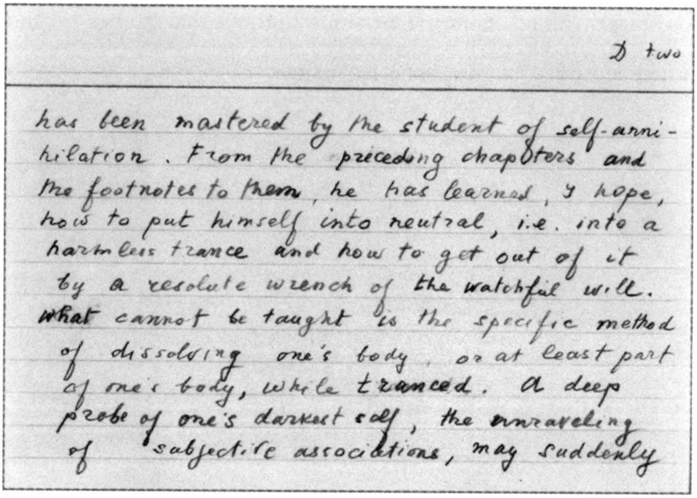
D two

has been mastered by the student of self-annihilation. From the preceding chapters and the footnotes to them, he has learned, I hope, how to put himself into neutral, i.e. into a harmless trance and how to get out of it by a resolute wrench of the watchful will. What cannot be taught is the specific method of dissolving one's body, or at least part of one's body, while tranced. A deep probe of one's darkest self, the unraveling of subjective associations, may suddenly

D two

has been mastered by the student of self-annihilation. From the preceding chapters and the footnotes to them, he has learned, I hope, how to put himself into neutral, i. e. into a harmless trance and how to get out of it by a resolute wrench of the watchful will. What cannot be taught is the specific method of dissolving one's body, or at least part of one's body, while tranced. A deep probe of one's darkest self, the unraveling of subjective associations, may suddenly

D 二

我希望他能从前面的章节，以及这些章节的脚注中学会保持中立态度，也就是说，进入一种无害的昏睡状态，并学会如何用一种警觉的意志，毅然从中挣脱出来。不能教的是在昏睡中消融躯体或至少部分躯体的具体方法。对一个人最黑暗的自我的深入探索，主观联想的瓦解，可能会突然

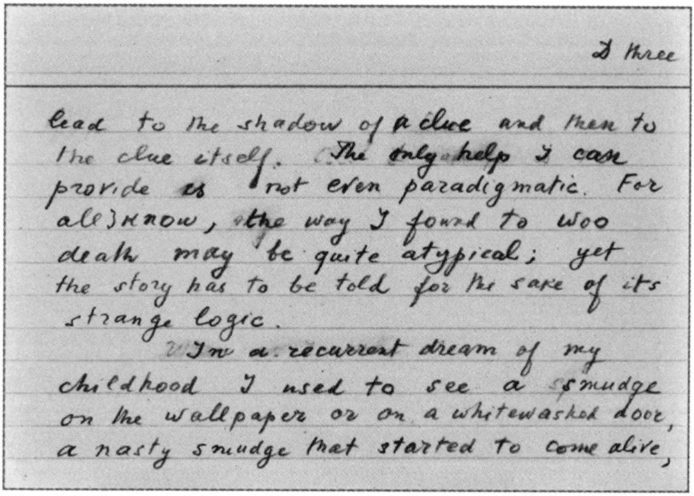

D three

lead to the shadow of a clue and then to
the clue itself. The only help I can
provide is not even paradigmatic. For
all I know, the way I found to woo
death may be quite atypical; yet
the story has to be told for the sake of its
strange logic.
In a recurrent dream of my
childhood I used to see a smudge
on the wallpaper or on a whitewashed door,
a nasty smudge that started to come alive,

D three

lead to the shadow of a clue and then to the clue itself. The only help I can provide is not even paradigmatic. For all I know, the way I found to woo death may be quite atypical; yet the story has to be told for the sake of its strange logic.

In a recurrent dream of my childhood I used to see a smudge on the wallpaper or on a whitewashed door, a nasty smudge that started to come alive,

D 三

指向线索的蛛丝马迹，进而指向线索本身。我唯一能提供的帮助甚至算不上范式。据我所知，我追求死亡的方式或许很另类，但就因为故事的逻辑诡异，所以必须讲给世人听。

在童年经常出现的梦境中，我总看到墙纸或刷白的门上有一个污点，那讨厌的东西开始动了起来，

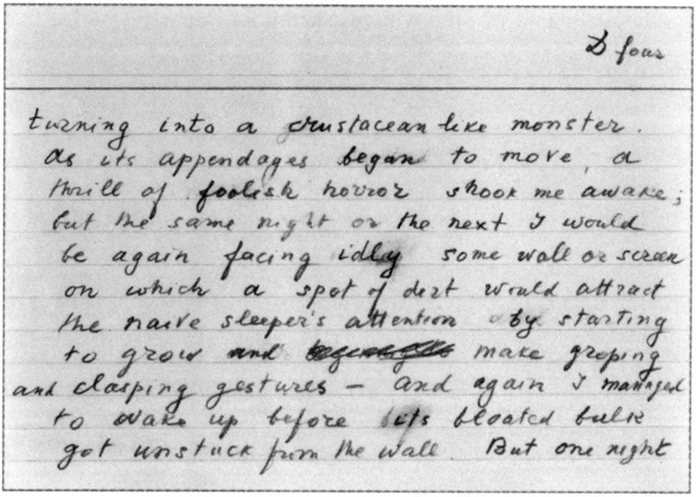

D four

turning into a crustacean-like monster.
As its appendages began to move, a
thrill of foolish horror shook me awake;
but the same night or the next I would
be again facing idly some wall or screen
on which a spot of dirt would attract
the naive sleeper's attention by starting
to grow ~~and~~ ~~[illegible]~~ make groping
and clasping gestures — and again I managed
to wake up before its bloated bulk
got unstuck from the wall. But one night

D four

turning into a crustacean-like monster. As its appendages began to move, a thrill of foolish horror shook me awake; but the same night or the next I would be again facing idly some wall or screen on which a spot of dirt would attract the naive sleeper's attention by starting to grow and make groping and clasping gestures—and again I managed to wake up before its bloated bulk got unstuck from the wall. But one night

D 四

变为一个类似甲壳纲动物的怪胎。它身上附属的肢体开始蠕动时，一阵可笑的恐慌令我哆嗦着从睡梦中惊醒；但同一天晚上或第二天晚上，我又会百无聊赖地眼看着某面墙或屏幕上的一个污点越变越大，逐渐显露出张牙舞爪的样子——又吸引了傻乎乎的睡眠者的注意力；我又一次在那个庞然大物从墙上挣脱之前设法醒了过来。但有天晚上，

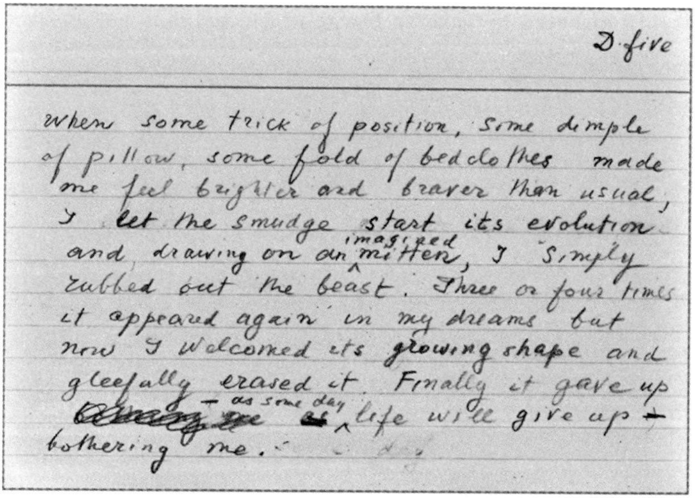

D. five

when some trick of position, some dimple of pillow, some fold of bedclothes made me feel brighter and braver than usual, I let the smudge start its evolution and, drawing on an imagined mitten, I simply rubbed out the beast. Three or four times it appeared again in my dreams but now I welcomed its growing shape and gleefully erased it. Finally it gave up ~~bothering me as~~ — as some day life will give up — bothering me.

D five

when some trick of position, some dimple of pillow, some fold of bedclothes made me feel brighter and braver than usual, I let the smudge start its evolution and, drawing on an imagined mitten, I simply rubbed out the beast. Three or four times it appeared again in my dreams but now I welcomed its growing shape and gleefully erased it. Finally it gave up—as some day life will give up—bothering me.

D 五

我睡觉的姿势、枕头的凹痕、睡衣上的褶皱，都让我感觉自己比平时要聪明和勇敢；我任由那个污点开始演变，戴上想象的手套，简单地擦掉了这个怪物。后来有三四次它又出现在我的梦里，而此时我对它的变形报以欢迎的态度，然后开开心心地将之抹去。最后，它不再来骚扰我，就像生命总有一天也会停止骚扰我一样。

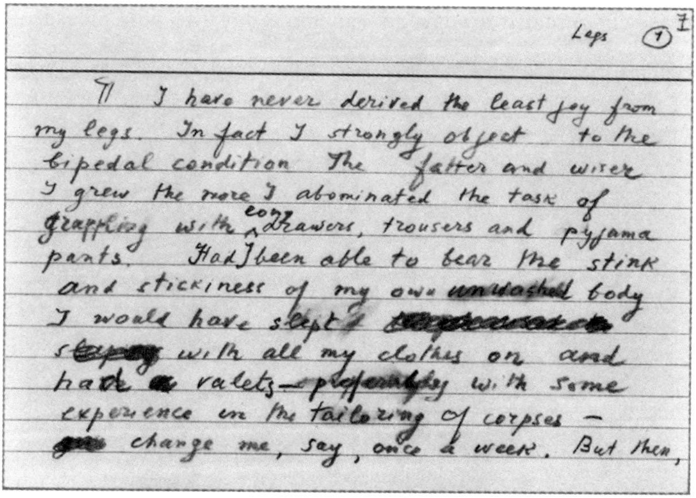

Legs (1) I

¶ I have never derived the least joy from
my legs. In fact I strongly object to the
bipedal condition. The fatter and wiser
I grew the more I abominated the task of
grappling with com drawers, trousers and pyjama
pants. Had I been able to bear the stink
and stickiness of my own ~~unwashed~~ body
I would have slept [illegible]
~~sleeping~~ with all my clothes on and
had ~~a~~ valets ~~preferably~~ with some
experience in the tailoring of corpses —
[illegible] change me, say, once a week. But then,

Legs 1　7

I have never derived the least joy from my legs. In fact I strongly object to the bipedal condition[.] The fatter and wiser I grew the more I abominated the task of grappling with long drawers, trousers and pyjama pants. Had I been able to bear the stink and stickiness of my own unwashed body I would have slept with all my clothes on and had valets—preferably with some experience in the tailoring of corpses—change me, say, once a week. But then,

腿 1　7

我从未获得过任何源自我的双腿的快乐。事实上我对拥有双足的现状持有强烈的反感，随着身体渐胖、智慧渐长，我对穿长内裤、长外裤和睡衣裤的厌恶与日俱增。假如我能忍受不洗澡的身体的臭味和黏腻，我会和衣而睡，让男侍——优先考虑具有为尸体裁剪衣服的经验的人——为我更衣，比如说，一周一次。但那时，

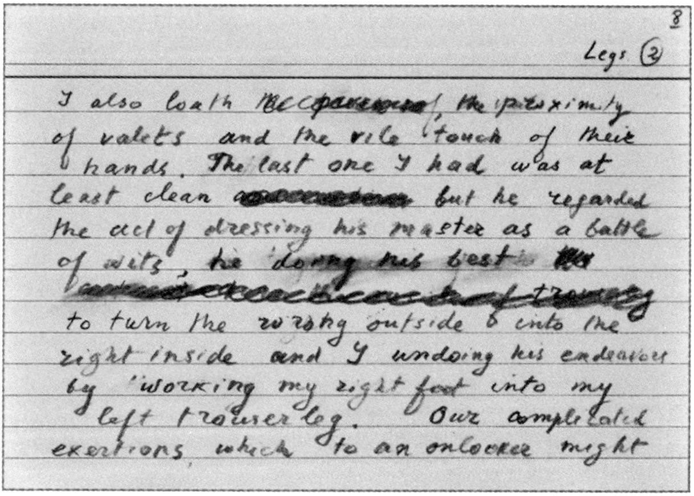

8

Legs ②

I also loath the proximity of valets and the vile touch of their hands. The last one I had was at least clean but he regarded the act of dressing his master as a battle of wits, he doing his best to turn the wrong outside into the right inside and I undoing his endeavor by working my right foot into my left trouser leg. Our complicated exertions, which to an onlooker might

legs 2 8

I also loath[e] the proximity of valets and the vile touch of their hands. The last one I had was at least clean but he regarded the act of dressing his master as a battle of wits, he doing his best to turn the wrong outside into the right inside and I undoing his endeavors by working my right foot into my left trouser leg. Our complicated exertions, which to an onlooker might

腿 2 8

我也厌恶男侍近身，讨厌他们肮脏的手的碰触。我用的最后一位男侍至少还算干净，但他把为主人更衣视为一场智力战争，他费了老半天劲把里子误翻在外面的裤子整理好了，我却将右腿伸入了左裤管，令他前功尽弃。我们的这番折腾，在一个旁观者的眼里也许

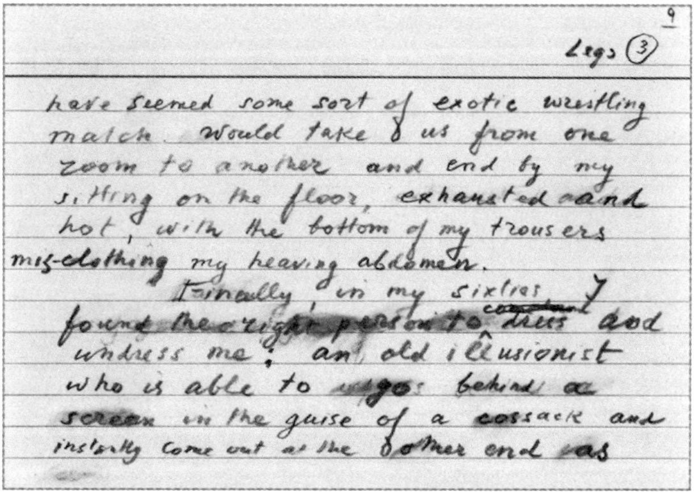
9

Legs (3)

have seemed some sort of exotic wrestling match. Would take us from one room to another and end by my sitting on the floor, exhausted and hot, with the bottom of my trousers mis-clothing my heaving abdomen.

Finally, in my sixties I found the right person to costume and undress me: an old illusionist who is able to go behind a screen in the guise of a cossack and instantly come out at the other end as have seemed some sort of exotic wrestling match[,] would take us from one room to another and end by my sitting on the floor, exhausted and hot, with the bottom of my trousers mis-clothing my heaving abdomen.

Finally, in my sixties, I found the right person to dress and undress me: an old illusionist who is able to go behind a screen in the guise of a cossack and instantly come out at the other end as

无异于某种具有异国情调的摔跤比赛，会让我们从一个房间转战到另一个房间，直到我精疲力竭地瘫坐在地板上，热得不行，长裤的臀部位置穿到了我隆起的肚子上，这才算告终。

最后，在我六十多岁时，我找到了一个合适的人为我着装和宽衣：一位老魔术师，他能够伪装成哥萨克人走到屏风后面，又即刻变身为山姆大叔从另一端走出来。

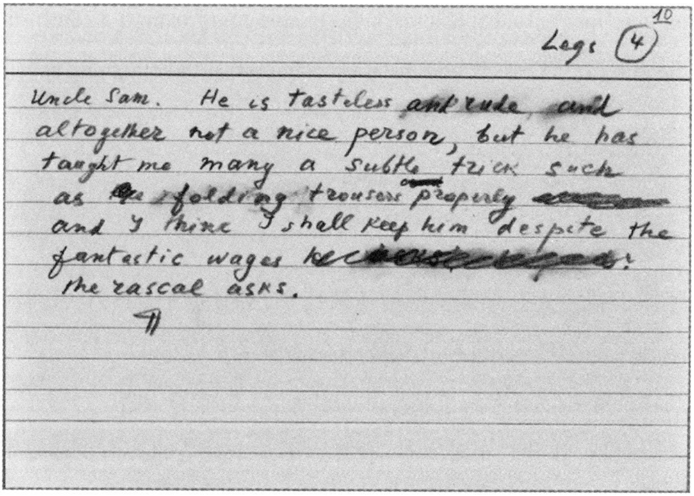

Legs (4) 10

Uncle Sam. He is tasteless ~~and rude and~~ altogether not a nice person, but he has taught me many a subtle trick such as ~~the~~ folding trousers properly ~~[illegible]~~ and I think I shall keep him despite the fantastic wages ~~[illegible]~~ the rascal asks.

Legs 4 10

Uncle Sam. He is tasteless and rude and altogether not a nice person, but he has taught me many a subtle trick such as folding trousers properly and I think I shall keep him despite the fantastic wages the rascal asks.

腿 4 10

他缺少品味，举止粗鲁，总之并非良善之辈；但他教会了我许多小窍门，比如如何把裤子叠得像样。尽管这无赖要价疯狂，但我还是决定继续雇用他。

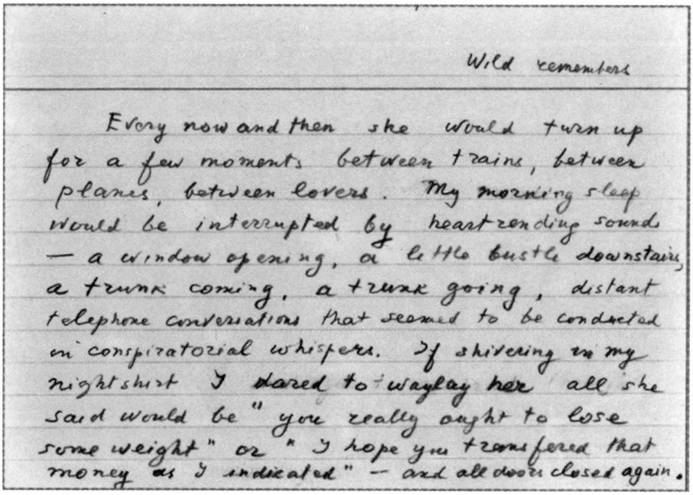

Wild remembers

Every now and then she would turn up for a few moments between trains, between planes, between lovers. My morning sleep would be interrupted by heartrending sounds — a window opening, a little bustle downstairs, a trunk coming, a trunk going, distant telephone conversations that seemed to be conducted in conspiratorial whispers. If shivering in my nightshirt I dared to waylay her all she said would be "you really ought to lose some weight" or "I hope you transfered that money as I indicated" — and all doors closed again.

Wild remembers

Every now and then she would turn up for a few moments between trains, between planes, between lovers. My morning sleep would be interrupted by heartrending sounds—a window opening, a little bustle downstairs, a trunk coming, a trunk going, distant telephone conversations that seemed to be conducted in conspiratorial whispers. If shivering in my nightshirt I dared to waylay her all she said would be “you really ought to lose some weight” or “I hope you transfered that money as I indicated” —and all doors closed again.

王尔德的记忆

她总是来去匆匆，在众多的火车、飞机与情人之间马不停蹄地穿梭。我清晨的酣眠总是被种种令人悲伤的声音打断——开窗子的响声、下楼时窸窸窣窣的动静、行李箱拖过来、行李箱拖走了、远处传来的电话交谈里似乎夹杂着密谋暗算的低语。如果穿着睡衣冷得直打哆嗦的我敢拦住她不让她走，她便会说“你真的应该减肥了”，或者“我希望你按我说的把那笔钱转到我账上”——说完，所有门再次关闭。

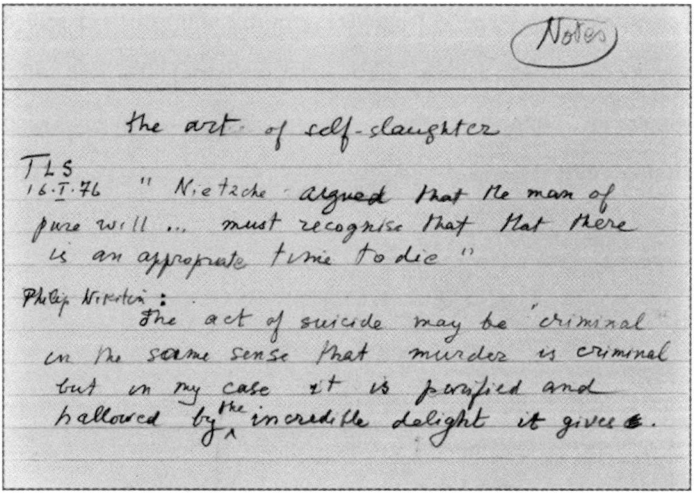

Notes

the art of self-slaughter

TLS
16·I·76 " Nietzche argued that the man of pure will ... must recognise that that there is an appropriate time to die "

Philip Wiertcin:
The act of suicide may be 'criminal' in the same sense that murder is criminal but in my case it is purified and hallowed by the incredible delight it gives.

Notes

the art of self-slaughter

TLS 16-1-76 “Nietz[s]che argued that the man of pure will... must recognise that that there is an appropriate time to die”

Philip Nikitin: The act of suicide may be “criminal” in the same sense that murder is criminal but in my case it is purified and hallowed by the incredible delight it gives.

笔　记

自杀的艺术

一九七六年一月十六日的《泰晤士报文学副刊》上记载：“尼采认为，一个有纯粹意志力的人……必须承认死亡有恰当的时机。”

菲利普·尼基京[①]：如同谋杀是犯罪一样，自杀行为或许也属同样意义上的“犯罪”，不过我的自杀行为是圣洁的，因为它给我带来了极大的乐趣。

① 菲利普·尼基京可能是指托尔斯泰的小说《安娜·卡列尼娜》中的Philip Ivanitch Nikitin，他是列文家的仆人、园丁以及车夫。

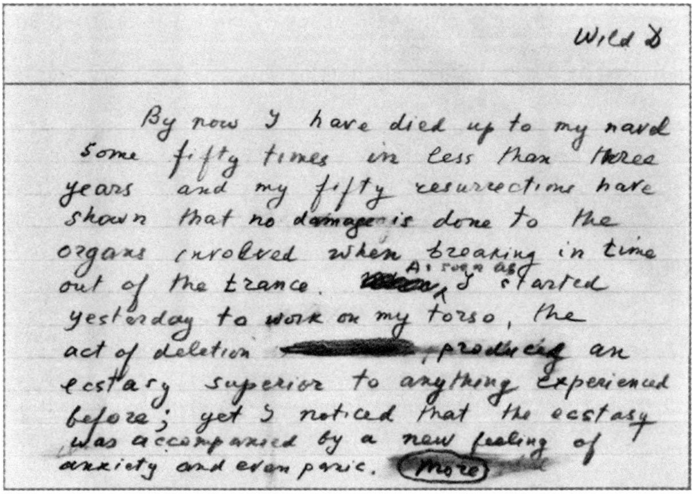

Wild 8

By now I have died up to my navel
some fifty times in less than three
years and my fifty resurrections have
shown that no damage is done to the
organs involved when breaking in time
out of the trance. As soon as I started
yesterday to work on my torso, the
act of deletion, producing an
ecstasy superior to anything experienced
before; yet I noticed that the ecstasy
was accompanied by a new feeling of
anxiety and even panic. (More)

Wild D

By now I have died up to my navel some fifty times in less than three years and my fifty resurrections have shown that no damage is done to the organs involved when breaking in time out of the trance. As soon as I started yesterday to work on my torso, the act of deletion produced an ecstasy superior to anything experienced before; yet I noticed that the ecstasy was accompanied by a new feeling of anxiety and even panic.

王尔德 D

迄今为止，我在过去不到三年的时间里死去了约五十次，死亡的感觉一直延伸到肚脐眼。五十次死而复生的经历显示，当我及时从昏睡状态中挣脱出来时，身体器官都完好无损。昨天，我一开始研究我的躯体，删除的行为就立即引发了一种以前从未体验过的狂喜。尽管我也注意到，伴随着这种狂喜的还有一种新的焦虑，甚至恐慌。

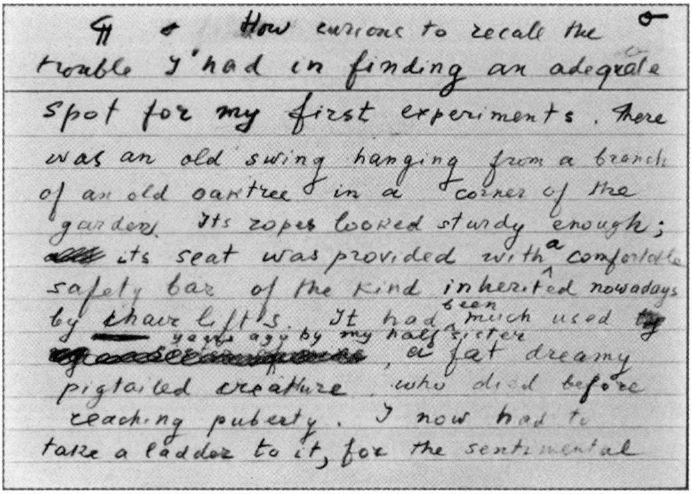

¶ How curious to recall the
trouble I had in finding an adequate
spot for my first experiments. There
was an old swing hanging from a branch
of an old oaktree in a corner of the
garden. Its ropes looked sturdy enough;
its seat was provided with a comfortable
safety bar of the kind inherited nowadays
by chair lifts. It had been much used
years ago by my half sister
, a fat dreamy
pigtailed creature, who died before
reaching puberty. I now had to
take a ladder to it, for the sentimental

O

How curious to recall the trouble I had in finding an adequate spot for my first experiments. There was an old swing hanging from a branch of an old oaktree in a corner of the garden. Its ropes looked sturdy enough; its seat was provided with a comfortable safety bar of the kind inherited nowadays by chair lifts. It had been much used years ago by my half sister, a fat dreamy pigtailed creature who died before reaching puberty. I now had to take a ladder to it, for the sentimental

O

第一次做实验时，为了找一个够宽敞的地方我颇费了一番周折，回想起来还真觉得奇怪。花园角落一棵古老橡树的树枝上悬挂着一个破旧的秋千，挂秋千的绳索看上去够结实的。秋千的座位上装有现在常用于滑雪缆车的那种舒适的保险杆。多年前，我同父异母的妹妹经常坐在这里荡秋千。她是个梳着辫子、心不在焉的胖孩子，可还没进入青春期就夭折了。如今的我得借助一个梯子才能爬到秋千上，因为这个伤感的遗物

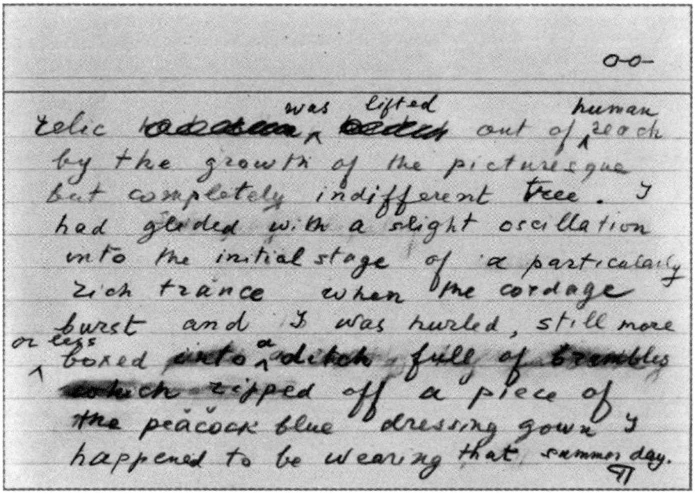

0-0-

relic [redacted] was [redacted] lifted out of human reach by the growth of the picturesque but completely indifferent tree. I had glided with a slight oscillation into the initial stage of a particularly rich trance when the cordage burst and I was hurled, still more or less boxed, into a ditch full of brambles which ripped off a piece of the peacock blue dressing gown I happened to be wearing that summer day. ¶

OO

relic was lifted out of human reach by the growth of the picturesque but completely indifferent tree. I had glided with a slight oscillation into the initial stage of a particularly rich trance when the cordage burst and I was hurled, still more or less boxed[,] into a ditch full of brambles which ripped off a piece of the peacock blue dressing gown I happened to be wearing that summer day.

OO

已跟随那棵古色古香但却冷漠无情地生长着的树一起到达了人无法企及的高度。在秋千上轻轻一荡，我陷入了一种极沉的昏睡状态的初始阶段。绳索崩断时，我多少有些像被一拳击中般摔了出去，掉进一条荆棘丛生的沟渠里。那个夏天我碰巧一直穿着的孔雀蓝睡袍也被撕破了。

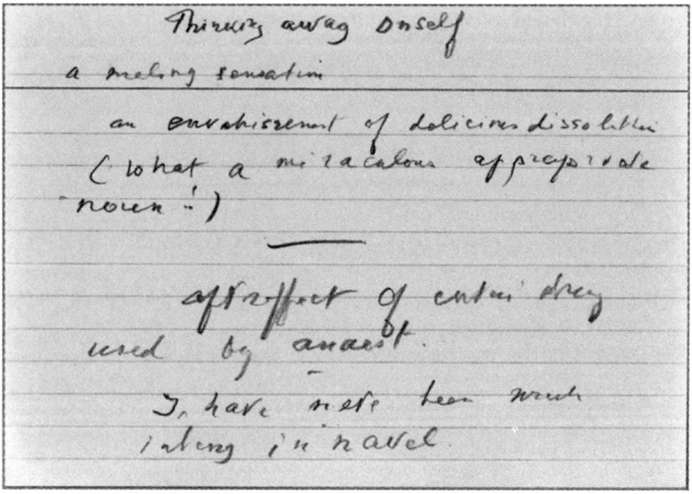
Thinking away oneself
a melting sensation
an envahissement of delicious dissolution
(what a miraculous appropriate noun!)

———

aftereffect of certain drug
used by anaest.
I have never been much
interested in navel.

Thinking away on[e]self

a mel[t]ing sensation

an envahissement of delicious dissolution (what a miraculous appropriate noun!)

aftereffect of certain drug used by anaest [hesiologist]

I have ne[ver] been much [interested] in navel

忘我的境界

融化的感觉

甜美的自我消融的入侵[①]（多么神奇又恰如其分的名词！）

麻醉学专家用过的某种药物的余效

我从未对肚脐有过多大兴趣

① 原文为法语。

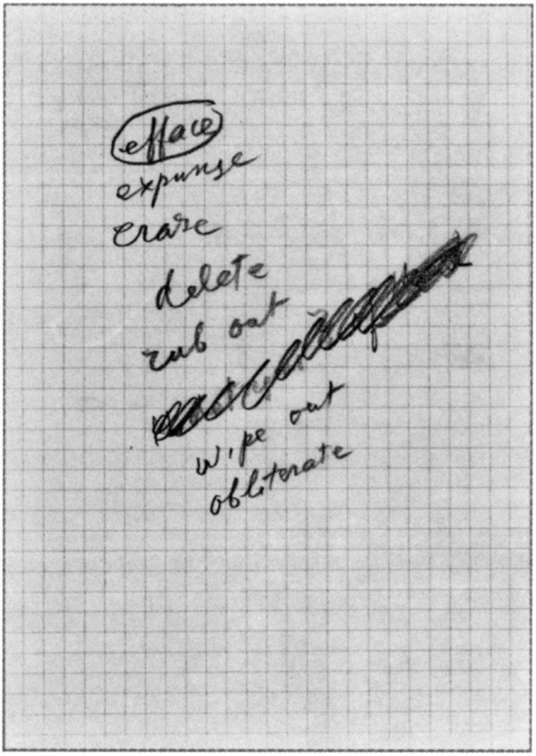
efface
expunge
erase
delete
rub out
wipe out
obliterate

efface

expunge

erase

delete

rub out

wipe out

obliterate

抹去

消除

擦掉

删除

磨灭

擦净

涂去

译后记

1. 纳博科夫——其人其作其译介

弗拉基米尔·纳博科夫（Vladimir Nabokov）是俄裔美国小说家、诗人、文学批评家、翻译家，公认的二十世纪杰出小说家和文体家。在美国，纳博科夫被视为二十世纪美国文坛继福克纳后最重要的作家之一，是一九四五至一九六五这二十年间最有贡献的美国小说家之一。

一八九九年四月二十三日，纳博科夫出生于俄国圣彼得堡莫尔斯卡亚大街四十七号的一户贵族家庭，这一天恰逢俄国大文豪普希金的百年寿诞，也正是英国文学大师莎士比亚诞生二百三十五周年纪念日。纳博科夫早年受父母影响很大。父亲弗拉基米尔·德米特里耶维奇·纳博科夫是著名的法理学家，作为政坛上的亲英派，他经常在家里为孩子们朗读狄更斯、福楼拜、司汤达、巴尔扎克等作家的作品。母亲艾莱娜·伊凡诺夫娜出生于上流社会家族，从小就受到良好的教育，通晓多国外语。她喜欢写诗，对绘画和音乐更是充满了兴趣。艾莱娜·伊凡诺夫娜出嫁时，纳博科夫的外祖父将维拉庄园作为嫁妆送给女儿，它后来成为纳博科夫童年和少年时期的乐土，留下了他许多难忘的经历和美好的回忆。母亲在维拉庄园里用英语给孩子们讲故事、读文章，纳博科夫六岁时就能用英语阅读，甚至早于他用俄语进行阅读。他五岁开始学习法语，六岁时就听法语女教师朗读《悲惨世界》、《基督山伯爵》和《八十天环游地球》等法国名著。早期优越的家庭教育环境使纳博科夫从小学起就鹤立鸡群，他的俄文作业里不时地夹杂英文和法文，这让老师非常头痛，他们甚至认为纳博科夫太喜欢表现自己，殊不知这是小纳博科夫脑海中自然闪现出来的。纳博科夫从小喜爱文学，年纪轻轻即以诗才见著，十五岁就出版了第一本诗集，十八岁出版了第二本，此后数十年雅咏不辍，这解释了何以他最朴实的散文段落里仍洋溢着浓郁而飘逸的诗意。一九一九年俄国十月革命后，纳博科夫随全家流亡伦敦，靠母亲变卖首饰和奖学金，进入剑桥三一学院修读斯拉夫语和罗曼语，并深入研究欧美先锋派爱伦·坡、乔伊斯、普鲁斯特等作家的作品。毕业后纳博科夫没有留在英国，而是去了德国柏林，德国在十月革命后成了俄国移民中心，这里出版的俄文书比俄罗斯本土出版的还多，这对当时一心想成为俄语作家的纳博科夫来说，无疑是一个很大的诱惑。

一九二五年，纳博科夫在柏林俄国侨民举办的一次慈善舞会上结识了犹太血统的女子薇拉·斯洛宁。薇拉身材瘦削匀称，光艳照人，生性幽默，思维敏捷，她与纳博科夫很快坠入爱河。嫁给纳博科夫后，薇拉任劳任怨地充当了他生活中的多重角色：妻子、速记、编辑、翻译、司机。一九三四年，她为纳博科夫家族添了一位继承人——儿子德米特里。

纳博科夫主要以其长篇小说作品著称于世。在西欧流亡的二十年里，他用俄语创作了九部长篇小说：《玛丽》（1926）、《王，后，杰克》（1928）、《防守》（1930）、《眼睛》（1930）、《荣耀》（1932）、《黑暗中的笑声》（1932）、《绝望》（1936）、《斩首之邀》（1938）、《天赋》（1939）。这些小说的主题多半为俄国流亡者的盲目生活或人们的盲目爱情，主人公除流亡者之外，大都是些畸形发展的天才或艺术家；他们为了摆脱精神空虚和受难的现实而沉浸在对往事的回忆、纯艺术、棋术或一些反常的行为中，作品流露出一种失落感、精神受压抑感乃至精神崩溃感。这些小说的现实背景感较强，主题较为明晰。纳博科夫结束欧洲流亡生活到美国之后，创作了八部长篇小说，包括《塞巴斯蒂安·奈特的真实生活》（1941）、《庶出的标志》（1947）、《普宁》（1957）、《洛丽塔》（1958）、《微暗的火》（1962）、《爱达或爱欲》（1969）、《透明》（1972）、《看，那些小丑！》（1974）。其中《普宁》、《洛丽塔》和《微暗的火》代表了他这一时期小说艺术的最高成就。这一时期的小说大多数仍沿袭了前期小说表现的主题、人物类型。但是，小说的现实感和背景感减弱了，而小说文本层面的虚构性、人为性、实验性则表现得更为突出。

二十世纪八十年代初，纳博科夫的作品随着西方一大批烙有“现代派”、“现代主义”印迹的作品一起来到了中国。翻译家梅绍武先生是国内纳博科夫研究领域的开拓者。他率先翻译出版了《普宁》[①]，一九八九年，国内突然掀起了“洛丽塔飓风”，

① 《普宁》，纳博科夫著，梅绍武译，上海译文出版社一九八一年版。

这一年国内至少出现了十一个《洛丽塔》的译本。

国内文学评论界对纳博科夫作品的探讨大多集中在《洛丽塔》、《普宁》、《微暗的火》和另外几部短篇小说上，对于其他重要的作品如《斩首之邀》、《爱达或爱欲》、《看，那些小丑！》等小说几乎尚未触及。鲜为人知的是，一九七五年，纳博科夫在着手创作一部名为《劳拉的原型》的小说。在纳博科夫生命中的最后几个月里，他仍在病榻上作最后的努力，但最终这部作品没能写完。纳博科夫弥留之际曾一再指示其妻子毁掉这部未完成的手稿，然而他的妻子却将手稿锁进了瑞士银行的保险箱。① 二〇〇九年九月，英国企鹅出版社终于将这部人们翘望已久的遗作以《劳拉的原型：（死亡是欢愉的）碎片小说》为标题出版。与此同时，美国兰登书屋旗下的克诺夫出版集团以《劳拉的原型》（*The Original of Laura*）为标题出版。

2. 作为“元小说”的《劳拉的原型》

“元小说”的英文“metafiction”由前缀“meta”加小说“fiction”组成。在希腊文中，“元”（meta）是作为前缀使用的，表示一种次序，因而也就带有表示结束、归纳、总结的意思。“元小说”这个小说叙事学研究术语，是由美国后现代派作家威廉·加斯一九七〇年正式提出的，但作为一种叙述技巧，“元小说”很早就用于不同历史时期的各种叙事作品中，比如，在流传

① Vladimir Nabokov, *The Original of Laura: (Dying is Fun) a Novel in Fragments*, UK: Penguin Modern Classics, 2009. p. x.
见弗拉基米尔·纳博科夫《劳拉的原型：（死亡是欢愉的）碎片小说》（企鹅出版社二〇〇九年版）。

于中东和南亚的民间故事集《一千零一夜》、欧洲最早的小说作品《十日谈》、英国古典作品《坎特伯雷故事集》中，这种有意在故事创作过程中揭示作者构思原始框架的技巧就已初见端倪。另外，《堂吉诃德》、《呼啸山庄》、《寒冬夜行人》等近代传世佳作也无不带有这种叙事结构的痕迹。加斯的“元小说”理论对于这一文学形式真正成为西方占主要地位的小说形态起了重要推动作用。一九八四年，约翰·巴思又将这种叙事策略解释为“故事中套着故事的故事”。

从结构上分析，带有“元小说”特征的早期叙述作品可定义为“故事中的故事”。但当代西方“元小说”作品不像现实主义或者现代主义那样关注文本虚构与现实世界的关系，而是充分借助现代语言学和哲学思潮理论，使作者思想和文本结构得到进一步深化，也由此推动了“元小说”理论研究的发展。纳博科夫正是美国“元小说”创作的代表人物之一，他特别关注“天才的个体与结构的问题”[①]“天才的个体”指的是那些具有强烈文学创新意识和自我意识的作家们，而“结构”则是纳博科夫本人一直都极为强调的文学形式的一部分，因为对结构框架的关注是元小说作家们遵循的一大创作基本原则。

《劳拉的原型》也是一部结构非常独特的“元小说”，表面上讲述的是有关菲利普·王尔德与他的妻子弗洛拉之间不幸的婚姻故事，但小说的深层次主题是男主人公的自我泯灭过程。为了帮助读者理清《劳拉的原型》的基本故事结构，译者试图对该

① 参见《文学讲稿》，纳博科夫著，申慧辉等译，上海译文出版社二〇一八年版。

小说“神秘的文学结构”进行一次“侦察”。[1]

男主人公菲利普·王尔德是“一名出色的神经病学家，一个颇负盛名的演讲者，一位拥有足够财产可以生活优渥的绅士”。他“可谓应有尽有，就是长相寒碜了点儿”。他娶了一位年轻美貌的妻子，即女主人公弗洛拉。弗洛拉出生于艺术世家。祖父列夫·林德是一位画家，一九二〇年他偕妻子艾娃和儿子亚当从莫斯科移民到纽约，但到了美国他相当失意，他的“一批极可悲的油画被运回了莫斯科，另一些则忧郁地游荡于租来的公寓里，等着在阁楼上展出，或是被偷偷运到集市上贱卖掉”。他的儿子亚当·林德比他成功，三十岁时就已成为时尚摄影师，并娶了一位名叫“兰斯卡雅”的芭蕾舞演员。在某种意义上，兰斯卡雅也是这部绯闻小说的主角，她有众多情人，而弗洛拉可能是其合法父亲亚当的女儿。弗洛拉出生三年后，父亲亚当成了同性恋者，他才发现自己爱恋的那个小伙子掐死了另一个他更爱的小伙子。亚当·林德喜欢特技摄影，在蒙特卡罗旅馆自拍他开枪自杀镜头的同时，他妻子的演出大获成功。兰斯卡雅带着女儿弗洛拉、一位英语家庭教师、一位俄国保姆，还有一个四海为家的情人，先在巴黎安顿下来，随后又搬到了佛罗伦萨，在伦敦小住一段时间后，又回到法国。她记不起自己的父亲了，也很讨厌她的母亲。接近四十岁时，兰斯卡雅被迫放弃芭蕾舞，跑到巴黎一所算不上一流的学校去教授舞蹈课程，随后嫁给了休伯特·赫·休伯特。

---

① “我的课程是对神秘的文学结构的一种侦察”，出自《文学讲稿》纳博科夫本人对全部讲稿的题记。

弗洛拉的出场与洛丽塔很相似："她常常独自与休伯特先生待在屋子里，休伯特总在她身边'转悠'，嘴里还哼着单调的曲儿，多多少少有些迷惑着她，可以说用某种黏糊的无形物质越来越紧地围困住她……"与《洛丽塔》中的亨伯特不一样的是，休伯特曾有个和弗洛拉一样漂亮的女儿，名叫黛西。她们都长着"比深蓝色鸢尾花更蓝的眼睫毛"，都长着"黄棕色或者说如帕洛米诺马般淡褐色光滑如丝的头发"，可怜的黛西在一条乡间小路上被一辆倒车的卡车碾死了，黛西的母亲也死于伤心过度。休伯特把对自己女儿的爱转移到弗洛拉身上，他愿意娶兰斯卡雅为妻，也因为她酷似他亡妻年轻时的明星样子。休伯特与这对母女过了几年幸福生活后，突然中风死在旅馆电梯里。几年后，弗洛拉嫁给了功成名就的菲利普·王尔德。

年轻的弗洛拉与年长的王尔德之间并无爱情可言，故屡屡背叛王尔德。"她到我灰暗的房间里来的次数超出每个月一次时（这是自我步入六十岁后她光顾我房间的平均频率），我就知道她在欺骗我，她又交上了新男友。"在以王尔德和弗洛拉婚后矛盾、弗洛拉婚外情为主线的故事后面，即产生了两个"元小说"。

小说开篇即明示，弗洛拉的丈夫也可以算得上是一位作家，他正忙于完成一份神秘手稿，这就是第一个"元小说"："哦，不，要知道那份书稿可不是为了挣钱草率写就的小说，而是一位疯狂的神经病学家的遗作，类似那部电影中的某种'有毒作品'。它已耗费了他多年心血，并且还将继续耗费下去，当然，这事绝对是个秘密。"这部作家不肯轻易示人的呕心沥血之作